MY
BROTHER'S
SECRET

MY
BROTHER'S
SECRET

DAN SMITH

Chicken House

SCHOLASTIC INC. | NEW YORK

First published in the United Kingdom in 2014 by Chicken House, 2 Palmer Street, Frome, Somerset BA11 1DS.

ISBN: 978-0-545-86869-3

10 9 8 7 6 5 4 3 2 1   15 16 17 18 19

Printed in the U.S.A.   40
First printing 2015

Book design by Yaffa Jaskoll

FOR MIKE — MY OWN BIG BROTHER

SUMMER 1941
WESTERN GERMANY

"I want a brutal, domineering, fearless, cruel youth.
There must be nothing weak and gentle about it."
ADOLF HITLER, 1933

WAR GAMES

We were the only ones left alive.

"It's up to us now," Ralf said. "We'll have to do it on our own."

We were lying in the shaded undergrowth at the edge of the woods, watching a small stone bunker at the opposite end of the clearing. Guarded by a group of uniformed boys, the derelict gray building wasn't much to look at, but it was our target; it was the difference between winning and losing. Every single one of the boys lying dead around us had lost their life either defending it or trying to take it.

I shook my head. "We'll never make it."

Martin grinned at me and his teeth flashed white against his dirty face. "It'll be easy." He was broad and strong — one of our best soldiers. Back in the woods, he'd lifted a boy right off his feet and thrown him down like a sack of potatoes before taking his life.

"But we can't just go running out there," I said. "What if there're others? What if they're waiting for us in —"

"You worry too much." Ralf nudged Martin and nodded,

then they stood and began moving back into the cover of the trees. "We'll distract them; you take the target. Divide and conquer. The only thing that matters is winning."

"What?"

"Just make sure you take the target," Ralf whispered as they disappeared into the forest. "And don't die — because if you do, I'll kill you."

It wasn't long before Ralf and Martin broke from the trees at the far right of the clearing. They came out running, and as soon as the guards at the bunker spotted them, two boys rushed down to challenge them.

Two more boys remained outside the bunker, standing beside the flagpole, scanning the tree line for other attacks. The last boy was still inside and I knew he would be watching, too.

I squeezed my hands into fists, fingernails digging into my palms. *Wait a little longer.*

The two boys who had gone out to meet Ralf and Martin sprinted across the field, giving chase as my friends turned to run, luring them farther away from the bunker. Close to the line of the trees, though, Martin stopped and turned. He lowered his head and rammed his shoulder into the first attacker. The boy went up in the air, over Martin's back, and landed in a heap on the grass. Ralf crouched, hit the fallen boy once, then tore his life away as Martin faced the second, who slowed and put up his hands, ready to fight. Martin shook his head at him and slammed a fist into his stomach, knocking him flat on his back. He leaned down, tore away the boy's life, then raised a hand to Ralf. "You ready?" he called.

"Ready," Ralf replied, and the two of them began walking toward the bunker.

Divide and conquer. Now I understood. With two boys down, and only three left, we would take the target with ease. We had won.

Ralf and Martin were halfway across the clearing, a hundred feet from the bunker, when I decided to leave my position. Before I could stand, though, I saw that we had underestimated the enemy.

They had a plan, too.

Without warning, a unit of ten boys emerged from the woods on the opposite side of the clearing. They came fast, shouting and whooping like devils. Martin and Ralf stopped, jerking their heads around to see the new attackers. Their bodies tensed as if their first instinct was to run, but they looked at one another, nodded, and turned to face the boys.

When the enemy force reached them, Martin was the first to wade in. He windmilled his fists, thumping anything that came close. He smashed noses and cracked jaws, and within seconds, three of the enemy lay flat on their backs. Ralf followed in his wake, bending to rip away the lives of the fallen boys. They took down the enemy group like perfect soldiers.

Watching from the bunker, the guards grew more and more agitated. The bigger of the two gestured at the ongoing battle, while the other shook his head and grabbed the first by the front of his shirt, trying to hold him back. The big guard pushed his comrade away, though, leaving his post and rushing down into the battle. Heading downhill, he picked up speed and crashed into Ralf from behind, knocking him off his feet, sending him flying into the mass of bodies.

I watched in horror as the enemy boy stooped to take Ralf's life.

Now. Go now.

I looked over at the bunker. Just one guard still outside, one inside.

You have to go now.

I jumped to my feet and broke from cover, tearing out into the sunshine. The remaining boys circled Martin like wolves. At the bunker, the guard was watching the battle. He hadn't noticed me.

Halfway there.

My chest was tight with exhaustion and my legs were burning.

"Go on, Karl," someone whispered as I ran past the bodies of my fallen comrades. "You can do it."

Martin was still flailing his fists, but he was weakening, too, and the circle was tightening around him.

"Win, Karl, win," another boy said as I came closer to the target.

Thirty feet from the bunker, the guard inside the building spotted me. His pale face appeared at the window and his eyes met mine, but he didn't react; he just watched me approach as if he didn't care.

The guard outside only saw me coming when I was just a few paces away, but he was too late. I was on him.

I swung my fist as if I were swinging a hammer, and the blow caught him on the side of the face, connecting with a solid thump that knocked him sideways. He collapsed in the grass without a sound and I took away his life before standing to face the final guard, who had left the darkness of the small building and come out to meet me.

In the clearing, the enemy boys closed in on Martin and overwhelmed him, forcing him down and taking his life, but they hadn't seen my attack.

I gritted my teeth and took a step toward the final guard, who had emerged from the bunker.

His shoulders were slumped and his eyes were red as if something had irritated them. He didn't seem to focus on me properly and stood motionless as I took another step closer and put up my fists.

The boy flinched, but did nothing to protect himself. I ripped away his life and pushed him to the ground, then turned to the pole and began raising the flag.

I looked up at the colors of the flag against the cloudless blue sky. Red, as bright as the blood we had spilled that afternoon. A white circle, so clean and crisp, and the bold black swastika at the center of it.

A single, earsplitting blast from a siren pierced the air, signaling the end of the game, then the clearing was filled with the sound of cheering.

"Heil Hitler," said a voice behind me, and I turned to see the area leader coming toward me. Flanked by two Hitler Youth squad leaders, he had been watching the game from a vantage point at the back of the clearing. He stopped in front of me and

looked down, tucking the thumb of his right hand into his belt. He was tall and strong with a square chin and a serious look in his pale eyes. His uniform was perfect in every way, his cap set just right.

"You did well," he said to me. "You'll make a good soldier. *As fast as a greyhound, as tough as leather, and as hard as Krupp's steel.* The words of the Führer himself."

I put my feet together and raised my arm in front of me. *"Heil Hitler."*

The other boys who had been lying dead in the field were on their feet now. Some groaned at their failure, others cheered our victory. They jumped up and down and hugged each other. Boys streamed out from the woods to see who had won, a few scuffles breaking out among them.

The boy at my feet sat up and watched me, biting down on his lip as if to hold back the tears. His name was Johann Weber, and he was in my class at school. He wasn't one of my friends, so I didn't know him well, but something about him had looked different today. Usually he was quick and smart, and when he was boxing, he could run rings around some of the bigger boys. I looked down at the red ribbon-of-life still tied around my right wrist, then at the blue ribbon I had just ripped from him, and wondered why he had given up so easily.

"Just in time," the area leader said, glancing at his watch. "A few more minutes and you would have lost."

"Yes, sir."

"How many did you get?" He gestured at the blue ribbon in my hand.

I pulled a fistful of them from my pocket and counted. "Seven, sir."

"Seven kills? You even have blood on your face."

"Not mine, Area Leader."

"That's good." A hint of a smile touched his lips and he nodded once at me. "Well done; you're exactly the kind of German we need in our army. Hitler would be proud of you. How old are you?"

"Eleven, sir. Twelve tomorrow."

"And what is your name?"

"Karl Friedmann, sir."

HONORED

The Hitler Youth boys marched us to the open-backed trucks and waited while we climbed up. Our uniforms were covered in grime and blood and grass stains, but that didn't matter. We had won.

There were two vehicles parked side by side, one for each squad, and we formed lines, waiting to climb aboard with our comrades.

We sat on the hard metal floor, packed tight together, hot and sweating, our bodies covered in cuts and bruises, but our spirits high.

"That was a good win." Ralf had to shout to be heard over the sound of the engine. "And just in time for your birthday tomorrow."

"Imagine what the British will be like," Christoph shouted. "They'll wet themselves when they see us coming."

"We'll win this war soon enough," Felix said.

"Not before we get there, I hope." I leaned forward to look at Felix. "I want my fair share of the enemy."

"My brother says there are millions of enemies." Martin

reached out and rubbed the top of my head with his knuckles. "Enough for all of us. Even for you, Karl!"

The truck jostled and bustled us for half an hour as it returned to the city, but I was so high on our victory and pleased with myself that I hardly noticed. The journey could have taken three hours and it wouldn't have mattered. My muscles ached with a pleasant tiredness, my skin tingled from the fresh air, and I was surrounded by my friends. To make things even better, our school had let the Hitler Youth take over physical training for a fortnight. The past week of school had been the best ever and there was still another to come. And tomorrow was my birthday, so I was going to spend the whole day with my friends.

When we finally arrived back at school, the truck clattered to a halt and we jumped down into the yard with stiff legs. By now my bruises were beginning to show, but I still felt on top of the world.

The area leader had put some of the older boys from the Hitler Youth in command, and they were shouting orders and organizing us into lines almost as soon as our boots touched the ground. On the adjacent field, to the left of the main school building, the girls were out in the sunshine, running through their exercises, dressed in white tops and black shorts. Most of us couldn't help looking over at them, and one of the boys even whistled, but when the group leader dragged him out and made him do twenty push-ups, everyone soon stood to attention.

As the trucks rumbled away behind us, the last few boys fell into line and the group leader, Axel Jung, began calling our names, ticking them off his list. He strode backward and forward along the line as he shouted the names, glancing up at each "here!" and when every last one of us was accounted for, he dropped his clipboard on the ground and faced us.

He stood with his hands behind his back, flanked by two other Hitler Youth boys, saying nothing for a moment, just casting his eyes along the ranks in front of him. There must have been at least a hundred of us but he showed no sign of being bothered by that.

He looked amazing in his uniform. Strong and brave. He held himself straight and proud like a true soldier, his dagger hanging by his side, and I knew I wanted to be like that — seventeen years old and almost ready to join the war. Trusted and reliable and ready to die for the Führer.

Eventually he sort of pressed himself up on his toes and relaxed back onto his heels before shouting, "Karl Friedmann, step forward."

I was surprised to hear my name called. I marched forward to stand in front of Axel Jung and saluted. He returned the salute, then nodded once before looking out at the other boys.

"Karl Friedmann showed great determination and cunning today. He made seven kills, took the flag, and was the last member of his squad still standing. He is to be awarded the silver proficiency badge."

My heart surged as Axel Jung leaned over and pinned the badge to my uniform. I had wanted one for a long time, and now it was finally mine. It was a single lightning bolt *s* in the shape worn by the Waffen-SS, with a small swastika in the center, surrounded by the words *"Für Leistungen im DJ"* — "for achievement in the DJ." "DJ" stood for Deutsches

Jungvolk, the group we joined before we were old enough for Hitler Youth.

Axel Jung looked down at me once more, then saluted, throwing his arm out straight and saying, *"Heil Hitler."* I did the same, then turned on my heels and went back to my place among the ranks.

As I went, the other boys clapped so loudly that all the girls in the other field turned to see what was happening.

"Well done." Ralf winked at me as I passed him.

I could barely stop myself from beaming as Axel Jung continued with other business, raising his arm and pointing to the far side of the yard, close to the fence. "Losers over there," he said. "Fifty push-ups each."

There were a few groans.

"A *hundred* push-ups."

No one groaned after that. Instead, they all ran over to the fence, dropped to the ground and began grinding out their push-ups. All, that is, apart from Johann Weber.

I noticed him right away, because he didn't run like the others. He half jogged to the fence and was last into position. Then, instead of doing push-ups, he lay prone, nose to the gravel, hands at his sides, as if he had no energy left in him.

"The rest of you, off to lunch," Axel Jung announced. "I will see you after lessons."

Ralf and Martin came straight to my side, wanting to see the badge, and a few others crowded around as we made our way across the yard.

"Get on with it!" the group leader shouted behind us. "No lunch until you've finished."

"You're so lucky," Felix said to me. "I've been wanting one of those for so long."

"Then you should be faster," Martin said.

"I *am* faster," Felix protested. "I beat Karl in the —"

"Not *faster*; you need to be *smarter*," Ralf told him, and I couldn't help feeling a slight tinge of guilt.

"It was your idea," I said to Martin and Ralf. "Divide and conquer."

"Yeah." Martin gave me a playful punch on the arm. "That's true. It was our idea and we put our lives at risk for you."

"But you took the flag." Ralf clapped me on the back and put an arm around my shoulder. "You took seven lives. And your shooting was better than mine yesterday. Anyway," he laughed, "we've got a gold one of those, remember; you haven't caught up to us *yet*."

He and Martin thrust out their chests and tapped the gold badges pinned to their uniforms.

"I don't know how a pair of dimwits like you managed it," I said with a shake of my head.

"You'll pay for that, Karl Friedmann." Martin grinned and waggled his eyebrows at me but I took off before he could make a grab for me.

I ran toward the school building, pumping my arms and legs as quickly as I could, but Ralf ran like a wolf and caught me before I reached the door. Martin was close on our heels, breathing hard, and he grabbed me in a headlock, rubbing his knuckles on the top of my head.

"Submit!" he laughed. "Submit!"

"I submit," I said.

When he released me, Martin put his arm around my shoulder once more. "Come on," he said, "I'm starving."

As we went inside, I glanced back at the losers to see that Johann Weber was still not moving. He was just lying on his front in the dirt.

"Are they letting girls into this group now?" Axel was shouting as he approached him. "Get on with it!"

The boys who had finished their punishment were standing now, laughing as Axel Jung kicked the tip of his boot into the ground, spraying a shower of gravel into Johann's face.

Johann recoiled and wiped a hand across his mouth, then put both palms flat on the ground and pushed himself up, but his head hung down and he was breathing heavily. His whole body looked as if it was wracked with some kind of seizure.

"Maybe you hit him too hard," Martin said beside me.

"I hardly touched him."

Either the effort of trying to do push-ups or the shouting was too much for Johann, because his arms gave in and he collapsed into the gravel once more, his whole body shaking.

Axel Jung grabbed the back of his shirt, pulling him to his feet and ordering him to stand on one leg while the others stood around laughing.

"Stop your sniveling or I'll make you eat this." The group leader scooped a handful of gravel and held it in front of Johann's face.

"Is he crying?" Ralf looked at him. "What the hell's he crying for?"

"Someone said his papa's plane was shot down," Christoph said. "He flew Heinkels or something. They got his death notice this morning."

"And he's crying?" Martin said. "I'd be proud if my papa died for the Führer."

"Me too." Ralf looked at me as if waiting for my opinion.

"Mm, yeah, of course," I said. "And me."

"Come on." Ralf turned me away. "We don't want to miss lunch."

"Yeah." But as I went into the school building, I glanced back at Johann Weber, standing on one leg, and wondered what he was thinking. Why wasn't he proud of his papa?

Lunch was some kind of soup, though no one was quite sure what. There were small pieces of meat and vegetables floating in the murky liquid, and we joked about it, but were all too hungry to complain much.

The dining hall was noisy with boys — the girls had their lunch before us — and we ate surrounded by army recruitment posters and front pages from *Der Stürmer* newspaper, which mostly had cartoons of big-nosed Jews on them. At the very far end of the hall, from a large frame, a picture of Hitler, the Führer himself, watched over us.

As I ate, I looked down at the badge pinned to my chest. I was so proud to have earned it; even though the divide-and-conquer idea hadn't been mine, I *had* been the one to take the flag. Except, I couldn't help thinking about the way Johann

Weber had done nothing to defend himself. Maybe I wouldn't have beaten him if he hadn't been feeling so bad.

I glanced around when the losing boys came in for their lunch, but Johann Weber wasn't among them. Nor had he come into the dining hall by the time we had finished our soup and left the room. He was in the classroom after lunch, though, sitting at the back, staring straight ahead. His eyes were still red, but now his face was covered in small scratches and angry marks.

I wanted to go and speak to him, to ask him what had happened to his papa, but none of the other boys would go near him and I knew it would look bad. Weakness was not allowed. Instead, I sat between Martin and Ralf, with Christoph and Felix in front.

"Why do you keep looking at him?" Martin asked.

"Hmm?"

"You keep looking back at Johann."

I shrugged.

"Don't feel sorry for him," Martin said. "He should be proud, not crying. There's no crying in the army."

"No," I agreed, turning back to face the front just as Herr Kappel came into the room.

We learned about trajectory that lesson. Herr Kappel set up a sand trap in a large box and used a miniature field gun to fire steel ball bearings at it. We took turns angling the gun to see if we could make the ball bearing land on a marker, and I was pleased with myself for being the first to hit the target.

"Must be your day today," Herr Kappel said, nodding toward

my proficiency badge. "And I understand it's your birthday tomorrow."

Thinking about the badge reminded me of Johann Weber, and I glanced over at him, standing slightly apart from the rest of us as if he were somehow different.

Racial science came after the lesson on trajectory, then we were outside again for more physical training. Axel Jung was waiting for us in the yard, flanked by the same two Hitler Youth boys who had been with him earlier. His uniform was still pristine and he stood tall and straight. He waited for us to form into lines, then called out for Johann Weber to come and stand in front of everyone else.

"Have you stopped crying?" he asked.

A few boys snickered but Johann nodded and kept his chin up and his shoulders back. He stared straight ahead as if there was nothing in front of him.

"We don't *cry*." Axel Jung raised his voice over the growing sound of laughter as he marched along the line of boys. "There's no crying in the army. What are you? A Communist? A *Jew?*" His words were thick with disgust.

Tears began to well in Johann Weber's eyes and it made me feel worse than it should have. I was supposed to be as hard as Krupp's steel — on the inside as well as the outside — but I wasn't laughing like the others. I felt sorry for him and had to tell myself not to be so weak.

I took a deep breath and held it in. I had won a medal today. I was going to join the Hitler Youth in two years. I had already learned the oath by heart. I would be like Axel Jung. I would make my family proud.

Jung stopped in front of Johann and looked down at him, staring until the other boys fell silent. "Your papa gives his life for the Führer, and you cry about it? How do you think that would make him feel, knowing how weak you are? You should be *proud*. If you want to be a soldier in the Führer's army, you have to be *strong*. Maybe we need to do something to toughen you up."

Johann lifted his arm and wiped his face with his sleeve. He wasn't standing so straight anymore. His shoulders had slumped and his head was hanging, and when he took his arm away from his face, a string of snot stretched from his nose to the cuff of his shirt.

"Disgusting," someone said from behind me, and a wave of laughter rippled through the ranks.

Jung stepped away from Johann as if he might catch some kind of disease from him. "Shirts off everyone. We're going to have a boxing tournament. Johann Weber against the rest of the class."

KNOCKOUT

We stripped off our shirts and stood bare-chested, with the sun warming our backs. When ordered, we formed a ring around Johann Weber, then Axel Jung stepped into the middle holding a pair of old brown leather boxing gloves in each hand.

He threw them down onto the gravel and turned around, inspecting the boys standing shoulder to shoulder around him. Already some were jostling others, trying to push forward, hoping the group leader would pick them to fight first.

Johann stood with his head bowed as if he didn't dare look up.

"Why don't we have today's champion up first?" Axel Jung had to shout to be heard over the boys begging to be chosen, and when I looked away from Johann, I saw that the group leader had his eyes on me. "You've earned it," he said. "Come on."

I must have hesitated without realizing because Jung furrowed his brow. "What's the matter? Don't want to fight?"

"Course he does." Martin put his hand on my back and pushed me into the ring. "Go on, Karl."

"Yeah, go on, Karl!" Christoph repeated, and then more of them joined in until most of the boys were chanting my name.

"Ka-arl! Ka-arl! Ka-arl!"

I looked around at them, feeling their admiration and excitement, then bent over to pick up the gloves. They were a little too big, but Ralf came forward to tie them for me, then he slapped me on the back and wished me luck.

Turning to face Johann Weber, though, I didn't think I was going to need much luck. He had picked up the gloves and put them on, but his arms were hanging by his sides, the laces trailing past his knees.

Axel Jung held up a hand, signaling for everyone to be quiet. "One-minute round each," he said. "Everyone will get a turn." Then he stepped back, saying, "Begin!"

I took up my boxing stance, left foot in front of right, fists raised in defense, but Johann just stood there.

"Put up your block!" Jung shouted at him.

Johann looked up at me and I saw something other than sadness there. Anger, perhaps.

"Put up your block!" Jung shouted again. He came forward and took Johann's wrists in his hands, dragging them up into a boxing defense.

Johann's eyes narrowed a touch and he snatched his arms away, holding them in place. His lips tightened and the muscles at the side of his jaw bulged.

"Just hit him," Jung said to me as he moved back. "Hit him hard."

I kept my block up and shifted to one side, watching Johann with a strange mix of sympathy and fear. I knew he was upset, and I knew he would be black and blue by the time he had fought everyone, but something was building in him. He stood with his chin tucked under, his fists up and his shoulders heaving as his breathing became heavier and heavier. His face turned red, snot rattled in his nostrils, and his eyes clouded over with tears, but he kept his fists up.

Around me, the others watched with interest. "Hit him," someone shouted from the ring of boys, and suddenly they all found their voices again and began chanting, "Hit him! Hit him! Hit him!"

I edged forward, testing Johann's reaction, but he did nothing.

The boys continued to shout.

I circled one way, then the other.

"Hit him! Hit him! Hit him!"

Johann didn't react to any of my movements. He just stood there, with his hands up, breathing heavily as the tears spilled from his eyes and ran down his cheeks.

"Hit him! Hit him!"

"For God's sake hit him!" Jung shouted.

That's when Johann moved. It was as if all of his emotions had reached boiling point and he opened his mouth to let them all out in one go. "HIT ME!" he screamed, then lunged forward as if to attack.

Almost without thinking, I sidestepped and threw a hard straight punch at his jaw. My fist connected with a jarring thud, snapping Johann's head to one side, and his legs buckled beneath him. He collapsed into the gravel, and for a moment, everything was silent.

I stared down at him, lying there with his eyes closed, then they blinked open and he looked up at me as if he didn't know where he was.

Around me, the other boys erupted in a volley of whoops and cheers, but all I could do was watch poor Johann Weber. With my teeth, I unfastened the glove on my right hand and shucked it off, offering my hand to help him up.

It was the second time I had knocked Johann Weber to the ground that day, and I didn't feel good about it at all.

"What's this, then?" Stefan said almost as soon as I walked into the kitchen.

My brother was four years older than me and we were complete opposites. Me with my uniform and my short hair; him with his long hair and his unruly friends and his terrible attitude. Mama was always telling him he should cut his hair and that his friends would get him into trouble if he wasn't careful. He'd already been arrested once for fighting with boys from the Hitler Youth.

"For achievement in the Deutsches Jungvolk?" He laughed and flicked at the badge pinned to my shirt. "How many times did you have to salute to get that? Or did you just have to jump over a few crouching boys?"

"That's not a game," I said, "that's for fitness."

"Ignore him," Mama told me. "He's just trying to upset you."

I was already feeling upset, though, because Axel Jung had shouted at me for helping Johann to his feet after I'd punched him. He'd said it was weak and made me look bad in front of my friends.

Mama came over and put her arms around me and I half hugged her back.

"I thought they told you not to be so attached to your parents," Stefan said.

"Ignore him," Mama whispered, and kissed the top of my head before going back to preparing supper.

"So what did you learn today?" Stefan sat down at the kitchen table and turned so he could drape one arm over the back of the chair and look at me. "How to click your heels? How to parade up and down the yard? Or maybe" — he helped himself to a piece of bread and pointed the corner of it at me — "maybe you learned about something *really* important, like how people with big noses should be —"

"That's enough, Stefan," Mama scolded him, and gave him a stern look before smiling at me. "What *did* you do today, darling?"

I watched Stefan for a moment, the way he slouched in his chair as he chewed the bread, and I wished he wasn't such a pain. "We had war exercises in the morning with the Hitler Youth —"

Stefan tutted.

"— then we learned about trajectory in class." I told her about the miniature field gun, and that we had talked about how to aim it and how we could use a real one on the battlefield.

"And that's what you want to do, is it?" Stefan brushed his hair from his eyes. "Bombard the enemy?"

"Leave him alone, Stefan."

"Of course that's what I want to do," I said.

"Well, they've done a good job on you." My brother shook his head and looked me up and down, sneering at my uniform —

brown shirt, black trousers, black scarf, and black hat. "Deutsches Jungvolk," he taunted. "More like an army of half-sized soldiers. The sooner you leave school the better."

"*Papa's* a soldier," I said. "Brave and strong, like he should be — fighting for the Führer in Russia, like he should be, isn't that right, Mama?"

"Yes . . ." She hesitated and looked away. "Yes, of course, but —"

"I want to be like *him*," I said to Stefan. "Not like you. I want to be a good German."

"You don't have to wear a uniform to be a good German."

"You only left school so you could get out of the Hitler Youth," I said. "Because you're a *coward*."

"One of those things is right," Stefan said, but he wasn't bothered by my accusation. "D'you know what, though?" He smiled. "Despite everything you just said and despite what you're turning into, you're still my baby brother and I still love you." He popped the last bite of bread into his mouth and stood up. "You *are* going to have to pay for it, though. Say it."

"Never." I took a step back.

"Say I'm the smartest and the best."

"You'll have to catch me first."

"Easy." He grinned.

As I dashed from the kitchen, with Stefan right behind me, I heard Mama calling after us. "Be careful, boys! Don't break anything!"

BAD NEWS

The next day was my twelfth birthday. The day Papa died.

When I came downstairs, there was a small present, about the size of a cigarette tin, in the middle of the kitchen table, wrapped in brown paper and tied with a piece of twine. Mama and Stefan were too excited to wait for Opa and Oma to arrive, and wanted me to open my gift right away, but then there was a knock at the door, and when Mama answered it and returned to the kitchen holding a letter, my birthday was over and my present was forgotten.

Instead, Mama sat and stared at the piece of paper as if she would never blink, then went to her bedroom, where she was quiet for a while before she started screaming.

After that, she screamed and screamed and screamed.

It was the most horrible sound, as if someone was murdering Mama in her room. I froze.

Stefan was quick, though. He was at the top of the stairs in just a few seconds, hammering at the locked door and calling, "Mama! Mama!"

Then other noises came from inside the room. Smashing

and banging and crashing. It was the sound of the world falling apart. My whole body was shaking with fear and I had no idea what to do.

Stefan stepped away from the door when the commotion started. His eyes were wide and he was just as afraid as I was. I crept upstairs and we looked at one another, but before we could do anything, the sounds died down and it grew quiet in the room once more.

"Mama?" Stefan asked.

When she didn't reply, he braced himself and took another step back.

He barged his right shoulder into the door with a solid thump that rattled the whole frame and shook the wall. There was a sharp crack, then he stepped back and did it again, splintering the wooden frame and smashing the door open.

It flew back into the room, slamming against the wall with a bang.

Everything was a mess. Mama had overturned the bedside table and shattered the mirror that had been on the chest of drawers. The wardrobe door was hanging from one hinge and the chair was on its back, one leg smashed.

Sitting on the edge of the bed, with her head in her hands, Mama looked wild. Her hair had come undone and was hanging about her face like a madwoman's. She didn't look up at Stefan when he went in. She didn't react when he sat beside her and held her.

"Help me get her into bed," Stefan said to me, but all I could do was stand and watch as he pulled back the covers and encouraged her to lie down.

*   *   *

"It's just us now." When we went back downstairs, Stefan spoke quietly and there was a distant look in his eyes.

I picked up the letter. It was just a single sheet of thin paper with Papa's name on it. Oskar Friedmann. There were other details, too, but all I could think about was that he had put on his smart uniform and marched away to Russia to fight for our Führer, and now he was never coming back.

"What are we going to do?" I asked.

Stefan squeezed his eyes shut. When he opened them again, he bit his lower lip and looked at me, shaking his head. "We have to take care of Mama." His voice caught in his throat as if it didn't want to come out. "We have to be strong." And then my brother hugged me.

He'd never done that before but I didn't try to stop him. Standing in the middle of the kitchen with my cheek pressed against my brother's chest, I wanted to hold back my tears but they came and came, just like Johann's had done, no matter how hard I tried or how pathetic it made me feel. So I buried my face into his checked shirt — the kind Mama told him not to wear because it was too colorful and could get him into trouble again.

"Maybe it's not true," I said, clinging to the tiniest speck of hope. "Maybe the letter is wrong. Maybe it's someone else."

Stefan said nothing.

"It's not fair. The war was supposed to be short," I sobbed. "It was supposed to be over. Everyone was supposed to give up when they saw us coming."

"That's what they want us to think," Stefan said. "That everything will be all right."

"I thought . . ." I swallowed and tried to organize *what* I thought. It was difficult with so many things spinning through my mind. I hadn't expected the overwhelming feeling of shock and emptiness. "I thought that . . . that I was meant to feel proud of Papa if . . . if . . ."

"If something happened to him, you mean?" Stefan leaned back to look at me, and his face darkened as if he were angry.

For a second, I thought he was going to say something else, but then he bit his lip and wiped his eyes and put his arms around me again, so I just stood and cried against his chest.

Stefan's movement, though, had pulled open his jacket, revealing a white flower embroidered on his inside pocket. It was small, perhaps the size of my thumbnail, and the stitching was crude, as if Stefan had done it himself.

At first, I didn't think anything of it, but it was right there, staring me in the face, and the longer I looked at it, the more I became aware of it.

"What's that?"

"Hmm?"

"That flower."

Immediately, Stefan stepped back and drew his jacket closed. "Nothing." He stared at me, eyes glistening, as if he were wondering what to tell me. When he spoke again, there was a defensive edge to his voice. "It's nothing," he said. "You didn't see it."

"What do you mean? I don't . . ."

"Just forget it." Then his face softened and he closed his eyes. He sighed, letting his breath come out through his nose in one long whoosh. When he opened his eyes again, he said, "Really, it's nothing. It's just a flower."

Stefan took the death notice from my hand, as if the paper were alive. He folded it and slipped it into his inside pocket, and I caught a glimpse of the white flower again.

"We have to tell Oma and Opa," Stefan said. "They're supposed be coming later, but we need them *now*. I'll go on my bike, it shouldn't take me more than an hour." He went to the door and began to pull on his boots.

"I'll come with you."

"No, you stay here. I'll be quicker."

Glancing over at the foot of the stairs, my gaze wandered to the top, and settled on Mama's bedroom door. Then I looked back at my brother. "I don't want to be on my own."

"I won't be long, I promise."

"But . . ."

"You'll be fine." Stefan came over and hugged me once more. "You're strong, remember. You're tough. You're a Friedmann."

"I'll be as quick as I can," he called as he slipped out of the front door and pulled it closed behind him.

I waited for a second, stunned by the speed at which everything had happened, then shook myself and went to the window.

Outside, Stefan was untying his bike from the place where it stood next to mine against the railing. When it was free, he threw one leg over and glanced up at the window. He nodded, then raised his hand and rode away along the pavement.

PAPA

It was deathly quiet in the house. Or quiet and noisy at the same time, which was strange. I could hear the air in the room, hear it moving in and out of my ears and circling my head. The thump, thump, thump of my heart was like the drums when we marched. The kitchen clock was like a ticking bomb, each click of the hidden cogs echoing in my head.

Waiting at the window, I watched the cars and people. A horse and cart went past, loaded with barrels and crates. I felt more alone than ever before. Out there, everyone was carrying on as usual. Ralf and Martin would be doing what they always did; they wouldn't know anything about what had happened to Papa. Then I remembered there was a photograph of Papa in the drawing room, so I went to look at it.

We didn't use that room much; mostly it was for if we had guests, and it smelled musty inside. Mama always kept it clean, but the furniture was old and the soft cushions soaked up the dust. If you banged them out on a bright day, when the sun was streaming through the windows, you could see the dust floating in the air.

It wasn't bright in there that morning, though. The heavy red blackout curtains were still pulled shut, and the only light that came in was from the open door.

My feet were quiet on the worn carpet as I crossed the room. Reaching the sideboard at the far end, I stopped and stared at the unframed photograph propped against an empty vase.

Not much bigger than a playing card, it was a close-up of Papa in his uniform tunic. He was looking just to his left and there was the slightest suggestion of a smile on his lips, as if he'd seen something funny and was trying not to laugh.

A hint of his close-cut hair was visible beneath the cap set at an angle on his head. On the front of the cap was the badge of the German Army; a bold and angular eagle clutching a wreath that circled the swastika.

I often used to sneak in to look at that photograph. Especially after the talks at the clubhouse. Sometimes someone would come from the army or the Nazi party to talk to us about racial theory or tactics or Nazism or just about how special we were. We were the youth, they told us: the future of our country. We were *important*. That always made me feel proud, and afterward, I would come home and creep into the drawing room to look at the photo of Papa, who was out there making the world a better and stronger place.

I wiped a tear from my eye. "I wish you were here," I said to the photograph.

When my grandparents arrived, they came in like a whirlwind. Well, Oma did, anyway.

I heard her before I saw her. The old car pulled up with a splutter and a squeak, and then her voice was there, filling the street, getting louder as she came to the door. If the other people in the neighborhood weren't already awake, they would be now.

". . . to be looked after. I won't take no for an answer," she was saying, and then there was a quick hard knocking at the door, just as I reached it and pulled it open.

Oma wasn't big — in fact, she was quite skinny — and if you saw her from a distance, you wouldn't think she was much of anything. She was neither tall nor short, but had settled somewhere in between. She didn't dress for attention and her face was creased with the same lines that anyone her age would have. But, close up, you could see the fire in her eyes. And when she opened her mouth to speak, you could tell, right away, that she was not a woman to be trifled with.

"Karl," she said, pulling me into her and pressing me against her chest. "You poor, poor boy. Now, where's your mama?" She released me and marched upstairs calling, "Hannah! Hannah! Where are you? Ah, there you are, my darling daughter. I'm so sorry. So sorry about Oskar. He was a good man."

Opa came in a few seconds later. A tall, thickset man who would always stand out in a crowd. He had been a boxer in the army when he was young and he still had something of his athletic build. He did fifty push-ups and fifty sit-ups every morning when he woke and another fifty of each every night before he went to bed. He didn't talk a lot — he always said Oma did enough talking for the both of them — and he had friendly creases around his eyes that stretched right back to his ears when he smiled.

31

He wasn't smiling now, though.

He closed the door behind him and put a hand on my shoulder and nodded. "Be brave," he said.

"Where's Stefan?" I asked.

"Waiting at home. Now go and get your things, you're coming with us."

A NEW HOME

Oma packed a bag for Mama while Opa sat on my bed as I wandered around the room in a daze, gathering a few things for Stefan and myself. I was already wearing my uniform, which I wore most of the time now, so I didn't have much to pack. A few spare clothes, my penknife with the broken handle, some schoolbooks, and my prized copy of the Führer's book, *Mein Kampf*.

Then we were back downstairs and Opa was carrying our bags to the car while Oma helped Mama into the backseat.

"We should never have let you stay in the city," Oma was saying. "The moment this . . . war started and Oskar went away, we should have brought you to live with us."

Mama was a nurse at the hospital and she hadn't wanted to be too far away from work; that's why we had stayed in the city. That, and because she said living with Oma and Opa would get on her nerves. Right now, though, Mama didn't say anything at all. She just stared ahead and let Oma do everything. Her face had taken on a blank expression, and she looked empty, like she wasn't Mama anymore.

"We'll organize everything," Oma said to me. "Don't you worry. Everything will be settled. You're coming to stay with us for a while and that's that. We'll let school know."

"And the Deutsches Jungvolk?" I asked, almost without thinking.

"Yes, yes, of course. We'll tell them, too."

Before we left, I sneaked into the drawing room and went to the photograph of Papa. Something felt final about the way we were going — as if we weren't ever going to come back to this house — so I snatched up the photograph and slipped it into my pocket. At least that way Papa would be coming with us.

In the kitchen, I picked up my present. There was something heavy inside.

"Karl!" Opa called. "We're waiting. Where are you?"

I stuffed the present into my other pocket and left the house.

"What about my bike?" I asked Opa as he turned the key in the front door. "Can't I take it with me?" I rode it to school every day, I rode it to the Deutsches Jungvolk clubhouse, and when I didn't have any meetings, I would go out and cycle around the streets just to make myself fit and strong.

"I'll never get it in the car with everything else," Opa said, glancing at the black vehicle at the side of the road. It wasn't much, but he'd had it as long as I could remember and he loved to tinker with it. He was always leaning over the hood to fix this or that.

When he turned back to me, he saw the look on my face. "I'll tell you what — I'll come back for it after I drop you off. How's that? I'll have to come back anyway to tell school why you're not there."

"And my troop," I reminded him.

"Yes. Them, too." He didn't look right at me, though, and I saw him share a quick glance with Oma.

When we arrived at the redbrick house on Escherstrasse, Oma and Opa took Mama up to the room she'd had when she was a girl. Oma settled her into bed while Opa drove back to get my bike.

"Will she be all right?" I asked Stefan. "She looks funny. Like she's not there."

The two of us were standing alone in the kitchen, not really knowing what to do.

"I think so," Stefan said. "She's . . . sad, that's all."

It was hard to believe that we would never see Papa again. It didn't feel real at all, and I began to imagine that someone would knock on the door at any moment and tell us it was all a mistake.

". . . look after her."

"Hmm?" I looked up at my brother.

"I said, Oma and Opa will look after her. Us, too."

I nodded.

"We'll be fine," he said, but I could tell he was being strong for my sake.

The rest of the day passed in a blur. Mama didn't come out of her room and I didn't eat anything.

Early that evening, I went up to the bedroom where Stefan and I slept when we visited. For years we had spent two weeks of every summer with Oma and Opa, but last year I had come alone because Stefan couldn't leave work.

I stood Papa's photograph on top of the chest of drawers, placing my unwrapped birthday present beside it, then said good night to Papa and climbed into bed.

It was still light outside when Oma pulled the curtains shut and kissed me good night.

When I woke up, though, it was dark. Not just dark, but *pitch-black*. There wasn't a shred of light in the room. And the worst thing was that I'd forgotten where I was. I had this horrible sense that something awful had happened but I couldn't quite remember what it was. My stomach felt empty but heavy. My heart was beating fast and my whole body was covered in sweat.

I sat up, pushing the sheet away. "Mama? Papa?" My voice was weak and scared, crackling from my dry throat.

"Karl?" my brother replied. "You all right?"

I heard Stefan's movement and felt his weight settle on the bed beside me.

"Don't be scared," he said, putting out a hand to find me in the darkness. "I'm here."

Then I remembered. Everything rushed back as if sleep had let it float away and now it was all being sucked back into my head.

Papa is dead. That was the first thought that slammed into me.

Mama is sick. That was the second.

And those two things welled up inside me, drowning me in a terrible, cold sadness that ached in the back of my throat and brought stinging tears to my eyes.

Out in the sunshine, with my friends, all the talk of soldiers and fighting was exhilarating, but everything felt so much worse in the dark, in the dead of night. "I hate this war."

"Me too." Stefan swung his legs up onto my bed and lay beside me, putting his head next to mine on the pillow.

For a time we just stayed like that, not saying anything.

"There's this boy in my class called Johann Weber," I said after a while. "His papa was in the Luftwaffe. No one important, just a —"

"Papa wasn't important," Stefan said. "Only to us. Not to your precious Führer. Not to the army."

"Papa was a sergeant," I reminded him. "An officer. He *was* important."

"Not so important they kept him alive."

"But that's . . . no . . . maybe there was nothing they could do." Stefan's comment made me angry. "He was probably doing something brave like rescuing his men or . . ."

"Maybe you're right," Stefan said to calm me down. "Just tell me about this kid . . . what's his name? Johann someone."

Only, I didn't feel like telling the story now. It didn't seem to matter anymore. "What's going to happen to us?" I asked.

"I suppose we'll stay here until Mama is better. Opa said he can get me a job."

"And I'll go to the local school? Join the town's Deutsches Jungvolk troop?"

"I don't know. I think Oma and Opa want to keep you here for a bit, make sure you're all right. Anyway, maybe some time away from all that stuff would be good for you."

"How would it be good for me?" I turned toward him but it was too dark to see him. I could feel how close he was, though.

"It'll give you some time to think about . . . I don't know," he said, "other things."

"What other things?"

He paused for a moment. "Maybe . . . maybe about what's important."

"The Deutsches Jungvolk is important."

"Yeah, well, it's just that maybe Oma and Opa think Mama's struggled a bit with us. You know, with me getting into trouble last year and then you being so . . ." He stopped as if he were trying to find just the right word. "Well, sometimes it's as if you like all that Nazi stuff a bit too much."

"Too much?" I pushed myself up onto one elbow. "What are you talking about? How can I like it *too much*? I don't understand."

"You will. One day, you will."

"What's that supposed to mean?" I was frustrated and annoyed that he was being so mysterious, and it reminded me of the flower I'd seen inside his jacket earlier that day. He'd been strange about that, too, avoiding my questions.

"And I want to know what that flower is," I said, thinking he might tell me now. "What is it? Does it mean something?"

"Mean something?" He sounded surprised. "Why should it *mean* something? No, it doesn't mean anything. It's nothing. Forget it."

After that, he wouldn't say any more about it, so we just lay there in silence until I fell asleep.

When I next woke, it was light and I could hear movement in the kitchen, so I dressed in my uniform and went downstairs to where Oma was preparing breakfast.

Before I went in, though, I checked the coat hook in the hallway. I opened Stefan's jacket and looked at the inside pocket.

A neat square of cloth had been cut away and the flower was gone.

PRISONER

Life at Escherstrasse was dull and I missed my friends. Oma and Opa wouldn't let me go outside or do anything I wanted to do. It was different for Stefan, though; Opa had a friend who owned the mill just outside town, so he gave Stefan a job right away.

"Stefan needs to be busy," he had said, but I think they just wanted to keep him out of trouble. They had even managed to persuade him to stop wearing his colorful shirts, telling him it was best for Mama and me if he didn't draw attention to himself. They were the kind of shirts that rebellious boys wore — boys who sometimes fought with the Hitler Youth. Stefan wasn't happy about it, but had eventually agreed and started dressing like everyone else.

Stefan left early every morning and came back at five o'clock in the afternoon, dusted with flour. For three days, he stayed at home in the evening, but on the fourth day, he went out on his bike after dinner.

"Where are you going?" Opa had asked him.

"To see some friends," Stefan told them.

"What friends?"

"People I met at the mill."

"People like you?" Opa asked.

Stefan shrugged and I could tell they wanted to stop him, but there wasn't anything they could do; he would have gone whatever they said, so they just stood at the door looking worried as he cycled away.

When *I* tried to go out, though, they told me I had to stay indoors where there was nothing to do.

I was beginning to feel as if I was in prison. It was like being in one of the camps out in the countryside where they kept captured enemies and Jews and other criminals. Stefan went to one of those camps last year, after he got into trouble when someone reported him for fighting with Hitler Youth boys. I was so ashamed when the police took him away, but felt bad about it, too. I didn't know they would shave his head and make him exercise for a whole week. When he came back, he was pale and hardly spoke.

But the worst thing about being at Escherstrasse was that Oma and Opa didn't send me to school or the local Deutsches Jungvolk. The frustration of that built up inside me, mixed with all the awful sadness about Papa and the worry about Mama, making me feel as if I might explode. I couldn't believe they hadn't even let the school and troop know I was there; I was a silver-medal holder, I should at least be going to meetings. I asked them about it a few times but they always said they were busy. The day after Stefan went out on his bike, though, I'd worked myself up into such a state, I couldn't help losing my temper with them.

"I'm supposed to join," I said. "I *have* to; it's the rules."

"I know." Opa looked up from his breakfast. "But . . . the local troop doesn't know you're here yet and . . ."

"I want to go," I said. "I'll get into trouble."

"Not if they don't know you're here, darling," Oma replied. "And anyway, they've got enough boys, so they can manage without you. We see them marching up and down the streets every weekend making all that racket. If you ask me —"

"Claudia." Opa held up a hand to stop her and they exchanged a serious look. "That's enough." He turned to me once more. "The truth is, we think you need a break from everything for a while, to give yourself time to think about Papa."

As soon as he mentioned Papa, an image of the photo popped into my head and my heart grew heavy. The last thing I wanted to do was think about him; that just made me feel worse.

I looked at the tabletop and shook my head. "I want to make some friends." When I'd been with my troop it was as if I had more brothers than I could count; without them, I felt lonely and bored, and upset with Oma and Opa for not letting me go.

"Maybe in a few more days." Opa smiled. "I think you should wait a while."

"But you let Stefan go out. It's not fair."

Opa softened his voice. "Stefan is older. He —"

"He gets into trouble," I said.

"He needs to be busy," Oma told me. "It's better for him." She reached across and put a wrinkly hand on mine. It was covered in small dark spots.

"Well, can I at least go outside, then?" I stared at those brown marks, wishing everything was back to normal. "On my bike?"

"You know we can't let you do that," Opa said. "You have to stay in the yard for now; that way —"

"No one will see me," I finished for him.

He looked at Oma again and then back to me.

"You're hiding me," I said, pulling my hand away. It was as if all my sadness was slowly turning into anger, and that felt much easier than being miserable, so I let it build up in me. "I'm not stupid, you know. You won't let me out in case someone sees me. Because I should have joined the school and the Deutsches Jungvolk. It's the *rules*."

Opa sighed and stood up. He went to the window and looked out at the street. "Karl," he said. "If someone reports that you're here, or if the wrong people see you, we'll all get into trouble."

"Then you should send me to school." My mood was growing blacker and blacker. My hands were shaking and I had to tuck them under my armpits to keep them steady. I felt lost and had no control over what was happening. My anger and frustration was drowning me and I *had* to do something or say something to make it all come out. "Or maybe *I* should report you." I stood up and looked at Oma. "I could walk out right now and go straight to the Gestapo myself —" I stopped myself and Oma recoiled in shock. Her eyes opened about as wide as I'd ever seen them and her mouth formed an O.

"I could —"

"That's enough!" Opa turned around and his face was dark like a thunderstorm. It was the first time I had ever seen him that way and it felt as if electricity had been shot through the room.

"Just . . . just give it a few more days," Opa said after taking a moment to calm himself. "You need to mourn your father. Give it a few more days and then we'll talk about it again. Now, why don't you go and check on Mama?"

I glared at them, lost for words, then pushed back my chair. "Fine," I said as I left the kitchen and stormed upstairs.

ESCAPE

Mama didn't even open her eyes when I sat on the edge of the bed.

She spent all of her time in that room, as if she had decided she didn't want to be alive anymore, and I thought that if we hadn't come to Escherstrasse, maybe she would be better. She wouldn't have been able to sleep all day because she would have had to look after Stefan and me, and I would still be with my friends.

As I watched her, though, the frustration of my conversation with Oma and Opa faded away, and I wondered if Mama didn't want to look at me because I reminded her of Papa. People always said I had his eyes and nose. The way I smiled was the same, too.

From where I was sitting, I could see through the window to the houses on the other side of the road. They were two-story redbrick buildings, just like Oma and Opa's, joined together in sets of three. We were at the end of one block, with a side road next to us, running off Escherstrasse and connecting with a back lane.

The middle house on the opposite block had window boxes just like this one, but Oma's were stuffed full with bright red geraniums while those were empty, and I remembered that when I had come to stay last year, no one had been living in there. Now, though, the front door opened and a woman came out onto the street. She was tall and fair-haired, wearing a plain blue dress and a white apron. She looked left and right, then turned and shouted something back into the house.

A moment later, a girl appeared, pushing a bicycle. It was the same kind as Stefan and I had — black, with a brown leather seat. The girl had a pretty face but didn't have fair hair like the woman at the door. Instead, she was dark-haired and dark-eyed, as if she might have been a second-degree *Mischling* — a person with one Jewish grandparent. She looked about the same age as me and was wearing a school uniform.

I went closer to the window and looked down, wishing I were going to school like she was, and that's when she glanced up and caught sight of me.

For a second, our eyes locked together and she stared right at me.

Then she smiled and waved.

I pulled away from the window as if I'd been caught doing something wicked, and terrible thoughts raced through my mind. Maybe she would report that she'd seen me. Maybe she would tell the Gestapo. Maybe they would come and arrest me for not going to school, and take me away in handcuffs to one of the camps.

I swallowed hard, trying to push the thoughts away as I looked again, edging closer to the window and peering out.

The girl was on her bike now, heading along the road to the right. Her mama was standing in the doorway, watching her ride down Escherstrasse and disappear from view. Seeing her cycle away made me want to go out on *my* bike. I hadn't been outside the house in four days, other than to help Opa with his car that was parked in the back where no one could see.

Even after the girl was long gone and her mama had shut the door, I stared out at the street. Not much happened, though. It wasn't like at home where it was always busy. In the city, there were cars and trams and carts to watch, and all the people going this way and that, but here it was quiet.

I waited a whole ten minutes, counting to sixty ten times in my head, but not one car went past. Not even *one*. The only thing I saw was an old man strolling past with his dog.

"So boring," I muttered, and sat down on the bed again. "Nothing to do."

But seeing the girl on her bike had given me an idea.

Downstairs, Oma was making bread and the kitchen was filled with the smell of the dough.

"I'm sorry for what I said earlier," I told her. "For saying I'd —"

"Never mind about that." Oma smiled. "Come and help me; it'll be fun."

"Cooking?" I asked. "Again?"

"Baking this time." She crushed the dough so that it squeezed out between her fingers. "It's a good thing to learn."

"It's for girls," I told her, as if she didn't know anything at all. "Boys don't cook."

"Is that right? Boys don't cook? So that's what they're teaching you at school these days, is it?" She stopped kneading and looked at me. "Tell me, then, what *do* boys do?"

"At school? Well, there's mathematics and science and how to fight our enemies."

"I see." Oma raised her eyebrows.

"And we learn about making weapons, about trajectory, and about racial theory. And there's running and boxing to make us strong."

"Don't you think Opa is strong?" she asked.

"Yes, but —"

"He sometimes helps me with the cooking. Does that make him weak?"

"It's different. The youth is the future, that's why we have to be stronger. We have to be *swift as a greyhound, as tough as leather, and as hard as Krupp's steel.*"

Oma turned away and sprinkled more flour on the table. "Those are the Führer's words," she said.

"Yes."

Oma lifted the dough to shoulder height and slapped it down on the table, sending a puff of flour into the air. "And the girls learn to cook?" She frowned and seemed to be kneading the dough harder than before.

"Yes," I said. "And how to look after our families, of course."

"I see." Oma stopped and looked me up and down. Her face softened into a sad smile and she came closer, wiping her hands on her apron before touching my cheek. "You know, Karl," she said, "you don't have to wear that uniform all the time."

"I like it."

"Well, it'll have to be washed sometime, you know. You'll have to take it off for that."

"It can be washed and dried overnight," I told her.

"Can it indeed?" she said, raising her eyebrows. "Now, if you don't want to help *me*, why don't you go and see if *Opa* needs some help? He's in the back with his car. Maybe you can do something to take your mind off all this exercise and war."

"But I don't want to take my mind off it. I *want* to exercise. I have to be strong and fit and ready," I said. "The Führer might need me."

"To go to war?" she asked. "Is that what you really want?"

"It's what every boy in my class wants. The teacher promised us we would get our chance."

Oma watched me with glistening eyes. "Even you? Even though you might be killed like . . . ?" Her words trailed into nothing and she put a hand to her mouth. "Oh, Karl," she said as she turned to face the window.

"What is it?" I asked, taking a step toward her. "What's the matter?"

"I'm fine." Oma held up a hand as if to wave me away. "Fine. Why don't you go and find Opa?" Her voice was tight in her throat and I stood for a moment, looking at her back, wondering what was wrong. She waved me away again, though, so I left her standing there and went to find Opa.

At the side of the house, Opa had built a shelter against the wall so he could park his car out of the rain. It wasn't much more than a timber lean-to with a rickety roof, and Oma hated it because their bedroom window looked out onto it. Opa spent a lot of his time under there, tinkering with the Opel Admiral he loved so much.

Right now, the hood was propped open and he was leaning over the engine, cigarette in the corner of his mouth. Oma didn't let him smoke in the house, she said it was dirty, which was probably why he spent so much time working on his car.

He looked like he was busy, so I left him to it. Anyway, I was sick of cooking and fetching tools, so instead, I sneaked down to the shed and wheeled out my bike.

Then I checked to see if Opa was watching and I did something that surprised me.

I broke the rules.

Wheeling my bike along the drive that ran up one side of the yard, I opened the gate and went out into the back lane.

Opa was still bent over the car, head under the hood, cigarette smoke curling around his head. I watched him for a long moment, feeling my heart beating harder. It wasn't too late. I could go back in. I could put my bike away and . . .

The gate clicked shut almost without me realizing I had done it.

Swinging my leg over, I pushed the bike away and cycled along the lane. Once around the corner, I followed the cut-through between Oma and Opa's house and the one next door, then I sped out onto Escherstrasse. Without stopping, I turned and headed in the same direction the girl had gone.

Something about being on my bike lifted my heart.

All my anger dissolved away and a great bubble of excitement and happiness and relief grew in its place. It started in my stomach and rose up my throat and filled me so full that it threatened to make me explode. I had to open my mouth to let it out, and when I did, the fresh morning air rushed in. It blew around my face and brushed over my short hair and swirled around my knees.

It was fantastic.

Amazing.

Brilliant.

For the first time in days, I felt free.

WORDS ON THE WALL

I didn't know where I was going. My feet just pedaled and my hands steered and my mind became blank. I forgot all about Papa dead and gone, and Mama lying in bed for days. I didn't have room in my head to think about Ralf and Martin, Stefan's white flower, or about Oma and Opa keeping me in the house like a prisoner.

The people in the street were a blur as I whizzed by. Men and women who hardly paid any attention to me at all. Everyone just going about their business.

I zipped along the main road, and turned down a side street before racing through a maze of alleyways running along the back of some large houses. The cobbled lanes jiggered me up and down so much that it blurred my vision, but I kept on and on and on. Faster and faster.

Until I saw the writing on the wall.

It was right there, on the bricks at the end of the alley, staring me in the face.

ETERNAL WAR ON THE HITLER YOUTH

As soon as I saw it, I squeezed the brakes and came to a stop.

Written in white paint, each letter was at least as big as my hand. I had seen things written on walls before, but they were always about the Jews, never something like this. Perhaps it was Jews who had written this, as some kind of protest. I stared at those letters, wondering what they really meant and who had written them, and the longer I stared, the more I felt as if they were saying something to me. I just didn't know what it was.

When I closed my eyes, the large white letters seemed to be burned onto the inside of my eyelids.

Eventually, I shook my head and pushed off once more, cycling right at the letters as if I were going to crash through them. I turned at the end of the alley, glad to leave them behind, but as I rode along the next lane, there were more letters painted on the wall beside me.

HITLER

I slowed down and read them as I passed.

IS

These letters were bigger.

KILLING

Written in the same white paint.

OUR

Shining as if they were still slightly wet.

FATHERS

My heart lurched at the message and then tightened at the sight of the symbol painted at the end of the slogan. As big as the letters, it clung to the wall like a giant period.

It was crude, not a very good painting, but I recognized the shape.

It was the same as I had seen on Stefan's jacket.

Once again, I squeezed my brakes and came to a standstill. I stared at the flower, realizing that these words had probably not been written by Jews. If they *had* been, then the symbol would have been a Star of David, not a flower. The star was their emblem.

I tried to make sense of it. It had to mean something. It *had* to.

And my brother, Stefan, was connected to it in some way.

I leaned my bike against the curb and stepped closer to the wall where I could smell the paint. I put out a hand and touched the center of the flower. The paint was still tacky, and when I pulled away, there were white spots on my fingertips. It was fresh; someone had just done this.

If I was quick enough, I might be able to see them.

I jumped back onto my bike and drove the pedals hard, leaving the letters behind. I didn't care about the cobbles now, and I juddered and jerked, the bike wheels slipping on the smooth, uneven stones as I rushed to the end of the alley. I looked each way, deciding to go right, and then I was off again, searching, searching, searching.

Riding up and down the streets and lanes and alleys, I didn't find whoever had painted the slogans. Instead, I found more flowers on the walls, more words telling me that Hitler was killing our fathers, and each time I saw them, I wondered why the Führer would want to kill our fathers. It didn't make any sense.

I must have been cycling for half an hour, maybe more, looking for the vandals, hardly thinking of anything other than those words, when I found myself in front of the school.

It wasn't as big as the school I went to in the city, but there were two large buildings with a good-sized yard and a wire fence surrounding the whole place. Where I was standing, there was a tall, thick pole with an air-raid siren at the top of it like two upside-down dinner plates painted red. When the sirens went off, they made the most terrible racket, so I moved farther along the fence, just in case.

The yard was filled with children. The boys on one side, all in Deutsches Jungvolk uniform and arranged into lines, the girls on the other side, wearing shorts and tops and doing their exercises.

The girls were swinging hoops over their heads and from side to side, but the boys were jumping up and down and doing push-ups. I watched the boys and wished I were with them, making myself fitter and stronger. The more I wished it, the more I felt my anger and frustration rising, as it had done before, and I remembered what I had said to Oma and Opa, that perhaps I should report them.

That would have been the right thing to do: what my group leader would have told me to do, and what my friends would have done — go to the police station or Gestapo Headquarters by the river and report Oma and Opa. Then they'd have to let me go to school and join the Deutsches Jungvolk.

As I was thinking about it, I glanced over at the girls and caught sight of the one I'd seen leaving her house this morning. She was standing in line with the others, twisting her hoop, but she wasn't looking ahead like she was supposed to. Instead, she had turned to watch me, and she was smiling.

I checked behind to make sure she really *was* watching me, and when I looked back, she let go of her hoop with one hand and lifted it — not high, but high enough for me to know she was waving at me.

Which was when the teacher noticed.

"Lisa Herz!" the woman shouted, then turned to see what Lisa was looking at, and caught sight of me right away.

The teacher was a short woman with her hair tied back in such a tight bun that it stretched her face. Her clothes were modest and smart — a dark skirt to her calves and a jacket that matched. As soon as she spotted me, she began marching across the yard in my direction, shouting, "You! Boy!"

I wasn't supposed to be out. I wasn't even supposed to *exist*. Not here. Not in this town. I was breaking so many rules it made my head spin and I froze to the spot. I'd just been thinking about reporting Oma and Opa, and now the reality of being caught was so close, I saw the truth of what might happen if the teacher stopped and questioned me. Maybe she would call the Gestapo and Oma and Opa would get into serious trouble. Maybe the SS would take us all away to a camp like they had taken Stefan.

"Boy!"

Now everyone was looking at me. All the children had turned to see what was happening, and the man who had been instructing the boys was starting to come over, too. As the teachers marched toward me, and all the children stared, an image came into my head. It was like the films we sometimes saw at the theater, except Oma and Opa were the stars of this one. They were sad: shoulders hunched, hands in chains, as they shuffled to the truck to be taken away to a camp. All because of me.

I glanced at Lisa Herz, the girl who had waved, and noticed that she was doing something with her hands. It was hard to focus because so many things were going through my head, but she was doing *something*.

What is it? What is she trying to tell me?

She kept her hands low so no one would notice, but she was flicking them at me as if shooing away a cat.

"Go," she mouthed. "Run."

And that was it. The spell was broken.

I grabbed my bike and began wheeling it away as fast as I could, putting one foot on the pedal as the teachers came closer to the fence.

"Stop!" the man shouted.

I swung my other leg over and used the momentum to push down hard on the pedal.

"Come back!"

I was rushing away now, the wind flying about me once again, my heart racing and thumping in my chest.

I pedaled hard and fast, but this time the excitement was long gone. Instead, I was filled with feelings I hardly understood as my thoughts twisted together: the fear of being caught, of Oma and Opa getting into trouble, the shame of imagining myself reporting them.

I put my head down, hunched over the handlebars and worked and worked and rode and rode and pedaled and pedaled and went faster and faster and faster.

I raced away from the school without glancing back, turning this way and that, hurtling through the streets and rushing down a cobbled alley that shook the bike and rattled my bones. The walls flew past on either side but I hardly noticed them as I bumped and jostled and headed for the end of the alley and shot out into the road.

The blast of the horn snapped me out of my confusion.

A loud, sharp, long blast that was too late to warn me.

Then everything was slow motion.

To my right, I saw a black Mercedes car heading straight for me. It was shiny and sleek, with a glimmering silver bumper that reflected the morning sunshine.

The driver's eyes opened wide in surprise and he leaned back in his seat, arms outstretched, fingers gripping the wheel as he jammed on the brakes.

The car screeched toward me and I closed my eyes and felt the shock of the bumper smashing into my bike.

Then I was in the air.

For what felt like a good ten seconds, I touched nothing and nothing touched me.

I was flying.

Floating.

Falling.

Hitting.

I landed on the road with a sickening crunch.

My hands touched the ground first, then my elbows and my knees as I skidded across the hard surface, scraping my skin and getting tiny pieces of grit in my flesh. My chin cracked against the curb, clattering my teeth together, and I came to a stop with an "oof" that shot the air out of my lungs.

". . . all right?" someone was saying. "Boy?"

I opened my eyes to see a pair of shoes close to my face. Shiny black shoes.

". . . hear me?"

Someone put a hand on my shoulder and shook me. He seemed fuzzy, my head was a jumble, and my vision was blurred.

"Are — you — all — right?" the smart-suited man asked as I turned onto my back and sat up.

There was blood on my palms and little black spots of grit under my skin. My knees were the same, and as soon as I looked at them, they started to throb with pain.

A few people had stopped on the opposite side of the road to see what had happened. Some had come to the windows of their houses when they heard the crash, or had ventured outside and waited by open doors, but none of them came to help. None of them came near except for the man in the suit.

"Do you always rush out into the road without looking?" Every word seemed to drip with poison.

I shook my head. "I'm sorry."

"Well, I don't think 'sorry' is going to fix my car, is it?" He waved a hand at the vehicle and I looked across to see a faint dent in the shiny bumper. Hardly much more than a scratch.

"Or your bicycle," he said.

My bike was lying ten feet away, at the side of the road, the front wheel bent out of shape.

"It can go for scrap," the man said. "To help the war effort." He turned around and looked at the people on the other side of the road. "Someone bring this boy a damp cloth and a glass of water."

For a moment, no one moved. They stared at the man in the suit, then glanced at one another.

"Come on," he snapped. "One of you. Get on with it."

It was as if the man in the suit had reached out and slapped them each on the face. Suddenly, they were breaking apart: some of them going back into the houses, others rushing toward the shop on the corner.

"We haven't met," he said, looking down at me. "So perhaps I should introduce myself. My name is Gerhard Wolff. Kriminalinspektor Gerhard Wolff."

The man from the Gestapo.

TRUTH AND LIES

Kriminalinspektor Wolff didn't help me to the car so much as drag me to it. He took one of my arms, hauled me to my feet, and marched me toward the glimmering Mercedes.

"Don't get in until you're clean," he said, opening the rear door and sitting me down on the edge of the rim. "This car was just washed this morning. Now, let me see your hands."

I hesitated.

"Your hands, boy, hold them out."

I put them both out in front of me, palms to the road, but Wolff continued to stare at me.

His eyes were like steel. Hard and gray and cold. His nose was slightly crooked as if it might have once been broken, and his lips were thin. He had a strong jaw and his forehead was lined with experience. His blond hair, flecked with gray, was neatly combed into a side part. His suit was clean and well pressed, and he gave off a strong sweet smell of aftershave.

When he looked down at my hands, he took a pair of black-rimmed spectacles from his pocket and put them on, leaning closer. "Turn them over."

I did as I was told.

"Tell me about this." He pointed at the white blobs on my fingertips. "Have you been painting?" He looked at me as if he could see right inside me.

"No, I . . ."

"The truth," he said.

"I touched the wall. In the alley. There was a flower."

"Was it you?" he snapped. "Have you been painting walls?"

"No, sir. I promise."

"Turn out your pockets."

I dug into the pockets of my shorts and pulled them inside out to show him they were empty apart from my penknife with the broken handle.

"How old are you?"

"Twelve, sir."

He stood straight and stared down at me, with his eyes narrowed and his thin lips held tight together as if he were deciding whether or not to eat me.

"Stay where you are."

Kriminalinspektor Wolff walked around to the front of his car to inspect the damage. Standing with hands on his hips, he shook his head, distracted only when a woman approached him, carrying a glass of water and a damp cloth.

"Over there, over there." He waved a hand in my direction, his voice thick with impatience.

The woman came and crouched beside me, offering the glass.

"Thank you." The water was cold and refreshing.

"Are you all right?" She spoke quietly as she put the damp cloth to my knee and wiped away the blood with short, gentle strokes. "That was quite a bump." She had blond hair tied back in a bun, and kind light brown eyes. "Nothing hurts too much?"

I thought I would look weak if I allowed even one tear to fall, so I wiped my sleeve across my face and shook my head. "I'm fine," I said. "Fine."

The woman nodded like she didn't really believe me. "Don't let him frighten you."

"I'm not frightened."

She glanced across at Wolff, who was bent at the waist, inspecting the front of his car, and as she watched him, her eyes flickered and her breathing quickened. The skin on her cheeks paled. It was the same thing I saw at school on the faces of boys who were singled out for punishment. It was a mixture of hatred and fear, and I wondered if she had done something wrong; perhaps she was hiding something from the authorities.

When she looked back at me, she forced a reassuring smile and finished cleaning one knee, moving on to the other. "I'll look after your bicycle for you," she said. "You can come back for it when you're ready. You'll be able to get back here? You know where you are?"

"I think so."

"Good. Try not to —"

"Enough of that," Wolff said as he came to stand behind her. "Give him the cloth and get out of the way."

She started to get to her feet.

"Well, come on." He grabbed her arm and pulled her up. "Out of the way. And you, boy, get in the car. Hurry up."

The woman pushed the cloth into my hands and took the glass without saying anything else. She backed away, turned, and walked to her house without so much as looking over her shoulder. It was amazing that this man Wolff could have such an effect on someone and I was both impressed and afraid at the same time. I could only imagine what it would be like to have people obey your every command without question.

"Get in," he said.

Wolff slammed the door shut behind me before settling into the driver's seat and starting the engine.

"Where do you live?" he asked as we drove away.

"Escherstrasse, sir."

"Speak up."

I told him again.

"Ah," he said. "Escherstrasse. It's not far."

I made no attempt to clean my elbows with the cloth. I just sat on the cold leather seat and stared at the back of Wolff's head. His hair was very tidy and there was a difference in thickness between where it was a little longer on top and closely shaved at the bottom.

"Your name?" he demanded.

"Karl Friedmann, sir." The inside of the car smelled strongly of his aftershave and it made me feel sick.

He nodded. "Well, Karl Friedmann, I find myself wondering why I don't know you. This is not a big town and I know all the faces. Especially the faces of young boys with silver medals pinned to their uniforms." He half turned his head, as if he were about to look over his shoulder. "You are, after all, the future of our great nation, are you not?"

I put a hand to the badge on my chest and a memory of better times flashed in my mind. "Yes, sir."

"So, why don't I know you?"

"I'm from Cologne, sir. Staying with my *Oma* and *Opa*."

I had told the woman that I wasn't scared of the Gestapo officer, and that was partly true. He made sure people didn't betray our country, and kept Germany strong, so that was something to admire. Everyone was at least a little bit afraid of the Gestapo, though, and there was something about Gerhard Wolff in particular that made me uncomfortable.

"And who is your grandfather?" he asked.

"Walther Brandt, sir."

"Ah. Herr Brandt." Kriminalinspektor Wolff nodded. "So your mother is . . ." He thought for a moment. "Hannah. Hannah Friedmann."

"Yes."

"And you father is Oskar Friedmann, correct?"

I nodded.

"So, tell me, Karl Friedmann, why are you not at school today? The school is open; you should be there. Even if you *are* just a visitor to our patriotic little town."

"I . . ." This was my chance to report Oma and Opa, but all I could think about was them being taken away to a camp and punished.

"Well?" he pressed me. "What do you have to say for yourself? Speak up, boy. Why weren't you at school?" He looked at me in the rearview mirror of the car, and when his eyes met mine, I saw a cruelty in his stare that made my insides turn to ice.

Now I felt afraid for Oma and Opa, but I had to tell the truth. What else could I do?

"Oma and Opa wouldn't let me. They said I needed time, sir, after what happened to Papa."

"And what was that?" Wolff asked.

I looked down at my knees. "He was killed."

"Where?"

"Russia, sir. He was in the army."

"Then you should be proud of him."

"Yes, sir."

"So tell me about this painting on the wall," Wolff said. "Do you remember where it was?"

"No, sir."

"You don't remember or you don't want to tell me?" He looked at me in the mirror once again.

"I was lost," I said, watching out of the window.

"I see. And what did it look like, this . . . work of art?" He said that last part with heavy sarcasm.

"It was words, sir. And a flower."

"What kind of words?"

"I . . . well, I don't want to say, sir."

"Something about the Hitler Youth? Or perhaps about our beloved Führer?"

"Yes, sir. Both of those."

Kriminalinspektor Wolff sighed and tapped his fingers on the steering wheel. "It wasn't you, was it? You're not one of those troublemakers, are you? Because, I should tell you, I don't like troublemakers."

"No, sir. I promise it wasn't me."

"And you don't know anyone who might do something like that? You've never seen the flower before?"

I tried not to think about what I'd seen in Stefan's jacket.

"No, sir." My mouth was dry when I spoke. The lie stuck to my tongue as if it wanted to give me away.

"You're sure about that?"

I could feel Wolff's eyes on me but resisted the temptation to look at him in the mirror. I was afraid he would know what I was thinking. Instead, I watched the streets and houses scroll past. "Yes, sir. I'm sure."

Wolff was quiet for a moment before he spoke again. "I believe you, Karl Friedmann. I think you're a good boy. I'm not wrong, am I?"

"No, sir."

"Let's hope not." After that, he remained silent for the rest of our short journey, but he felt like a dangerous monster sitting in the front of the car and all I could think about was how afraid I was for Oma and Opa, about how maybe this man didn't deserve any of my admiration at all, about the expression on the woman's face when she had looked at him.

She had been terrified of Gerhard Wolff.

WOLFF IN THE HOUSE

When Opa came to the door, he looked at Wolff with surprise and alarm, but as soon as he saw the state I was in, his expression changed. He reached out with one hand, and was about to speak to me when Wolff marched me into the house, making Opa stand aside.

"Who is it, Walther? Who —" Oma's face fell when we entered the kitchen and she laid eyes on the Gestapo officer. "Oh. It's you."

"This boy is your responsibility?" Wolff said, throwing a glance at her.

"Yes," Opa said, coming in behind the officer. His voice sounded tight and tense. "What happened?"

Once Oma had overcome her shock, she came straight to me, wiping her hands on her apron and bringing me to sit down at the table. "What happened, my darling? What happened to you?"

"Not at school," said Wolff. "Racing through the streets on his bicycle, is what happened to him."

Oma glanced at him for just a second before looking back at me. She opened her mouth but it took a moment for the words to come out. When they did, she had to clear her throat and she spoke quietly. Her tongue clicked as if her mouth were dry. "Let's get you cleaned up, shall we?" She took the cloth from my hands and dropped it into the trash before taking a medical kit from the cupboard beneath the sink. Oma used to be a nurse, just like Mama, so she always had a few things under the sink for emergencies.

"Does it hurt?" she asked. "Can you walk all right? Can you move your arms?"

"He's fine," Wolff said. "He's a strong —"

"He's a *child*," Oma interrupted him. "A twelve-year-old child."

Wolff's expression hardened. "He's lucky to be alive. And you two have some explaining to do. A child of this age should be at school."

Oma and Opa exchanged a look of worry.

"His papa was killed," Oma said as she wet a cloth and wrung it out. "His school and troop know about it. He needs time to —"

"Whatever happened to his papa, he shouldn't be out on the street where he can damage my car," Wolff said.

"Of course," Opa agreed. "I'm very sorry. It won't happen again."

Oma's fingers shook as she cleaned my cuts and bruises. Wolff strode around the kitchen, looking in the drawers as if he owned the place. He didn't ask for permission, he just put his nose into everything. He seemed to fill the room, and the smell of his aftershave overpowered everything else in the kitchen.

He removed a can from one of the cupboards, opened the lid, and sniffed. "Coffee," he said. "*Real* coffee. And plenty of it."

"From Herr Finkel's shop," Oma said.

Wolff looked across at Oma. "How is it that you have so much coffee and I have none?"

"It's from Herr Finkel's shop," Oma repeated as she dabbed disinfectant onto my knees. "We paid for it with —"

"Cigarettes, too," he said, taking four packs from the back of the cupboard. "German. Good ones."

"They're from Herr —"

"— Finkel's shop, yes, yes, so you say." Wolff waved a hand. "How lucky that Herr Finkel's shop is so well stocked. He must be quite a resourceful businessman. For me, these things are not so easy to come by." It was as if Wolff were trying to sound pleasant, but there was a suspicious and accusing edge to his voice.

Wolff put two packs in each of his jacket pockets and turned his hard gray eyes on Oma. "We are becoming a nation of black marketeers even without the Jewish influence," he said.

"They're not black market," Oma protested.

"You know, some people are already hoarding, filling their cellars like little hamsters," Wolff said. "It's the kind of behavior that undermines the strength of the Fatherland."

"You'll find nothing in our cellar but old furniture."

"Hmm." Wolff stared at Oma for a moment, then put the coffee can on the table and replaced the lid. "You *are* a member of the party are you not, Herr Brandt?"

"Yes," Opa said.

"Card and badge."

Opa nodded and left the kitchen. Wolff looked around once more, then followed him, their footsteps receding along the hallway to the drawing room.

"What were you thinking?" Oma whispered when he was gone. "We were so worried about you. Why did you run off like that?" Her voice was trembling.

"I'm sorry." I'd never seen Oma look so frightened. "What's going to happen?"

"I don't know," she said, fumbling with the bandage she was putting on my knee, "but you're all right and that's what's important. Everything else can be dealt with."

When Opa came back into the kitchen, Kriminalinspektor Wolff was close on his heels.

"I want you to go upstairs." Opa was now wearing a Nazi party badge, pinned to his shirt, and I wondered why he hadn't been wearing it before. "Don't come down until we call you," he said in a near whisper. "And don't be afraid. Everything will be fine."

"I'm sorry," I said.

"You have nothing to be sorry about," he replied. "Now, upstairs."

I turned to do as I was told but Wolff blocked my way for a few long seconds, as if he wasn't going to let me leave. He stared down at me with almost no expression at all, unblinking, his eyes fixed on mine.

I couldn't look away from him. My mouth went dry and my heart quickened. He wasn't a big man like Opa, but he *seemed* bigger, as if he could squash me with one swipe of his hand.

Then he grinned, showing me a flash of teeth, and moved aside so I could hurry upstairs to Mama's room.

I wanted, more than anything, for Mama to comfort me but she was fast asleep and didn't even move. I watched her for a moment, feeling lost, then went into my own room and changed out of my dirty uniform, putting my silver medal on the chest of drawers beside the photograph of Papa.

Wearing a white shirt and nonuniform trousers, I stood at the window and listened to the mumble of voices from downstairs. On the road below my bedroom window, Wolff's Mercedes was hunched at the roadside like a sleek and brooding beast. The sunlight glinted from the silver-colored bumper and I couldn't see any scratches from here. There wasn't much damage at all. My bike was in much worse condition. I'd probably have to ask Opa to help me get it, because the front wheel was all buckled and I'd never be able to ride it in that condition. In fact, I might not be able to ride it ever again if I couldn't find a new wheel.

I sighed and was about to move away from the window when Wolff emerged into the street. I pressed my face closer, pushing my nose against the glass so the top of Opa's head was just visible, too.

Wolff stood straight with his shoulders back and his head up. He was so stiff, he looked as if he might have a plank of wood stuck up the back of his suit jacket. As he spoke, he lifted his right arm and pointed a finger at Opa. He shook it as he spoke, punctuating each word, then he turned and strode to his car, yanking the door open.

"I hate you," I whispered, remembering how he'd spoken to me when he knocked me off my bike. "I hate you."

And he looked up.

Gerhard Wolff stood beside his gleaming car and looked up at the window and saw me when it was too late for me to pull away.

So I forced myself to stare back at him.

He kept his eyes on mine and grinned like before. Then the grin was gone, as quickly as it had appeared. It just fell from his face as if it had never been there, and he climbed into his car and pulled the door shut.

The engine started with a growl and Wolff's car pulled away from the side of the road and sped along Escherstrasse. When it reached the end, it turned left and I stared at the empty road, hoping I would never meet Wolff again.

TROUBLE

When Kriminalinspektor Wolff had gone, I crept down to the kitchen. Oma was sitting at the table, still in her apron, staring at the tabletop like Mama had done when we received Papa's death notice. For the first time in my life, I thought Oma looked old. I'd never known her so tired and gray.

Opa was standing beside her, hands in his pockets, also staring at the tabletop, as if there was something on it that was enormously interesting.

Oma turned her head and shifted her gaze to look at me, but the two motions didn't happen together. She had to *tear* her eyes away, and she didn't focus at first, as if she wasn't sure who I was, then she shook her head and made a smile come to her lips. "Darling," she said, holding out both arms. "Come here."

I thought they might have shouted at me, and her actions took me by surprise.

"Come," she said again, so I went to her and let her hug me.

She crushed me against her bosom and I looked at Opa, who smiled in a way that didn't reach the corners of his eyes like it usually did.

"Am I in trouble?" I asked.

"No, no," Opa said. "Everything's fine. You're not in any trouble."

"I shouldn't have gone out," I said. "I'm sorry."

"Nothing to be sorry about." Opa, glanced down at the tabletop again.

Now that I was closer, I could see what he was looking at: his Nazi party membership card.

"I didn't mean to . . ." My thoughts were all muddled. "I didn't want to . . ."

"It's all right," Oma reassured me.

"What did he say?" I asked.

Opa pulled out a chair and sat down. "Well, he said that you will start at the school here in a week. And the Deutsches Jungvolk at the same time. Isn't that good?"

I shrugged.

"Aren't you pleased?" Oma asked. "I thought it's what you wanted. You'll be able to join the other children your age and —"

"What about you?" I asked. "Did you get into trouble?"

"It's nothing," Opa said. "I have to go to more meetings, that's all."

"Meetings?" My eye was drawn to the badge he now wore on his shirt. It was a perfect white circle surrounded by a red border that was fine-lined with silver and printed with letters proclaiming *National-Sozialistische D.A.P.* The Nazi Party.

Right in the center of it all, black as coal, was a swastika.

"The Party has meetings at the town hall," Opa said. "I haven't been for a long time, so . . . well, I have to go and come back with a signed document. Then I have to report to Kriminalinspektor Wolff once a month to show that I've been."

"Why haven't you been going? Don't you want to?"

"Don't ever say that." Oma spoke quickly and quietly as if she were afraid of something. "Don't ever say Opa doesn't want to go to those meetings. Don't *ever* say that. Of course he wants to go."

Lunch was boiled potatoes with herring sauce and a small dollop of sauerkraut. I didn't like any of it, and wasn't hungry after everything that had happened, so I pushed it around my plate, not saying much.

"Eat up," Oma said, and I took a forkful, swallowing the sauerkraut without chewing.

"And drink your milk. It'll keep you strong. Mind you, I'm sure they're taking out more and more of the fat. It's getting more watery as the days go on."

Picking up my glass, I looked across at them sitting side by side and thought about what it would be like if Oma and Opa weren't here, if I were alone with Mama, silent and deathlike, upstairs. When I was at school with Ralf and Martin, the idea of people being punished for not following the rules felt right, but I wasn't so sure now.

When lunch was finished, I helped Oma in the kitchen for a while, then tried reading a book in the drawing room but I couldn't settle or concentrate on anything.

"Is it all right to go outside?" I asked.

"Of course," Oma said. "Opa is in the back —"

"I mean out the front. I thought I'd sit on the doorstep for a bit."

"Watch the world go by?" Oma asked.

"It's warm there. It's right where the sun lands."

Oma thought for a moment. "Well, I don't suppose it can do any harm. You have permission not to be at school now for another week, so it doesn't really matter."

That's what took me to the front step. I told myself it was because I wanted to sit in the warm rays and watch the cars and the people pass by, but there was another reason why I wanted to go out. Something I hadn't even had time to think about.

I wanted to see *her*.

I wanted to be sitting there when the dark-haired girl came home from school, so I could wave at her the way she had waved at me.

WOODEN FLOWER

Escherstrasse was long and straight, and right at the end of it, a white-and-black blur was coming toward me. That's all it was — a blur — but as it came closer, I could see it was someone on a bicycle.

Closer still and I knew it was a girl in a white shirt and black skirt.

Then she was just ten feet away, and I lifted my hand and waved.

The girl slowed and came to a stop on the other side of the road. She raised a hand and waved back, and I thought that would be it. I thought she would knock on her front door, disappear inside, and that I'd wave to her again another time. It hadn't been that difficult.

She didn't knock on her front door, though. She *looked* at it, but then she looked at me again. She climbed off her bicycle and leaned it up against the wall beside her front door.

And then she was coming toward me.

A girl.

I hardly ever spoke to girls. At school we were separated,

and the Deutsches Jungvolk was just for boys. The girls had their own groups; Jungmädel for girls my age, then the Bund Deutscher Mädel for when they were older. We were even told not to mix with girls, so I didn't know what I would say if —

"Hello," she said.

I must have looked like a simpleton, the way I stared. "Uh. Hello."

"What happened to you?" she asked, pointing at my bandages.

"Oh. I . . . I fell off my bike."

"Not surprised, the way you rushed off like that. What were you doing anyway? If you want to skip school, it's not a good idea to come and stand by the fence."

Close up, her hair was even darker than it had seemed from farther away. It was braided into pigtails, just how most girls wore it at school. She had dark eyebrows and dark eyes, too. Her uniform was quite dirty and her socks were ruffled at her ankles, revealing shins that were covered in bruises — old and new. Both her knees were grazed, but not as badly as mine.

She stood on the pavement, with her hands on her hips, and looked down at me with her brow furrowed. "What's your name?"

"Karl Friedmann." I stood up with the step against my heels, stopping me from moving any farther back. It felt as if we were very close and I could smell her. It was a mixture of soap and the outdoors.

"I'm Lisa," she said.

I didn't know what to say after that. "Umm . . ." I thought for a moment. "Umm . . ." I was stuck for something to say so I said the first stupid thing that popped into my head. "Are you a *Mischling*?" I asked.

Lisa's face darkened as if a storm cloud had passed over it. "That's a bit rude, isn't it?"

"I didn't mean to . . . I just . . ."

"No, of course you didn't mean to. You're just a silly boy who thinks girls are from another planet and doesn't know how to talk to them."

"I . . ." I looked at the pavement, feeling my cheeks flush. They grew hot and I was sure my whole face had turned beet red.

Lisa sighed. "Well, Karl Friedmann, no I am not a *Mischling*. Not even second-degree *Mischling*, and if you're going to talk to girls, then you need talk to them exactly the same way you talk to boys."

"Sorry." I made myself look her in the eye.

Lisa waited for a moment, still with her hands on her hips, then the storm cloud vanished as if it had been wiped away. "I forgive you, Karl Friedmann." She put a hand in her pocket. "Do you have any money?"

"No."

"Well, never mind. I've got ten *Reichspfennigs*." She pulled out two silvery coins and showed them to me, as if to prove it. "Come with me." She turned and began walking back along the road, in the direction she had first arrived from. "Come on."

I looked from Lisa to the front door and then back again, wondering what to do. If I was going to go somewhere, perhaps I should let Oma and Opa know.

"Come *on*," she said. "We're just going along here. It's not far. It's not as if you're running away."

So I jogged to catch up and we walked side by side with the warm afternoon sun on our backs.

"It's good to see you're not wearing that silly uniform for a change," she said.

I tried to think of when she might have seen me. Oma and Opa had been so strict about keeping me inside that I'd hardly been out at all over the last few days.

"I see you at the window sometimes," she said, as if she knew what I was thinking. "And when you went to the shops with your *Oma*. She *is* your *Oma* isn't she?"

"Yes."

"Anyway, I like the white shirt better. Your brother sometimes wears a blue one and it looks smart. Maybe you should get a blue one."

"What do you know about my brother?" I asked.

"He waves to me in the morning, which is more than you managed. Until today, that is."

"I'm not supposed to be here," I said. "Oma and Opa are hiding me. Or, they were until the Gestapo man hit me with his car."

"The Gestapo man?" She stopped walking and turned to look at me. "You were knocked off your bike by the man from the Gestapo? Kriminalinspektor Wolff?"

"Yes."

Lisa's face darkened. "I hate him," she said. "He's a pig."

I was shocked by her insult, and looked around to see if anyone had overheard, but the street was more or less deserted here.

"Do you know him?" I asked.

"Everyone does. Someone at school said he worked for the baker when he was our age. Delivered bread on his bicycle before he joined the police. Now he's just a Gestapo pig."

"Shh." I looked around once more.

"What did he say to you?" She lowered her voice.

"Umm . . . he was just angry that I damaged his car, and —"

"So do you have to go to school now? Is he making you go to school?"

"He said I could stay off for a few days because —"

"Lucky you." She turned and carried on walking.

I watched her for a moment, braids bouncing on her shoulders, arms swinging, then I trotted to catch up. "Why?" I asked her. "Why am I lucky? At school we learn about —"

"School's boring."

"What?" I'd never heard anybody other than Stefan say that and I looked around again to make sure no one was listening.

"So why did he say you could stay off school? Is your mama ill? My mama said she looked ill when she arrived and that she hasn't seen her since. Is she ill?"

"I . . . Yes, I suppose. I don't really know. She's sad, I think."

"Sad?"

"My papa died," I told her. "The enemy killed him."

"Oh, that's horrible."

"We should be proud of him, though," I said, remembering the words of my squad leader. "He was doing his duty for the Führer."

Lisa looked at me as if she was giving that some serious thought. "Before he went away, my papa said the war was the Führer's fault."

"Well, that's not true, he's *winning* it for us."

"Hmm. Mama never says it's his fault, but I think she's too scared."

"Of what?"

"Well, everything. Sometimes I even think she's scared of me."

"You?"

"Uh-huh. Scared that I'll report her. Some children do that, you know."

I felt a stab of guilt when she said that, and tried not to think about what had happened to Stefan, or the thoughts I'd had about reporting Oma and Opa. We fell into a silence that lasted all the way to Herr Finkel's shop.

There was a line of women outside the shop, all of them holding empty baskets. Two of Oma's friends from farther along Escherstrasse were there, Frau Amsel and Frau Vogel, deep in conversation as they waited. The lines seemed to be getting longer every day.

"You want to see if he's got any chocolate?" Lisa asked, joining the line and pulling the coins from her pocket once more. "I have enough."

The silver coins looked big in her small hand, and the sun glinted off them, highlighting the eagle holding the swastika.

I looked at Lisa's dark eyes, which now I thought about it, were almost the color of chocolate. She had a round face, emphasized by the way her hair was pulled back into those tight braided bunches, and a nose that the doctors probably said was a bit too big when they measured it at school. It was a nice nose, though, all the same. Despite being dark-haired, Lisa's skin was quite pale, and that made her rosy cheeks stand out all the more. She looked pretty — not in the proper German way that we learned about at school, but in a different way. In a more *real* way.

"You always stare at people?" she asked.

"Hmm?"

"You're staring."

"Oh. Sorry. It's just, I don't know, I suppose I was thinking it's kind that you said you'd share."

"Well, that's what friends do, isn't it?"

So, just like that, Lisa and I were friends. No oath, no swearing-in ceremony, no rituals or exchange of punches. Just a few words, and that was that. Friends.

I couldn't help smiling.

"What?" she asked.

I shrugged. "Friends. It's . . . nice." I held out my hand for her to shake. I don't know why. I just felt as if I needed to fix the friendship in some way.

Lisa glanced at my hand, then smiled and looked me in the eye. "Really? A handshake?" She shook her head. "You're funny, Karl Friedmann."

The line moved in front of us as two women left the shop, so we shuffled closer toward the door. One of the women was Frau Oster, who lived over the road from Oma and Opa, a few houses down from Lisa. She was younger than Mama, slim and with mousey hair held back from her narrow face. Her husband was fighting in Russia, just like Papa had been, except he was a panzer driver in the SS. Oma said that you'd think he was a general, the way Frau Oster talked about him.

"It's not getting any better," she complained to her friend as she passed. "There's still not enough to go around. I don't know how long this can go on." She was carrying a folded copy of *Der Stürmer* at the top of her basket.

"Not much longer, Monika. Hitler will win this war for us soon enough and then . . ." The rest of the conversation was lost to me as the women moved along the street.

The man on the radio told us that everything in Britain had been rationed since the beginning of last year. Things were better here, but they were getting worse. There was never quite enough in the shops anymore and you had to have the right stamps to buy certain things — white for sugar, blue for meat, green for eggs, yellow for dairy. I didn't hold out much hope of there being any chocolate in the shop, but didn't say that to Lisa. She looked so delighted at the prospect, I didn't want to spoil it. I just enjoyed her excitement and shuffled a little closer to the shop every time someone came out and another went in.

When it was our turn, Lisa opened the door and we entered to the sound of a tinkling bell.

The walls were lined with wooden shelves. Some were empty, but others were heavy with jars and bottles and tins. There were boxes of vegetables on tables, but they were small and few, and most of them could only be bought if you had the right stamps. On the counter, a huge pot of sauerkraut sat beside a set of scales, and next to that was a pile of *Der Stürmer* newspapers.

On the front of the paper, there was a scary cartoon of a dark Jew holding a knife and standing over a blond German woman who was screaming. At the bottom the words "The

Jews Are Our Misfortune" were printed in bold letters. I had seen lots of these papers before — they put them on the walls at school so everyone could read them. They were also displayed in special glass-fronted notice boards in the city.

There were a few women inside the shop, passing bags and containers to Herr Finkel, who stood behind the counter. He filled them and weighed them and took stamps and money as he chatted to his customers.

Herr Finkel had sparkling blue eyes and ruddy cheeks speckled with tiny red veins, and his dark blue apron bulged around his large stomach. He looked older than Opa, with hair that was almost completely white. He showed me a sad smile when he looked down at me from behind the counter. "Karl," he said. "It's nice to see you, but I'm so sorry about your papa. He was a good man."

"Thank you."

"I remember when he used to bring you in here and you were only this high." He held one hand at waist height. "I liked him; he always had a smile on his face and a good word to say."

I nodded.

"How's your mama holding out?"

"She . . ." I struggled for the right words.

"It's all right," Herr Finkel said. "Don't mind me. It's none of my business. What can I get for you?"

Lisa rescued us both by asking if he had any chocolate.

"Your lucky day," Herr Finkel said with a wink as he passed the small bar over to Lisa. "It's getting harder and harder to find things like this."

On the wall behind the counter, there was a poster with Hitler on it, wearing his brown jacket and red armband and looking very serious. Beneath him were the words "One people, one nation, one leader." It had been there for just about as long as I could remember, but had now been joined by two other posters. One showed a hamster, carrying full baskets in each paw, warning housewives not to hoard food. The other was a poster, printed in black and white that showed a house, at night, with the lights on and the front door open. Above the house a terrifying skeleton sat on top of a British plane, about to throw a bomb.

"THE ENEMY SEES YOUR LIGHT!" it said. "BLACKOUT!"

The skeleton was frightening but fascinating at the same time and I could hardly take my eyes off it.

". . . grandparents?"

"Hmm?" I turned to look at Oma's friend, Frau Vogel, standing beside me. She was leaning close, inspecting me with dark blue eyes.

"I said, how are your grandparents? I haven't seen them for a few days. They seem to be keeping themselves to themselves at the moment."

"Oh. They're fine, thank you." I glanced around to see that some of the other women were still looking at the food, but had stopped chattering and were listening in.

"I saw they had a visit today." She raised her eyebrows and waited for me to tell her what it had been about, but I didn't say anything. I felt as if I were in a cage, being watched.

"You haven't been causing trouble, have you?" she asked, widening her eyes.

I took a step back and shook my head. Oma and Opa had tried to pretend that Wolff's visit hadn't bothered them too much, but I knew they were scared of him, so it was probably better if I didn't say anything at all. Especially with all those people listening.

"I don't think Karl wants to talk about it," Herr Finkel said. "I can understand that." He winked at me. "Boys will be boys, eh?"

I backed away to the door and went out into the street, feeling all those eyes watching.

Lisa came after me asking, "Are you all right? What's the matter?"

"It's just all those women looking at me."

"Take no notice," Lisa said. "I never do." She put her arm through mine as we set off along Escherstrasse toward home.

"Don't." I pulled my arm away.

"Why not?"

"We're not supposed to. It's not . . . it's not allowed. People will see."

"I've seen your brother do it," she said. "With that girl. They think no one can see, but I saw them."

"What girl?"

Lisa carefully unwrapped the small chocolate bar and broke it in half. She held up the pieces and closed one eye as she checked they were the same, then handed one piece to me and took a bite from the corner of her own. More of a nibble, really, like a mouse.

"What girl?" I asked again, letting the chocolate melt in my mouth. It was delicious, the best thing I'd tasted all week.

"The girl he walks home with. She goes all the way to the end," she said, pointing to the far end of Escherstrasse, "then turns right. They were arm in arm yesterday, just for a moment, but I saw. She's very pretty. Blue eyes and shiny blond hair. I bet all the girls are jealous of her."

"But not you?"

"I like mine just how it is." She reached back to run a hand along one of her braids.

"Me too," I said before I could stop myself.

"What's that?" Lisa looked at me with a smile.

"Nothing." My cheeks reddened. "Must be someone he works with," I said, changing the subject.

Lisa eyed me suspiciously for a moment, then shook her head and gave me a playful nudge. "You're funny, Karl Friedmann." She laughed and bit off a chunk of chocolate. "So what's his name, then? Your brother?"

"Stefan."

"How old is he?"

"Sixteen."

"Nearly old enough for the army."

"One more year," I said, but I was still thinking about the girl Stefan was with. I couldn't help feeling a little annoyed that Lisa knew things about my brother that I didn't.

"But he doesn't go to school?" Lisa asked. "Left when he was fourteen?"

I nodded and took another bite of the chocolate.

"You know, some boys and girls leave at fourteen so they

don't have to go into the Hitler Youth or the Bund Deutscher Mädel. D'you think that's why your brother left?"

"Uh-huh. There was a group of them all left at the same time and they used to hang around wearing colorful shirts, trying to look different. Mama got so upset with him."

"Hang around?"

"On the corner of our road or sometimes in the café or the park. They used to go hiking at weekends, too, boys and girls together. Ended up getting into trouble with the Gestapo."

"The *Gestapo*?"

"Yeah. Him and his friends used to fight with the Hitler Youth boys. One time . . . well, the Gestapo caught him and shaved all his hair off."

"Honestly?" Lisa couldn't hide her admiration.

Talking about it made me feel a bit guilty, because of what had happened to Stefan, but I'd started now and I didn't want to disappoint Lisa. She looked so excited.

"He went to boot camp for a week, and when he came back, they'd cut all his hair off," I said. "It just made him angry, though, so Mama stopped him from seeing his friends. She didn't let him out of the house for a long time and then told him to get a job to keep him out of trouble."

"And now?" Lisa asked. "Does he still get into trouble?"

We had reached my house, so I stopped and looked at Lisa "No. Now he has to look after us because Mama's not well."

Lisa nodded as if she was letting that sink in. "We have boys a bit like that here, sometimes. Girls, too."

"Like what?" I asked, running my tongue around my mouth to savor the last taste of the chocolate. When it touched a small chip on my front tooth, I remembered Wolff and his shining silver bumper coming toward me on the road.

"Ones who get into trouble. I once saw two boys fighting with Hitler Youth in the town, but it wasn't their fault. They didn't start it. I saw the Hitler Youth boys attack them." She paused. "They were making fun of them for wearing colorful clothes, and started calling them names and pushing them around. The boys tried to fight back but there were only two of them and they ended up running away." She shook her head as if it had all been a terrible tragedy.

"Stefan wouldn't fight like that," I said. "Not anymore."

"How did he get caught? Did someone report him?"

I shrugged.

"It happens here all the time — people reporting each other." She took a bite of her chocolate. "Anyway, one of them dropped this." She fished into her skirt pockets and rummaged for a second before tugging out her fist. When she opened it, stretching her fingers, there was a flower resting on her palm.

It wasn't a real flower, of course, but had been made from wood. No bigger than the tip of my little finger, the carving was crude, as if someone had done it with their penknife, but it was recognizable. Most of the color was scratched, but the short stalk was painted green and the petals were white. The center of the flower was a faded yellow.

As soon as I saw it, my stomach tingled and other images of the same flower exploded in my mind.

"It's some kind of badge I think. It's pretty," Lisa replied, but her voice seemed far away. It echoed as if it was coming to me down a long, dark tunnel. My stomach was tumbling over and over, and my mouth had gone dry.

I picked the tiny wooden object from her hand and turned it around in my trembling fingers. "What does it mean? What sort of flower is it?"

Lisa shrugged. "It's hard to tell.

"Lisa!" Her mama had opened the door across the street and was beckoning for her to come home.

"Maybe a daisy." Lisa took back the carving and stuffed it into her pocket.

"Lisa!"

"Better go," she said, turning and checking for cars before looking back at me.

"No wait, I want you to tell me about —"

"See you tomorrow? It's Saturday. No school."

I tried to think past all the visions of the flower that spun around in my head. "Tomorrow? Um . . ."

"We can go for a bike ride." She stepped onto the road and began to cross. "Take a picnic."

"My bike's broken," I said, suddenly remembering the buckled wheel and the shining bumper that had crashed into me.

"Then we'll fix it," Lisa called. "Together."

"I'll need to get it first," I shouted after her, but she had already turned and was running across the street toward her mama, who greeted her with open arms.

I watched them hug, then Lisa turned and waved and the door closed behind her and she was gone.

TRUST

The strong aroma of coffee drifted out of the kitchen. "I saw you talking to Lisa from over the road," Opa said, leaning to one side so he could see into the hallway.

"We just went to the shop," I said, taking off my boots. "I didn't —"

"It's all right; I know. I watched you. Are you hungry?"

"Not really. Just going upstairs for a bit."

"Stefan will be home soon." Oma poked her head from the kitchen. "We've got sausage and bread tonight."

I smiled and pretended it sounded delicious, then hurried upstairs, taking them two at a time. What Oma had said about Stefan coming home soon was already on my mind, and I wanted to see if he was with the girl Lisa had talked about, so I went straight to the window and pressed my face against it, looking as far as I could along Escherstrasse. The angle was all wrong, though, so I opened the window and stuck out my head.

At the moment, the street was clear apart from a flock of starlings that had settled on the rooftops. I glanced across at

Lisa's house. It looked like every other house on the street, but it felt special now.

My friend lives there.

I'd made a bit of a fool of myself with all that *Mischling* talk and shaking hands business, but Lisa had shared her chocolate with me and called me her friend. Even though boys and girls weren't really supposed to mix together, I'd liked it when she'd put her arm in mine.

I lost myself in those thoughts, imagining that Lisa would come to the window on the other side of the road and wave to me, but I was distracted by the sound of laughter. Looking along the street to my right, I saw Stefan, walking side by side with a girl.

There were one or two other people on the street now, coming back from work, but there was something different about Stefan and the girl. They stood out from everybody else, even though Stefan didn't wear the colorful clothes he used to.

Since coming to Oma and Opa's, he was more careful about being noticed, so he was wearing a plain white shirt under his jacket, and a pair of black trousers. The girl was wearing a dark skirt, and a bright turquoise blouse. She was almost as tall as Stefan, and had fair hair that had been left loose in a care-free way.

Something made them different from everybody else, though. They were smiling, passing a cigarette between them and looking right at each other when they spoke. Instead of walking, they seemed to almost *flow* along the street as if they lived in a different world from everyone else.

They stopped a few doors away and turned to each other. Stefan flicked the cigarette into the street, and for one moment, it looked as though they were going to kiss, because they suddenly became very serious. They stared into one another's eyes and stood as close to each other as they probably dared. Their hands came together, touching just at the fingertips to begin with, then closer until Stefan was holding the girl's hands right there in broad daylight for everyone to see. My own breathing quickened just at the sight of it.

Then the moment was gone and they broke apart. They walked on, side by side, and when they reached our house, Stefan waved good-bye to her and came inside. The door slammed and voices floated up from downstairs while I watched the girl walk farther along the street.

Just as she disappeared from view, Stefan came into the bedroom bringing the smell of tobacco and perfume with him. He looked me up and down with concern. "Opa told me what happened; are you all right?"

"I'm fine." I was still thinking about what I had just seen.

"You're sure?" He came closer and took hold of my arm to inspect it.

"I chipped my tooth."

"Let me see."

I opened my mouth and he peered in. "Doesn't look too bad."

He made me recount the accident blow by blow, and wanted to know all about Kriminalinspektor Wolff coming to the house. He looked very worried, but started to relax when I told him about Lisa, and about how we had become friends.

I didn't mention the writing on the wall and I didn't say anything about the hole I'd seen cut into his jacket.

When I finished, Stefan smiled and took a cigarette pack from his shirt pocket. "It's good you've got a friend," he said, throwing it down on the windowsill and unbuttoning his work shirt.

"Since when do you smoke?" I asked.

He looked up at me and shrugged.

"And where did you get them? Are they black market?"

"Black market?" He stopped what he was doing and pretended to look shocked. "As if I would."

"You'll get into trouble."

He smiled. "Don't worry about me, little brother."

"So who's that girl you were with?" I asked.

"A friend from the factory." He took off his shirt and dropped it on the floor. "She's pretty, don't you think?" Stefan started humming as he took a clean shirt from the wardrobe and slipped his arms into the sleeves.

"What's that you're humming?" I asked, coming to sit on the bed.

"Just some song."

"I've never heard it."

"Of course you haven't," he said, fastening the buttons. "You're one of the Führer's little soldiers, aren't you? You're — wait a minute." He looked up through his long bangs and narrowed his eyes at me. "I can't believe I didn't notice. Who are you and what have you done with my little brother?"

"What? I *am* me," I said.

"So where's your uniform?" He took a step back and made a show of looking me up and down. "What the hell have they done to you?" He walked around me, prodding my back and sides, making me giggle. "Who did this to my brother?"

"Get off." I couldn't help laughing, and then I was trying to prod him back but he was too quick and strong and eventually I collapsed onto the bed, saying, "I give up!"

"Say I win."

"You win."

"Say I'm the best and the smartest."

"Never!"

"Say it." He started tickling me again. "Say it."

"All right, all right. You're the best and the smartest!"

"Quite right, too." He released me and sat next to me on the end of the bed and we were quiet for a moment, catching our breath.

"Oma said Mama didn't get up today."

"No." I shook my head.

"Maybe tomorrow, then."

"Yeah. Maybe." I looked at him.

"You still haven't opened your birthday present." He tipped his chin toward the chest of drawers. "I reckon you'll like it."

"I was waiting for Mama to get better." I hung my head. "Is she going to be all right? It feels like she's fading away."

"That's why I need you to help me by being strong." He nudged me. "Strong as Krupp's steel, isn't that what you all say?"

"I don't feel strong as Krupp's steel." I rubbed my face and wiped my eyes.

"Well, maybe you should just open your present now." He went over and picked it up, holding it out to me.

I tried to protest, but he was insistent, so I untied the twine and carefully took off the brown paper. Inside, there was a plain cardboard box.

The lid slipped off easily, and a few pieces of shredded paper fell out onto the floor. The box was full of the strips, but nestled among them was a pocketknife.

"Where did you get *this*?" I said, taking out the knife and admiring the dimpled brown handle. "It's like a real soldier's!" I opened the biggest blade and held it up to the light.

"Well, every boy should have a good pocketknife, and we knew yours was broken," Stefan said. "Mama and I saved up."

I folded the blade back into the handle and wondered if I deserved it.

"I was paid today," Stefan said before he sat down for supper in the kitchen. "And I want to give some to you." He looked at Oma when he spoke. "To help with looking after us."

"Oh, you don't need to —"

"Please," Stefan interrupted. "It's only right." He put his hand into his pocket and pulled out a fold of notes.

But as he did it, something else came out of his pocket and fell to the floor at his feet.

We all saw it.

A small square of black cloth embroidered with a flower.

Yellow center. White petals.

Stefan quickly bent over to pick it up and stuff it back into his pocket.

"Be careful," Opa said to him with a serious voice. "Please be careful, Stefan."

"What is it?" I asked. "The flower. What does it mean?"

All three of them turned to stare at me.

"What?" I said. "Why are you looking at me like that?"

"Don't let anyone see that." Opa took his eyes off me and spoke to Stefan. "Not *anyone*." He looked at me once more. "And don't you breathe a word of it to anyone, Karl."

"Why won't you tell me what it means?" I asked. "Why won't —"

I stopped because Lisa's words came back to me, about children reporting their parents, and everything was suddenly very clear to me. I knew *exactly* why they wouldn't tell me. It was the same reason why they never mentioned that Papa didn't want to fight the war.

"You think I'll tell someone," I said, backing away toward the kitchen door. "None of you trust me."

I ran upstairs and went straight into the bedroom, closing the door behind me. I felt angry and sad and frustrated and confused and everything was muddled in my head. But underneath it all, I couldn't blame them for not trusting me.

INTO THE CELLAR

That night, I woke to an awful sound.

One moment I'd been lying in bed, trying to think of a way to make Stefan tell me what the flower meant, and the next I was jarred awake by the nightmarish wailing and screeching of the air-raid sirens.

My whole body felt numb, and cold fear gripped me in a tight fist as I flung back the bedcovers and turned, looking for Stefan. It was too dark to see anything, though, and the darkness danced and sparkled in my eyes.

"You all right?" My brother's voice was filled with urgency.

"Yes."

"Good. Everything's fine. We'll be fine. We'll get to the cellar and . . . Mama," he said, and I knew what he meant. We had to get her up.

I fumbled for my flashlight and switched it on, then we rushed across the landing, stumbling into Mama's room, just as Oma and Opa were coming out of theirs.

"Mama. We have to get down to the cellar," Stefan said as he pulled back her sheets. "Quick. They're coming."

There wasn't much time. The sirens had been wailing for a few minutes already; the planes would be here soon.

Mama stirred just enough to open her eyes. "Oskar? Is that you?"

"No, it's us. Stefan and Karl."

"What's happening?" She started to sit up, looking around and sounding confused. "A raid, is it? Oh, well, just . . . just leave me. I'll be all right."

"We're not leaving you here." Opa came in to help but Stefan just grabbed her arm as she tried to lie back down.

My thoughts were wild with images of bombs falling toward us. A thousand of them raining from the flying beasts, all of them coming right at us and in just a few seconds they would hit us and we would be engulfed in a storm of fire and rubble. "Please, Mama," I begged her. "*Please*. You have to come."

"Oskar?" Mama said.

"It's Karl." I took her hand. "Please get up."

"You're afraid?" she asked.

"Yes. Please get up."

"Of course, my darling. Of course."

Mama climbed out of bed and Stefan put his arm around her waist to lead her from the bedroom and down to the hallway.

Opa went straight to the door under the stairs. It stuck in the frame, so he had to yank it hard, and then he lifted the cellar trapdoor.

"In," he said. "Come on, quick."

*   *   *

The cellar was a musty, higgledy-piggledy mess of unwanted junk and forgotten treasures. An ancient wooden sea chest with thick iron bands around it. A stack of chairs with flaking paint. There was an old bicycle and a kerosene heater that gave off an oily smell.

There was the boiler, too: a dark demon that skulked at the far end of the cellar. It was quiet now, hardly alive in the summer, but in the winter months, Opa fed it glinting black chunks from the coal pile in the corner and it would roar with life. Its heat would clatter and clank through the house, rattling the pipework and banging in the night, hissing steam from the radiators.

Stefan and I used to dare each other to go down the rickety steps and stay there, in the dark, for as long as we could manage. It had been a place of monsters and ghosts. Now, though, it was our place of hope. Somewhere that might save our lives.

Opa had cleared an area directly under the single naked lightbulb, and put out a few chairs and a table so there was somewhere to sit during a raid. He had put up shelves that were lined with tins of nails and screws and assorted odds and ends, and Oma had brought down packets of food in case we were stuck here for a long time. There were buckets of emergency water, as well, changed every few days to keep them fresh.

The sirens were nothing more than a faint droning now the door was shut, but we'd feel the bombs when they came.

I'd only been in an air raid once before, when we were in the city. It had been the most terrifying and the most exciting night of my life. The bombs had fallen forever and we had felt the ground shake. We had huddled in the communal shelter under our building and, afterward, we'd seen the flames and lights in the distance. The next day at school, we talked about the damage and how we hated the enemy more than ever.

Right now, though, I felt nothing.

"Is it a false alarm?" I whispered, because whispering seemed to be the right thing to do.

Opa shook his head and held up a finger. "Listen."

Boom b-boom boom-boom. B-boom.

It was faint, but we could all hear it.

Boom b-boom boom-boom. B-boom.

"Eighty-eights," Stefan said. "That's not bombs."

Opa nodded. "You're right."

It was the sound of the 88-mm flak guns that protected the city. There were a number of them put in along the route that bombers were expected to take, but they could be moved anytime — towed away by a tractor or a half-track. They fired clouds of hot metal into the sky, to rip through the enemy planes and bring them howling to the ground. Often, it was the Hitler Youth boys who manned them, desperate to shoot down the enemy. I had always hoped I would get the chance to fire them one day.

"I don't hear any bombs," I said.

The eighty-eights continued to boom and cough their flak into the sky and I knew that even if there weren't any bombs dropping, it wouldn't be safe to be out in the streets. The flak would be falling back to the ground like hot, sharp rain.

"It's the roads and the railway they want," Opa reassured us. "Factories and things like that. They don't drop bombs on people."

"They did at Münster." Oma sounded afraid. "Just dropped them like there wasn't any target at all. The radio said they didn't know how many people were killed."

"Münster's much bigger than here." Opa narrowed his eyes at her and shook his head in a tight movement. "They're not interested in us."

I didn't want to think about it. I wanted it all to stop. The war wasn't exciting anymore. It wasn't about being the best anymore, about Germany making everywhere else as good as it was here. It wasn't about being proud of Papa. Now it was about people dying and being scared. It was about Mama being sad. And I didn't want that. I didn't want that at all.

I moved closer to Mama and put my arms around her, and there was a scary moment when it was like hugging a doll. It was as if she hadn't noticed me at all, and that was worse than any bombing or being stuck in any damp old cellar. Her words came back to me — the ones she had spoken not long ago, when we'd tried to get her out of bed.

"Just leave me," she had said, as if she hadn't wanted to come. As if she didn't care about the raid.

As if she didn't care if she died.

"Mama," I whispered, and hugged her again, tighter this time. "Mama, please."

Then a breath of life ran through her — as if she woke up from a long sleep. She lifted her arms and gathered me to her. She put her face to the top of my head and breathed deeply. She kissed me and squeezed me. "We'll be fine," she said. "I promise."

A mixture of surprise and hesitant relief washed through

me, and I glanced over at Stefan, who was watching her, wide-eyed. Oma and Opa seemed just as shocked to hear her speak.

"I'm sorry I've been so useless," Mama said with a croaky voice. "But I think I'm going to be better now." She looked around at everyone. "I'm so sorry. I've been . . ." And then she burst into tears as if she'd been holding it in for all these days, allowing it all to build up.

"Oh, darling." Oma sounded pleased and sad at the same time, and tears sparkled in *her* eyes. "Let it out," she said, getting up from her seat. "Let it out and you'll feel so much better."

I didn't want to let Mama go, but Oma moved me aside so she and Opa could get close to her.

"I miss him so much," Mama sobbed. *"So much."*

Oma held her tight. "We all do. But we have to remember the good things, not . . ."

"You mean like when he used to chase me and Karl around the yard with a bucket of water in the summer?" Stefan looked over at me. "Or when he used to come back and tell us to check his pockets and there'd be chocolates in there — one for each of us."

I couldn't help smiling when I remembered that, picturing Papa coming to the door and making a show of pretending he'd lost something in his jacket pocket, patting himself down. He'd laugh so much sometimes, running away as we tried to grab him, to pin him down and check him for candy. Eventually he'd trip over on purpose so we could jump on top of him.

Despite Mama's tears, her change had a great effect on all of us. It lightened the mood in the cellar. Even with the air-raid sirens outside, and the distant booming of the guns, we all felt better. When she heard us talking about Papa, she listened to the stories and even managed to smile a little. It was odd that it had taken an air raid and being cooped up in the half darkness to breathe some life back into her.

She wasn't back to normal just yet, but at least it was a start.

When the raid had passed over and everything had been quiet for half an hour, Opa decided it was safe to venture out.

"Strange we didn't feel any bombs," Stefan said as we climbed the steps.

"Maybe they were too far away," I suggested, but I was beyond caring much about that now. I was so pleased Mama was talking again.

"We should have at least heard something," Stefan said. "It doesn't make sense."

Opa led us into the hallway. "Maybe we should go outside and look."

"Is it safe?" Oma asked.

"I would think so. I don't hear any sirens, do you?"

I clung to Mama like I wasn't going to let her go, and we all went to the front door and out into Escherstrasse.

There were other people at their doors, too, and many had come out into the street, so there were men and women and children standing in the road. They hardly spoke at all, and it was unnerving to see everyone like that — motionless, like stunned ghosts, all looking up at the sky, all of them gawping, just as we did.

None of us had expected this.

CONFETTI

No bombs had been dropped.

The planes had left something else instead.

Amid glowing red parachute flares and the piercing beams of the searchlights, the sky was alive with the confetti of a million leaflets that flickered and flashed as they caught the light. They spun and sailed and fell and floated and buzzed and rattled as they came to earth. Then the gentle wind snatched them up again, before leaving them to fall like a magical rain.

They landed on the rooftops, on the road, the pavement. The wind pressed them to windows and deposited them on cars and blew them along the street like the aftermath of a great celebration.

Above the leaflets, the rods of the searchlights touched the ceiling of clouds, creating huge shimmering circles that rippled bloodred from the color of the parachute flares that floated and fizzled, dropping as if through water. It was mesmerising and terrifying all at once, to see the night filled with a glow that was both hellish and beautiful.

I couldn't stop staring at the sky and the strange storm of lights and paper.

"Isn't this exciting?" said a voice beside me.

I tore my eyes from the spectacle and rubbed my stiff neck as I looked around.

"It's like a giant party." Lisa was wearing pajamas almost exactly the same as mine and had a huge smile on her face.

"What are they?" I asked her. "What's going on?"

Some of the younger children started to chase the confetti along the road, laughing and spinning in circles as they gathered handfuls of the paper, but their parents were quick to call them back. They took the leaflets from their children's hands and threw them down as if the paper burned their fingers.

"It's all lies." Frau Oster was standing close by, shaking her head. "Just horrible lies."

"Of course," said the woman beside her. "Your husband is quite safe, I'm sure." She patted Frau Oster on the arm and gave her a sympathetic look.

"Hitler's definitely got them on the run if they're trying tricks like this," Herr Finkel agreed. "Don't you worry, we'll have the Russians soon enough." He crushed one of the pieces of paper in his hand and threw it down. "Then the British will surrender and your husband will be home."

"They can't fool us with this nonsense." Frau Oster grabbed her young son's hand and ushered him home.

Herr Finkel watched her go, then turned to walk back to his apartment over the shop. When he was away from the crowd, though, he snatched up one of the leaflets, glanced around, then folded it in half and slipped it into his pocket.

As I watched him, the wind blew one of the leaflets against my foot, so I bent to pick it up. When I stood up again, Herr Finkel had disappeared into the darkness and I stared for a while at the place where I had last seen him.

"Mama says it's propaganda," Lisa whispered, breaking me from my thoughts. "Things to make us feel bad about the war."

The piece of paper in my hand was about twice the size of a postcard but printed on flimsy paper. The image on the front shimmered in the reddish glow of the dying flares and I turned it so I could see it better, wanting to know why it had upset Frau Oster so much, why Herr Finkel had slipped one into his pocket.

It flapped a little in the breeze, but I recognized the figure in the picture right away.

The Führer looked smart. He was wearing his military cap, his long leather coat and his shiny black boots. His hands were clasped together in front of his chest as if something had pleased him very much.

At his feet, and all around him, lay a pile of dead soldiers wearing German uniforms. Some had their arms outstretched; others were curled up as if they were asleep. Three of the dead men, right at the Führer's feet, were on their backs with their mouths open. Their unseeing eyes stared up at their leader.

In the sky, beside the Führer's head, words were printed in bloodred ink.

Hitler is killing your fathers

"That's like what it said on the wall." Lisa leaned close to get a better look at it. "And see who it is," she whispered, and raised a finger to tap the Führer's head. "Look at him smiling."

I stared at the picture.

"What's on the back?" Lisa nudged me and made me turn over the leaflet where there was a whole page of print. "What does it say?" she asked, leaning closer still.

Her hair wasn't braided like it had been when I saw her earlier, and the breeze played with it, blowing it across my cheek. It tickled and I brushed it away so I could read the words.

". . . put it down."

"Hmm?" I turned to see Stefan looking at me.

"Put it down," he said through clenched teeth. "Now."

Oma and Opa were watching me. Mama, too. All of them staring at me.

"Put it down," Stefan said again, and he reached out to swipe the leaflet from my hands. It snapped from my fingers with a crack, and dropped to the pavement before it was caught by the wind and tumbled away.

"Ow." I furrowed my brow and watched the leaflet flutter down the street to join the others. "Why did you do that? What are you —"

"Someone will see," he said, looking around.

"I was just reading it. I want to know what it says."

Lisa stood beside me, watching Stefan. She looked almost as if she was in awe of him and I couldn't help thinking I would like her to look at *me* that way.

"We should go back inside," Opa said. "You too," he spoke

to Lisa. "Someone will be along to clear this up soon enough. Best not to be outside when that happens."

I started to complain, but Stefan grabbed my arm and I knew there was no point. I could struggle, but I'd only embarrass myself even more in front of Lisa. My brother was much bigger and stronger than I was.

"See you tomorrow, then?" Lisa said. She looked disappointed but I couldn't decide if that was because I was leaving or because my brother was.

I nodded, saying, "Tomorrow," and then Stefan whisked me into the house and closed the door behind us.

"Ow!" I snatched away from him. "What's that for? Why did you make me —"

"Because you don't want people to see you reading those things, you idiot."

The way he raised his voice at me made me flinch and take a step back.

"You don't want anyone to think you kept one. If they tell someone, then who knows what would happen to us? To *you*." He stressed that last word with a finger pointed at my chest. "If the Gestapo finds out you've even *read* it . . ." He took a deep breath and shook his head. "Everyone's probably already watching you. Going out on your bike and getting caught by that man. Do you know how much trouble you've already caused for Oma and Opa?"

"That was an accident. I didn't mean to —"

"Then try thinking about someone other than yourself for a change." Stefan's voice was getting louder and I took another step back.

"You're scaring him," Oma said.

"Good," Stefan told her. "Maybe he needs a good scare. Maybe I can scare some sense into him."

"Please." Mama spoke so quietly her words were almost inaudible, but everyone stopped and looked at her. "Please," she said again. "No more shouting."

"You're right," Opa agreed. "I think that's enough." He put a hand on Stefan's arm.

"Why don't you boys go into the kitchen?" Oma said. "I'll take your mama upstairs and then come down and make us a hot drink. I think we've had enough excitement for one night."

Stefan was as agitated as I'd ever seen him. He didn't sit down, but paced the length of the kitchen, hair hanging over his eyes, watching his feet. Up and down on the black-and-white checkerboard tiles. Up and down. Up and down.

I sat at the table, beside Opa, and watched Stefan.

When he finally stopped, he leaned back against the sink and put his hands behind him. "I'm sorry," he said, looking up at me as if he were about to burst. "I didn't mean to shout. It's just . . . No. Actually I'm not sorry. I don't think you understand what's going on." His voice grew louder with each word. "I don't think you know how much trouble you can get into for the smallest things." He lifted a hand and squeezed it into a fist. "They take people away just for saying what they think, Karl. Or because their nose is too big or their hair is too dark or because they keep their children away from the Deutsches Jungvolk."

"I know about —"

"Well, did you know they took away your new friend's papa?"

"What? Lisa? No." I leaned away from him. "I thought he was a soldier, fighting in the —"

"He was a schoolteacher," Stefan shouted, and slapped his fist into the palm of his left hand. "Not a soldier, a *schoolteacher*. He refused to join the party and said things he shouldn't have — things about your Führer — so they called him a Communist and took him away and nobody has seen him again."

"He was a *Communist*?"

Opa shook his head. "No, Karl, he was a teacher, until Wolff took him away."

"Then he must have done something to —"

"He didn't do *anything*," Stefan snapped. "When are you going to get that into your stupid, thick head?"

"That's enough Stefan." Opa held up a hand.

"No, he needs to hear this." Stefan glanced at Opa, then focused on me again. "It's time to stop pretending. He needs to know that you don't have to do *anything*. You just have to *say* something, *think* something. All it takes is for one person to tell the Gestapo and that's the end of it. Some people even report their own family."

He stared at me and I felt myself shrivel inside as he continued to shout.

"And do you know what happens to the people they take away, Karl? People like Lisa's papa? They torture them at Headquarters. They make them sign their own imprisonment orders, and they torture them, then they send them to camps, but they're not like the one I went to. They're worse. Much worse. People don't come back like I did; they starve to death in those places. *That's* what your Führer does to people who think the wrong thing."

"Starve? No." I shook my head. "No. They come home. They just go there to learn how to be better Germans. To exercise and . . ."

"They go there to *die*, Karl." He slapped his fist into his palm again. "Just like the poor soldiers are sent to Russia to die. Soldiers like Papa. *That's* how much your Führer loves us." Stefan sniffed hard and looked away for a moment before turning back to me. When he spoke again, his voice was softer. "Do you really think Papa wanted to go and fight?"

"I . . ."

"Of course he bloody *didn't*. Papa didn't want to go away; he wanted to stay here with us. He can't take care of us when he's thousands of miles away, can he?"

"I don't understand . . ."

"The Nazis made him fight. He had to go. He wanted to stay here with us but they took him away, don't you understand that? Your Führer made him leave us. *He* sent him to fight. *He* killed him. The leaflet is right."

When he stopped, silence hummed in the room and my brother's words echoed in my ears.

Stefan took a deep breath and squeezed his eyes shut. When he opened them again, he looked at me and shook his head. "Please tell me you understand now."

I nodded, but my mind was spinning with thoughts of guilt and betrayal and the idea that I had been a part of something terrible. I was thinking about how awful Lisa must have felt when her father was taken away, that it was too horrible for her to even talk about, and what must she have thought of me in my uniform? I was thinking about Johann Weber's tears and about Axel Jung kicking dirt in his face. I was remembering how Stefan had been taken away, and I felt a chill run through me at the thought that he might never have come home. And I was seeing those words, over and over again, spinning in my head. Those white words that had turned bloodred.

Hitler is killing our fathers.

LEAFLET

I didn't mention any of it to Lisa when she came to call for me the next morning. I didn't know what to say or how to feel; everything was such a muddle in my head. I could hardly even think straight.

"Good to see you're not in that uniform again," was the first thing she said.

"Not such a little soldier anymore, eh?" Stefan came up behind me and tousled my hair, making me pull away from him. It was Saturday and he had the morning off work.

"What's the matter, little brother? Am I embarrassing you in front of your girlfriend?"

"She's not my girlfriend."

Stefan whistled and raised both hands in surrender. "Sor-ry." He rolled his eyes at Lisa, which made her giggle.

"Come on." I stepped outside. "Let's go."

"Don't do anything I wouldn't do," Stefan said before he closed the door on us.

The street was clear, the sky was blue and there was only a wisp of cloud. Everything was so different from how it had been last night; we might have been on another planet. There were no leaflets fluttering around, so someone must have come in the dark and cleared them all away. The only hint that anything had happened were the odd corners of paper that protruded from the guttering, or the ones that had stuck in the roof tiles and chimney pots.

As we set off, I looked back at the kitchen window to see Mama standing there with Oma. She still looked tired and ill, but at least she wasn't stuck in her bedroom.

"Your mama's feeling better?" Lisa asked.

"I think so."

"That's good." She smiled. "Come on, then, let's go and get your bike. You remember what street it was on?"

I only knew the names of a few streets other than the one I now lived on, so we decided to go back to the school and walk from there.

When we were just past the alley running alongside Oma and Opa's house, Lisa took my hand and pressed something into it. "I brought this for you. Put it in your pocket."

"What is it?" I glanced down at the folded piece of paper.

"One of those leaflets from last night."

It was as if she'd given me a small lump of electricity. The piece of paper seemed to come to life and tingle in my palm. I wanted to open it up right then and discover its secrets. I wanted to know what was written on the back and I wanted to see that picture again, the one of the Führer standing among the bodies of our dead fathers.

"Don't look at it now," she whispered, speaking as if she was trying not to move her lips.

Remembering what Stefan had been so angry about last night, I looked around to see if we were being watched, then jammed the piece of paper into my pocket and stuffed it right down to the bottom where it lay like a dark secret.

"Don't you have a meeting today?" I asked, trying not to think about the leaflet. "Jungmädelbund?"

"There's one this afternoon, but I could not go if you want."

"Not go?"

"I do that sometimes. "

"Don't you get into trouble?"

"Usually, but it's not too bad. They make us parade up and down the yard for a while if we miss a meeting, but that's no worse than all that exercising and talking about motherhood." She looked at me and made a face. "Bo-ring. You boys get to play war."

Ralf and Martin and the others would probably be playing one of those war games right now, but I didn't feel as if I was missing out. Not anymore.

"I don't want to play war," I said. "I want to fix my bike and go for a ride."

Lisa smiled at me. "Good idea."

"But maybe you should go this afternoon," I said. "I don't want you to get into trouble because of me."

"Because of you? Who says it's because of you?"

"No one, I just thought . . ."

"I'm teasing." She nudged me. "Of course it's because of you."

"Oh."

"You're funny, Karl Friedmann." She laughed and hit my

arm, saying, "Come on," then made as if to take off down the street, but I grabbed her sleeve to stop her.

"Look," I said, feeling my mouth go dry. "Over there, outside Herr Finkel's place."

At the end of Escherstrasse, a group of five or six people had gathered close to the shop. By the side of the road was a small gray truck with a hard, enclosed back, and behind it, glinting in the summer sun, Kriminalinspektor Wolff's Mercedes was hunched at the side of the street.

Just the sight of it made everything Stefan said to me last night come flooding back, the way he had shouted at me about the Gestapo and torture and camps and people never coming home.

"Something's happening," Lisa said. "Something bad."

A shiver ran through me and my scalp prickled. "Like what?" And even though I wanted to know, I was also afraid to find out.

"Let's see."

As we moved closer, more people began to stop near Herr Finkel's place. There must have been at least twenty of them on the street now. Frau Amsel and Frau Vogel were there, standing with Frau Oster among the bystanders, shopping baskets in hand and —

We stopped when we saw the SS soldiers.

Two of them, stationed right outside the shop. Tall and menacing in their black uniforms, they stood to attention with submachine guns slung from their shoulders. Their faces were set like stone, their eyes staring straight ahead.

"You think Herr Finkel's in trouble?" There was a tremble in Lisa's voice.

"I don't —" Then it hit me. After the raid last night, I had seen Herr Finkel pocket one of the leaflets. Perhaps I was not the only one to have seen it. Perhaps someone had reported him.

Without thinking, I put a hand to my pocket, where the folded leaflet lay like a guilty secret.

As I touched it, a voice called from inside Herr Finkel's shop. The two SS soldiers left their post and entered the building.

For a moment, there was an eerie hush over the onlookers, then came the harsh sound of a man's voice shouting inside.

Nobody dared move on the street, and I felt very frightened for Herr Finkel.

The voice shouted once more, loud and vicious, followed by a brief pause, then the terrible sound of things being smashed. It was impossible to see what was happening inside the shop, but the noises made my blood run cold: the repeated crashing of glass, the clatter of breakables, and the thunder of wood splintering.

And beneath it all, I was sure I could hear an old man begging to be spared.

The bystanders on the street started to push back, as if the windows might explode outward at any moment, showering the pavement with glass. Or as if they were afraid they might be drawn into the terrible things happening inside the shop, but then the sounds stopped almost as suddenly as they had started.

A quiet hush fell over Escherstrasse once more.

When the shop door opened, the soldiers reemerged into the street with Herr Finkel between them.

The shopkeeper's right leg dragged beneath him as he shuffled across the pavement. His movement was slow and difficult, and when he slipped, the soldiers grabbed him, shaking him and shouting at him.

"Hurry up!" they ordered. "Walk straight!"

Herr Finkel's head hung between slumped shoulders as he tried and failed to do as they instructed, and eventually he collapsed to his knees. For a moment, he knelt on the hard stones, with his head bowed. He swayed for a moment, then keeled over to one side, hitting his head on the pavement.

"Stand up!" the guards shouted at him. "On your feet!"

They took hold of him with a tight grip, holding an arm each as if they were going to tear them right out of their sockets, and dragged him to his feet.

That's when I saw what they had done to him.

Herr Finkel's left eye was swollen shut and there was blood smeared around his mouth and nose. When I looked closer, I could see spots of it on the pavement where he had collapsed.

"They've beaten him," Lisa whispered in disbelief. "Beaten him in his own shop."

Behind the soldiers and poor Herr Finkel, Wolff emerged into the day, dressed in his dark suit, hat placed neatly on his head, and I imagined I could smell his aftershave. He stopped in front of the shop and studied the crowd with his steel-gray eyes.

"This shop is no longer in business." He spoke clearly so everyone could hear. "The contents are now the property of the Reich. Anybody found breaching these orders will be arrested."

I felt numb. Seeing someone I knew arrested and manhandled

out of his own shop was horrible. I'd heard about these things, I knew it happened, but I had never *seen* it. And I always thought it happened to the right people, to people who deserved it. But after what Stefan had said last night, and how angry he was about people being taken away for just saying something or thinking something . . . Herr Finkel was a *shopkeeper*. He sold chocolate. What could he have done to deserve this? Had it been like this for Lisa's Papa?

I glanced at her, seeing her watching in a kind of daze, as the driver of the truck jumped down from the cab and hurried around to open the back of the vehicle. A heavy clunking sound drifted to us on the warm breeze as the lock unfastened and he swung the door open.

Then something appeared from the corner of my eye. A flash of movement.

I turned my head to see the two boys run across the road to stand by the truck. They huddled close together, one of them turning his head this way and that, while the other pulled something from his pocket that looked like a brown paper bag. He fiddled with the gas cap for a second, then tipped the contents of the bag into the fuel tank before replacing the cap. It was no more than a few seconds before the boys had finished whatever they were doing and ran back across the road to stand as they had been, as if nothing had happened.

I watched them for a moment, confused, then looked back at the other side of the street, seeing the soldiers drag Herr Finkel to the rear of the truck.

The old shopkeeper raised his head and looked around as if he were seeing everything for the first time, as if he didn't know where he was, or why his face was covered with bruises and his nose was bleeding.

With one eye, Herr Finkel looked at the people in the crowd — people he had known and served for years. But no one could help him.

We were all too afraid.

"Take him away," Wolff snapped.

The soldiers forced Herr Finkel into the back of the truck and slammed the door shut, and then Herr Finkel was gone.

I couldn't believe what had just happened. Neither of us wanted to see any more, but it was hard to just walk away, so we stayed for a while as the vehicles drove off, leaving the two soldiers to close up the shop, hammering boards across the door.

On the opposite side of the street, the two boys hung around for a few minutes. They looked disappointed.

"We should go now." I spoke quietly and turned to Lisa, but she didn't respond.

The color was completely drained from her face. Hardly blinking, her eyes welling up, she stood as if rooted to the pavement and stared at the spot in the road where the truck had been parked. She looked, for that moment, as if she were lost to the world.

I watched her, not knowing what to say, and wondered again if it had been like this when her papa was taken away. I wanted to ask, but it didn't feel right, so I just stood with her.

When the soldiers fixed the last board in place, they shouldered their submachine guns and walked back along the street. The bystanders began to drift away, and soon it was almost as if nothing had happened.

"Come on." I touched Lisa's arm and she blinked hard, squeezing tears onto her cheeks. "We should go."

She looked at me and nodded, then wiped her eyes with her hands.

By the time we went back to the task of trying to find my bicycle, the only evidence of the event was that Herr Finkel's shop was boarded up.

And the old shopkeeper's blood on the pavement.

Lisa and I walked in silence as we followed the route I had taken the day I met Wolff. I glanced at her from time to time, checking she was all right, but she just stared ahead and kept walking, as if she didn't know I was there.

After some time, Lisa led me into a narrow lane, similar to the ones I had cycled along the day of the crash. "This is where *I* saw it." They were her first words since leaving the site of Herr Finkel's arrest, and her voice was hoarse. "The writing and the flower."

I stood beside her and looked at the white smear on the wall. It was the only sign that anything had been there at all. "I don't think I saw it here. It was somewhere else."

"But it said the same thing? *Hitler is killing our fathers?*" Her eyes were red and puffy from the tears.

"Shh." I put a finger to my lips. "Someone might hear."

"I don't care." Lisa was standing with her hands in her pockets and her shoulders hunched, studying the wall as if something might appear if she stayed there long enough. She was wearing the same dress as yesterday and her hair was in braids again. It had looked better last night, though, when it wasn't all tied back. The braids made her look like every other girl in the Jungmädelbund and that didn't seem right. Lisa was different, so she should look different.

"Why are you looking at me like that?"

"I . . . Come on." I blushed. "We should keep going."

Our footsteps were loud on the cobbles. The alley was empty, and the walls were high on each side, so we left an echo as we walked.

"Do you think Hitler killed your papa?" Lisa's question took me by surprise and I turned to look at her, but she just stared straight ahead.

"I don't know," I said, still watching her. "I mean, *he* didn't do it, but if the war is his fault, like Stefan says, then . . . well, he wouldn't have gone away, would he?"

"My papa said it was wrong to fight," she sniffed, "so they put him in a camp."

I hesitated. "Do you know where?"

She shook her head and took a deep breath, then stopped and leaned against the wall, folding her arms over her chest. "Wolff came in the night and took him away." She stared at the ground as she spoke. "He said Papa was spreading lies about the Führer, so he took him away like he just took Herr Finkel away. I'm scared they might have killed him."

An image of the Kriminalinspektor popped into my head. The cold gray eyes and the thin lips. The strong, sweet smell of aftershave. I could imagine him killing someone, and I didn't know what to say to Lisa. What *could* I say that would make any difference? I felt useless.

"I read the back of the leaflet," she said after a while. "I didn't understand most of it, but it says he's lying to everyone.

That Hitler started the fighting and could stop the war whenever he wants. Lots of German soldiers have been killed, it says. *Thousands* of them in Russia."

Soldiers like Papa.

"I thought we were winning," I said.

Lisa shrugged. "I don't know if it matters. They should stop anyway. Fighting is stupid and I hate Hitler as much as I hate the people who are bombing us."

I'd never heard anyone other than Stefan say something like that, but it didn't shock me as much as it might have a few weeks ago. I felt as if a layer of cloud was moving away from everything, and that I was finally seeing things as they really were.

FRAU SCHMIDT

We went to the school, which was deserted now except for a pair of magpies sitting on top of the air-raid siren. They chattered at us as we approached, then flew off across the yard.

From there, I tried to retrace my way to the spot where Kriminalinspektor Wolff had bumped into me. It didn't take us long to follow the route I'd taken, and it turned out I hadn't even traveled very far. I recognized the street where the woman who'd helped me lived as soon as we came to it, but the houses were all in a row and looked identical.

"We'll knock on a few doors," Lisa suggested. "Someone will remember you."

No one answered at the first house but, at the second, the woman recognized me right away. She directed us to number forty-three, just along the street.

Number forty-three was the woman who had brought me a damp cloth and a glass of water. She was named Frau Schmidt, and she let us into her house and offered us milk and cookies.

She ushered us into the kitchen and we sat at the table, both of us silent while she poured milk into two short glasses.

"I was so frightened when I heard the crash," she said. "Such a loud bang, and when I came to the window and saw you on the road like that, I thought you were . . ." She shuddered and brought the glasses to the table. "You're very lucky you weren't killed." She opened a tin, saying, "Help yourselves. I made them fresh this morning."

Lisa didn't hesitate. She dipped right into the tin and took a cookie. When she bit into it, crumbs scattered everywhere.

"I hope you didn't get into too much trouble," said Frau Schmidt. "I know what that man can be like. He's a . . ." She stopped herself. "Anyway. I hope you're all right. The injuries not too bad?" She pushed the cookie tin toward me.

"Not too bad, thank you." I took a cookie and had a small bite. It was plain and didn't taste of much, but I was hungrier than I had thought. "Thank you for helping me," I said with my mouth full.

"You're welcome . . ." She waited for me to tell her my name.

"Karl," I said. "And this is Lisa."

"Well, I'm Frau Schmidt and it's very nice to meet you both."

"Do you have any children?" Lisa asked. "I might know them from school."

Frau Schmidt shook her head. "My children are older now." She was staring over my shoulder as she spoke, and when I turned around, I saw a collection of photographs on the sideboard. Three of them were pictures of men in uniform and were arranged in a line in front of the others.

"Is that them?" I asked. "Are they in the army?"

"My son Joseph was killed last year in France. He's the one in the middle. The other one is my younger son, Max. He's in Russia, fighting for Hitler."

"And the other man?" I asked. "Is that your husband?"

Frau Schmidt sighed. "Yes. Another one I lost in France."

When I looked back at Frau Schmidt, her eyes were glistening and there was something about her that reminded me of Mama.

"My papa was killed," I said.

"Oh, you poor boy." Frau Schmidt blinked hard. "And your poor mother. It gets better with time, but you never forget."

"I don't want to forget." Since getting the news about Papa, Frau Schmidt was the first person I had spoken to who knew someone killed in the war. "Do you think they wanted to fight?" I asked.

Frau Schmidt put a hand to her mouth and looked away as if she might be about to cry, so I glanced at the pictures once more and was drawn to one in particular.

It was a picture of a girl and two boys, holding guitars and standing in front of what looked like an orchard, but I didn't look at their faces because something about one of the boys had caught my attention.

His badge. Pinned to the right side of his jacket, I noticed it right away.

"What's that?" I said, before I could stop myself. "There." I pointed. "What *is* that?"

Lisa leaned closer to see it, then looked at me. "It's the same," she whispered.

"What's that flower?" I asked, turning around, determined to know. "What does it mean? I've seen it painted on the walls."

Frau Schmidt came over and took the photo from my hands. "It's nothing. Just some silly thing Max made." She held the picture tight to her chest so we couldn't see it anymore.

"And my brother had the same thing sewn into his jacket —"

"Then you should ask your brother what it means." She returned the photograph to its place with the others and stood with her back to us, both hands on the sideboard.

"I did. But he wouldn't tell me. And the next thing I knew, he'd cut the flower off his pocket."

Frau Schmidt turned around but seemed flustered. She glanced around the room as if she didn't know what to say or where to look. "Then . . . then perhaps he doesn't want you to know about it," she said eventually. "Perhaps he doesn't trust you."

Frau Schmidt might as well have slapped me hard across the face, and my guilty feelings rose to the surface. "I . . ."

"And we have this." Lisa stepped forward to rescue me just like she did that day in Herr Finkel's shop. She was holding out her hand, and in her palm was the carved wooden flower she had found. It was almost exactly the same as the one the boy in the photograph was wearing.

Frau Schmidt stared at it. "Where did you get that?" She reached out as if to grab it, but then clutched her fingers tight and snatched her hand away.

"One of his brother's friends," she lied. "What is it? A daisy?"

Frau Schmidt looked at it for a long while. "An edelweiss," she whispered.

"An edelweiss," I repeated, suddenly seeing it. Of *course* that's what it was. "And what does it mean?"

She looked up at us as if deciding whether or not to tell us.

"Please," I asked.

Frau Schmidt sighed and opened her mouth to speak, then closed it again and shook her head. "You'll have to ask your brother. He'll tell you if he wants you to know."

PARADE

We walked on either side of my bike, with a handlebar each, lifting the front wheel off the ground. It was so buckled we had to take the weight and let it roll on just the back wheel.

"She was going to tell us." I could hardly contain my frustration. We had been *so close* to knowing.

"She was probably scared." Lisa was annoyed, too; I could hear it in her voice. "But at least we know what flower it is."

"Except now I've got about a million other questions. Like what does it mean? And why did her son have a badge just like it on his jacket? It was almost *exactly* the same." I stopped. "And I didn't like what she said about my brother not trusting me."

"She doesn't know you," Lisa said. "And last time she saw you, you were all dressed up in your stupid uniform." She looked at me for a moment and frowned as she chewed the inside of her lip. "Anyway, no one trusts anyone — this whole place makes me want to scream sometimes." She shook her head. "Come on, Karl Friedmann, let's go home."

Lisa knew the way from here, so we headed toward the main street, and as we came closer, I heard the sound of drums in the distance.

"Marching again." Lisa grumbled and her frown deepened. "As if today wasn't bad enough already."

The noise grew louder and louder as we neared the main street. We could hear trumpets, too, though they weren't being played very well, and when we turned the final corner, we saw the boys from the Deutsches Jungvolk and the Hitler Youth parading, just like I used to during weekends in the city.

The boys were all in uniform — black trousers, black scarf, and brown shirt. Their belt buckles glinted in the sun and their black boots were tromp-tromp-tromping on the road like the beat of an approaching army.

Men in hats and suits and women in dresses lined the pavements to watch them. There were very young children, too, pushing through for a better look. Some people clapped and cheered, while others were not so excited, as if they were just keeping up appearances.

Most of them were strangers to me, but I recognized some of the faces of people who lived on Escherstrasse — Herr Ackerman, the butcher, was there, and Frau Oster was wearing her best hat. She was holding on to her son with one hand and waving her flag with the other. There were a few people whose names I didn't know but whose faces I had seen passing by the house or waiting in line at the shops. Several of the girls in the crowd waved to Lisa or said hello, but she ignored them and plowed on.

"Don't stop," she muttered to me, and put her head down, tightening her fists around the handlebars as the day's frustration and anger grew in her.

There weren't as many boys parading here as in my group in the city, but what they lacked in numbers, they tried to make up for in noise.

The first group of nine was marching three abreast, and each of them held a pole with a flag draped from it. Bloodred, with a white circle and a black swastika in the center of it. There wasn't much of a wind that day, so the flags just hung there like limp rags.

A second group of boys — another nine marching three abreast — was right behind the flag bearers, but each of these had a drum and was beating it furiously. Behind them, three boys were blowing into trumpets. Their faces were red with effort and their cheeks were puffed out as if they'd been stuffed with bread.

Behind the flag bearers and musicians, another fifty or sixty boys marched, black boots stomping hard on the road. They had been arranged so that the younger boys from the Deutsches Jungvolk were at the front and the older Hitler Youth boys were at the back.

It was the older ones who started singing first.

"Hang the Jews! Line the fat cats up against the wall!"

The younger ones started to join in, but they didn't know the words so they just said the same thing over and over again.

"Hang the Jews! Line the fat cats up against the wall!"

Not so long ago, marching like this had seemed like the best thing in the world, but now I felt a stab of shame that I had shouted such hateful things.

I glanced at Lisa, seeing that she was glowering at the boys and shaking her head.

"Stupid parade," she said. "Stupid *Nazis*."

"Shh."

As the flag bearers approached, many of the people at the side of the road stood straight and raised their arms in salute, but Lisa and I kept going, struggling with my bike among the bystanders.

Boots crunched, drums banged, trumpets blasted, and the boys continued to sing.

"Hang the Jews! Line the fat cats up against the wall!"

One group of spectators had clustered so tightly together that they blocked the pavement. To get past, we had to bump the wheel down the curb and make our way along the edge of the road. Lisa tugged harder on the bike than necessary and jostled past two women as we went. When I looked across at her, her jaw was tight, and her expression was like thunder.

"Stupid Nazis," she muttered again, and I willed her not to say it any louder.

I was taking the weight on the right side of the bike — the side that was closest to the approaching parade — and, as the boys came closer and closer, I knew there would be barely enough room for them to get past.

"I'll take it," I said to Lisa. "I'll bring the bike. You get behind me." A great sense of urgency was building in me. There wasn't much time. A few more seconds and the marching boys would be right here.

"No. Just keep going." Lisa raised her voice and her knuckles whitened as she gripped the handlebars harder.

The sound of boots grew louder.

"There's not enough room," I told her. "Please. Just get behind me."

"Why should I?" She scowled at the boys who were now only a few steps away. "It's not their road."

"Just —"

"Get out of the way, you idiots!" shouted the flag bearer closest to us.

"Who are you calling idiot?" Lisa snapped back at him.

"Get off the road, Lisa!"

As soon as I heard the boy call her by name, I realized that Lisa would know him from school. In fact, she would know most of them, but that didn't change anything. She just made a face at the boy and lifted the front of the bike. "Keep going," she said to me. "Come on."

"No. Wait." I let go of the handlebars and hurried around the front of the bike, going to Lisa's side. The bicycle was like a barrier between us and the parade. "Please," I said to her. "What's the matter with you?"

"It's our road, too." There was such a frown on her face now that I thought she might explode as she tugged on the bike, trying to make me go on.

"Salute!" one of the boys shouted at us, but we could hardly hear his voice over the sound of the trumpets and drums that were now just a few steps away. Their rhythm pounded in our ears like the heartbeat of an angry beast.

More of the boys had noticed us now. As we wrestled with the bike, most of the drummers turned to glare at us as they passed. Their hands worked like pistons, the drumsticks rising and falling like hammers.

To one side of us, the bystanders stood on the pavement with their arms outstretched in salute. On the other, the boys marched and drummed.

Lisa and I were sandwiched between them, and I felt more and more trapped as the boys paraded past and more faces turned to watch us.

"Move!" said one as he jostled past.

"Out of the way, you idiots!" said another.

"Salute!"

The closest drummer glared over his shoulder as he passed, and then the trumpeters were alongside us, each of them with his head facing forward, but his eyes turned to watch us.

Lisa nudged me aside and pulled at the handlebars, lifting the front wheel of the bike. "Come on," she said. "Keep going."

"Just wait." I reached across her and put my hand on hers, but she struggled, trying to snatch away, and for a moment, neither of us was holding the bicycle.

The trumpeters trumpeted. The drummers drummed. The marchers marched and sang with their boots thump-thump-thumping on the road.

And the bicycle toppled.

There was nothing I could do. Even though my eyes saw it in slow motion and my mind knew what was going to happen, my body just couldn't keep up.

I tried to grab it. I stretched out both arms, but Lisa was too close to me, blocking me. The end of the handlebars brushed my fingertips as the bike went down. It fell sideways, toward the parade, just as the fifth row of Deutsches Jungvolk marched past.

The closest boy saw that it was going to collapse right into his path. He was about my age, but smaller, with cropped hair beneath his cap. He had a round face that was mottled with light freckles, and his pale eyes widened as soon as he realized what was happening. He tried to adjust his step, breaking time with the rest of the boys so that he could avoid the falling bicycle. The boy directly behind him hadn't noticed, though, and he barreled into Freckles, pushing him hard enough to reach the bicycle at exactly the right time for his foot to come down on top of the front wheel as it collapsed on the road.

His ankle twisted on the spokes and he crumpled like an infantryman cut down on the battlefield. The boy behind couldn't do anything other than crash into him, falling over his comrade as the next boy stumbled and tripped.

The three of them went down in a bundle of arms and legs, causing the boys in front to turn and wonder at the commotion, while the ones behind toppled over them in a heap.

After that, the parade collapsed into chaos.

EDELWEISS PIRATES

Boys were bumping into boys. They were falling over one another and jostling for space as the march came to a confused halt. The trumpets petered out with a few squeaks and squawks and the drums stopped banging. The air was filled with the cursing and shouting of angry boys and there was a sharp intake of breath from the crowd behind us, followed by a long moment of silence that was punctuated by one or two giggles and people stifling their laughter.

Lisa and I could only stare.

"You!"

I shook my head and looked across at one of the older boys pointing right at us.

"You! Lisa Herz!"

He was a big boy, probably seventeen years old, almost a man really. Taller than Stefan and thicker set. His uniform was pristine, making him look like a real soldier.

"You did this!" he shouted as he began to work his way through the collapsed boys, who were trying to get to their feet. He took off his cap as he came, gripping it hard in his left fist, and I knew what was on his mind. He wanted to hurt someone for ruining his parade.

I started to look around, searching for a way out, but there was nowhere to go. The road in front of us was blocked by the chaos that had once been a well-organized parade, with many of the boys now looking at Lisa and me — and they didn't look happy. Behind us, the crowd of bystanders was jostling for space, trying to see what was happening.

There was no escape route.

The boy was coming closer now, pushing others out of his way, his eyes fixed on us like he couldn't see anything else. Anger burned in his eyes. He stepped over boys still on the ground, his head lowered like a bull about to charge. His thick shoulders were raised and his face was set hard like concrete.

Beside me, Lisa planted her feet firmly on the ground and waited for him to come. She was preparing to fight him, but she was a girl. She wasn't supposed to fight.

As the boy came closer, I stepped in front of Lisa and put up my fists.

He was far too big and bullish for me, though; I didn't stand a chance.

"You stupid weakling," he said as he stepped over the nearest boy and swung his fist.

To my surprise, I deflected the first strike. I feinted to the left and knocked his fist aside, sending it swinging wildly into thin air. His other fist came in right away, but I leaned back and managed to deflect that, too, then I stepped toward him and punched straight up at his face.

He was too tall for me to reach my intended target, but I was shocked when my fist connected with the underside of his chin. There was a clatter of teeth for him and searing agony for me. Pain exploded in my knuckles, ballooning out across my hand and right up my wrist.

The boy stepped back to steady himself, and I shook my hand to wave away the pain, but it blinded me. It was like my hand had been plunged into a furnace. I looked at my fingers, half expecting to see flames licking around them, and that's when the boy came at me with his third punch.

It was like being hit with a steel bar. The Führer would have been proud of that boy's strength. His fist caught me on my left cheekbone, jarring my head to the right, shooting pain down my neck and shoulders. I spun to one side as my legs gave way and there was a moment when my head filled with darkness. The shadow swallowed me up, and when it spat me out again, I was lying on the floor beside my bicycle and the big boy was standing over me.

I looked up at him, wondering, for a moment, who he was.

As it came back to me, the boy lifted one foot and cocked his leg back as if he was about to kick a football. Except instead of a football, his boot was aimed at my head.

"No!" There was a cry from behind me and Lisa came into view, flying at my attacker, flailing her fists in front of her. Slamming straight into him, she forced the boy backward so that he bumped into one of the Deutsches Jungvolk who was struggling to his feet.

The boy who had hit me lost his balance. His arms whipped

141

out in front of him as if he might be able to grab Lisa and stop himself from falling, but he was too heavy and too far gone. His fingers raked along the front of Lisa's dress as he dropped, his right hand catching in her pocket and ripping it off, and then he hit the ground.

Even from where I was lying, I saw the carved flower spin away from Lisa's torn pocket.

Up and up, it went, around and around, turning in the air as it arced upward before tumbling toward the ground. Except it didn't ever reach the ground.

Instead of hitting the road and bouncing away where it could cause no harm, the small wooden edelweiss dropped right onto my attacker's chest.

For a moment, Lisa stood over him, triumphant, while I lay behind her, dazed and shocked.

Then the boy noticed the flower lying on his chest, and some kind of recognition flashed in his eyes.

He lifted a hand and picked up the carving, holding it between his finger and thumb so the petals were pointing toward the sky.

He stared at it for what felt like a very long time, then looked at us once more as a clear expression of distaste spread across his face. His lip curled and he took a deep breath before pointing a finger and shouting two words.

"Edelweiss Pirates!"

He might as well have shouted "British soldiers!" or "Russians!" or even "Spies!"

First the boys around him looked at their comrade lying on

the floor at their feet. Then they looked at his finger pointing in our direction. Then they looked at us.

Lisa took the chance to help me to my feet as the boy who had hit me drew himself up to his full height. He held the carved flower out toward us as if it were some kind of accusation, and spat the words again.

"Edelweiss Pirates."

He threw the wooden flower at me so that it bounced off my chest and landed on the road at my feet.

Lisa put a hand on my arm and together we stepped back so that the curb was against our heels.

The crowd pressed up against us, blocking our escape, and I glanced left and right, seeing no way out.

Other boys fell in behind the one who had hit me. First two, then three, four, five, six, until it was impossible for us to count how many boys were standing in a semicircle around us.

The world closed in on me. My heart pounded like a black-smith's hammer. My vision swirled and brightened and became crystal clear. It was as if there were nothing in the world but me, Lisa, and those boys in front of us. My body was preparing itself for what was about to happen. There were only two things for me to do. I could either run or I could fight. But there was nowhere for me to run. No way out.

I would have to fight.

My tongue was as dry as summer dust and it stuck to the roof of my mouth as I edged in front of Lisa. I knew I couldn't beat these boys, but I had to do what I could. I had to put myself before Lisa. They would have to deal with me first. Except Lisa disagreed. She moved out from behind me and stood by my side, shoulder to shoulder.

She raised her fists when I raised mine.

The boys didn't laugh at our defiant stance, though; they didn't even smile.

They advanced.

THE WOLFF GROWLS

It was Kriminalinspektor Gerhard Wolff who saved our skins.

He appeared as if from nowhere, stepping into the small patch of empty road in front of Lisa and me.

He stood with his back to us and held up a hand, making the boys stop and glance at each other.

"Stay where you are." Without taking his eyes off them, Wolff crouched and picked up the little wooden flower. He slipped it into his pocket as he stood up.

"You saw what they did," said the one who had hit me. His fists were still tight, and he took a step closer. "This girl —"

"I said, stay where you are." Wolff didn't raise his voice; he lowered it. And there was something about it that reminded me of the way a dog drops its head and snarls. Not a loud bark, but a low and dangerous growl.

The boy stopped in his tracks.

"Good." Wolff's tone returned to normal, as if he were wishing the boy a good morning. "I'm surprised at you, Erich Mann; I shouldn't have to remind you who I am."

Erich took a step back now. The grim expression fell from

his face, to be replaced with surprise. His fists loosened. "I . . . sir . . ." Then he seemed to remember himself. He snapped his heels together and raised his arm. *"Heil Hitler."*

The others followed suit.

"Yes, yes. *Heil Hitler.*" Wolff half raised his arm in much the same way as I had seen the Führer do on the newsreels. A sort of half salute, as if he couldn't be bothered to extend his arm completely.

"Sir," Erich said, "I know this girl. She's called Lisa Herz, and I have reason to believe these two are Edelweiss —"

"I will make that decision for myself."

"But you know what that badge is? The one that —"

"I'm perfectly aware of what it is," said Wolff. "But this is no concern of yours. I will get to the bottom of this."

The boys stayed where they were, but the leader was looking past Wolff, staring right at me.

"You need to move now," said Wolff. "Organize yourselves and carry on. This is supposed to be a parade."

Some of the boys shared a few glances.

"You're not hooligans," Wolff warned. "You think the Führer wants street brawlers in his army? No, no, no. He wants disciplined soldiers."

Erich continued to glare, but the others looked at the ground and started to move away, helping their comrades to reorganize the parade. Many of the Hitler Youth had reformed their lines and the group leaders were bringing the younger boys into formation.

"I know who you are." Erich pointed at Lisa. "I know where you live."

"And I know where *you* live." Wolff lowered his voice again and fixed Erich Mann with his steely stare. "Now, off you go. Unless you wish to pay a visit to Headquarters."

Erich swallowed hard and saluted once more before heading off to help with the reorganization. As he gave his orders, though, he couldn't help looking over in our direction.

"Pick up your bicycle," Wolff said without taking his eyes off Erich.

My hands were shaking as I pulled up the bike, and my arms felt full of energy.

Once it was upright, Lisa grabbed the handlebar nearest to her and we lifted the front wheel off the ground before moving back onto the pavement. It was only then that we realized we had such a large audience. A large crowd had formed around us, all the people straining to see what was going on, but not one of them had come to our help. Some of them had probably been too afraid to do anything, but others would have been glad to see us beaten up by the Hitler Youth.

They parted in front of us, and I glared at all the adult faces around me, faces of people who had done nothing to help us. I was sure I caught a glimpse of Frau Oster, shaking her head in disapproval.

Wolff followed us through the crowd, leaving the parade and the onlookers behind as we broke through onto the clear pavement and headed home.

"You were lucky I was there." Wolff was wearing the same suit and the same shiny shoes as he had been on the day of our crash. His hat was pulled low so that it almost covered his eyebrows and there was the same smell of aftershave around him.

"You have a good punch, though. I imagine you've practiced it a lot."

I shrugged, feeling the ache in my neck, and put a hand to my cheek, where it was sore. I imagined I'd have a black eye tomorrow.

"And you've got spirit," Wolff went on. "But it seems you also have a gift for getting into trouble." He put his hands in his pockets and we continued along the main street.

Being so close to him made me prickle with fear, and despite everything that had just happened, I couldn't help thinking about poor Herr Finkel, bloodied and beaten.

"So are you going to thank me?" Wolff said after a while. "For saving your skins?"

"Thank you, sir," I muttered.

"Well." He stopped and looked around. "I think this should be far enough. You'll be safe now."

Lisa and I came to a halt beside him and he leaned closer to me. "If I walk you all the way home we might scare your *Oma* and *Opa* again — and we don't want to do that now, do we? They might think you've been telling me their secrets." He winked, making me shudder inside, and stood back as if he were about to leave. "*Do* you have any secrets you want to tell me?"

"No, sir."

"Hmm." Then a puzzled expression crossed his face and he held up a finger. "Oh, there is one thing you could tell me," he said. "You could tell me about *this*."

He removed his other hand from his pocket and showed me the little carved flower that had caused so much trouble.

I stared at it and wondered what I should say.

"I found it," Lisa said. "Some boys dropped it." There was hatred in her voice.

"And would you recognize them if you saw them again?" Wolff asked.

"It was a long way off," she muttered. "They could have been anybody."

Wolff nodded as if he'd expected her to say that. "And there's nothing else you want to tell me?"

"I . . ." I was almost afraid to ask. I didn't want to give anything away.

"Yes?"

"Well, it's . . . something those boys said. About the badge."

"Spit it out."

I couldn't help myself. I had to know. "What are Edelweiss Pirates?"

For a second, Wolff's face darkened like a storm, then it lightened and he smiled. He took a deep breath and looked along the street before turning to me once again. "Criminals," he said. "Reprobates. They are long-haired thugs who hang around on street corners and loiter in cafés doing nothing but spreading lies, the kind of young people you should avoid at all costs. Do you understand?"

I nodded. Lisa just stared at the pavement.

"Edelweiss Pirates are the lowest of the low," Wolff went on. "Maybe worse even than Jews." He leaned closer. "You see, Jews can't help being Jews. It's what they are. But these Edelweiss Pirates are Germans who hate the Führer. They are traitors and troublemakers, writing on walls, distributing leaflets, attacking the Hitler Youth."

I swallowed hard and remembered the leaflet Lisa had given to me on the way to Frau Schmidt's house. The same kind that Herr Finkel had taken. It was now folded into a square and pushed deep in my pocket, but if Wolff asked us to turn out our pockets, he would see it and arrest me.

"A group of them put out the windows in the factory on the other side of town just this morning," Wolff said. "And we have a problem with them pouring sugar into gas tanks." As soon as he said it, it made me think of the boys I'd seen outside Herr Finkel's shop. "It doesn't do any permanent damage, but it's a nuisance, and one thing leads to another; before we know it, there will be anarchy on the streets." He fixed me with those cold gray eyes. "You *are* a good German, aren't you, Karl Friedmann?"

"Yes, sir."

"Then I want you to tell me if you see any of these." He held the little wooden badge up and snapped it in half before dropping it on the road. "Do you understand?"

I nodded.

"Good boy." Wolff ruffled my hair and I had to stop myself from recoiling. "Off you go, then. Stay out of trouble."

Lisa and I didn't look at each other as we took the weight of the bike between us and headed to the corner of Escherstrasse.

"One other thing," Wolff called after us, making us stop and turn around. "Give my regards to Frau Schmidt next time you see her."

He must have seen the surprise on our faces because he looked very pleased with himself.

"There's not much happens in this town I don't know about," he said. Then he half raised his hand in a lazy salute, turned on his heels, and walked away in the opposite direction.

THE FÜHRER'S BOOK

What do you think he meant by that?" I asked. "About Frau Schmidt?"

We had turned onto Escherstrasse in silence, both of us lost in our thoughts.

"He's a pig." Lisa shivered. "I hate him."

I couldn't blame her — and after what we'd seen him do to Herr Finkel and what he'd done to Lisa's papa, I was starting to hate him, too.

"He was just showing us that he knew we'd been there," Lisa said. "He thinks he knows everything, but he doesn't know who these Edelweiss Pirates are, does he? But we do."

I looked up at her. "You mean Stefan? You really think he's one of them?"

"He had the flower, didn't he? I reckon that girl's one, too."

"You can't tell anyone. Not *anyone*."

"Don't worry," she said. "Your brother's secret is safe with me."

"Anyway, he might not even be one. Maybe he just had the flower . . . I mean . . . Do you really think they're criminals? Worse than Jews?"

"Jews are just people like everyone else," Lisa said. "You can't believe *everything* they tell us at school." She shook her head. "It's a good thing I met you when I did, Karl Friedmann. Any longer and there'd have been no hope for you."

When we arrived at the entrance to the alley beside Oma and Opa's house, I looked back along the street. "Do you think he followed us? Maybe he's following us now."

"He can't follow us all the time." Lisa was looking along the street, too, though, scanning the windows as if she thought someone might be watching us right now. "But he said he saw the whole thing, didn't he? At the parade, I mean. And he knew you hit Erich, so he must have seen that."

An image of the boy popped into my mind and I remembered what he had said to Lisa. "Does he really know where you live?"

"Erich?" Lisa said. "Yes, but I'm not scared of him. He's just a bully."

She was afraid of Kriminalinspektor Wolff, though, and so was I, and it made me even more scared to think that he might be watching us. Suddenly I felt exposed, standing in the mouth of the alley like that, the leaflet in my pocket. I imagined what would happen if Wolff appeared at the corner now, running up to us because he'd forgotten to make us turn out our pockets. "Come on," I said. "Let's get inside."

I had to get rid of it. Put it somewhere safe.

Opa was tinkering with his car when we let ourselves in through the back gate.

"That doesn't look good," he said, coming toward us, cleaning his hands on an oily rag.

At first, I thought he must have been talking about my face, and I put a hand to my cheek, but he was looking at the bicycle.

"You'll never ride it like that."

He stood with the rag in one hand and shook his head at the state of the buckled wheel. When he looked up at me, though, his face fell.

"What happened to you?" He came forward and put his fingers on my chin, turning my head to one side. "Have you been fighting?"

"You should see the other boy, Herr Brandt," Lisa said.

"It wasn't my fault, Opa." I told him what had happened, but left out the part about Frau Schmidt and the Edelweiss Pirates. I didn't tell him about Wolff, either; it was best to keep that to myself. Instead, I told him that we ran away from the boys.

"Well, that's not a bad option," he said. "Live to fight another day. And fighting is for boys who don't know how to use their brains."

"You were a boxer," I said.

"That's a sport. Controlled. It's not the same as fighting in the street. Come on, we need to get you cleaned up, and seeing as Stefan's gone out with friends, and your mama and Oma are visiting Frau Dassler, it looks like it's going to be my job."

"I can help," Lisa said.

"You need to be getting home for lunch, young lady. I think we've had enough excitement for one day, don't you?"

"What about my bike?" I asked. "Can you fix it?"

Opa looked down at the buckled wheel and took a deep breath. "Not much hope for it, I'm afraid. It'll need a new wheel and that's not going to be easy to find."

"There's one in the cellar," I said. "I saw it last night during the raid."

Opa thought for a moment. "You know, I think you're right. There's a whole bike down there — it was mine when I was about your age. We'll bring it out after we get you cleaned up."

"There's something I have to do first." I moved past him and headed toward the house.

"And what's that?" he asked.

"Nothing." I raised a hand at Lisa, saying, "See you later," then ran across the yard and jumped up the steps into the house.

I hurried through the hallway and up the stairs to my bedroom where I closed the door and scanned the room, looking for a good place to hide the leaflet. Under the mattress was too obvious. In a shoe? Maybe at the back of the wardrobe? Or under my pillow?

As I tried to decide on a safe place, a voice crept into my head as if from nowhere.

Get rid of it.

I put my hand into my pocket and touched the folded paper.

Get rid of it.

But I wanted to keep it. Not just because I needed to read what it said, but because Lisa had given it to me. She had kept it especially for me and it would feel wrong to just throw it away.

Get rid of it.

I snatched it out of my pocket and went to the chest of drawers where Stefan and I kept our underwear and the few belongings we'd brought with us. Above it, hanging on a nail, was a small mirror, my reflection looking back at me. I looked pale and there was a bruise forming around my eye. I touched the angry red skin and winced.

Papa looked at me from the photo.

"Where should I put it?" I asked him.

Then, as if he had answered, I saw the perfect hiding place, right behind him.

On top of the chest of drawers, pushed back against the wall, I had arranged a line of books, with the smallest at the left side and the biggest at the right.

I slid Papa's photograph to one side, moved my silver medal, and slipped one of the books from the line before laying it faceup on the top of the chest of drawers. It had a black-and-white picture of the Führer on the front, looking very stern, and a red banner across it with the words *"Mein Kampf"* printed in white.

I had pestered Mama and Papa to buy me a copy of the Führer's book but they had said I would never read it, so I did odd jobs for the neighbors until I'd had enough to buy it for myself. I'd been so proud, coming back from the shop with my very own copy, but Mama and Papa were right. I didn't read it. I tried, but it was too complicated. Too boring.

The Führer looked up at me from the chest of drawers, with his shiny black hair and his neat moustache and his dark eyes accusing me. It was as if he could see me. Wherever he was right now, giving his orders, conducting his war, he could look through this picture, right into this room, and see me standing in front of his unread book, holding a leaflet dropped from a British bomber.

"Oh, shut up," I whispered. Then I unfolded the leaflet and put it over his face so I could see the new picture of the Führer.

In the bright sunlight that streamed through the bedroom window, the piles of dead German soldiers lying at Hitler's feet were easier to see. The one closest, with his face turned toward me, had his mouth open in a silent scream, and his eyes were wide and dead. His body was twisted, his machine gun lying just out of reach as if it had fallen from his hands as he was killed.

He looked like Papa. Whoever had drawn this might have been drawing my own father. I had to shake my head and rub my eyes before looking more closely to see that it wasn't Papa. It was a nameless soldier, dead at the Führer's feet.

Hitler is killing your fathers.

I stared at the picture for a long time. It drew me in, sucking me right into its world. I could smell the smoke from the gun-fire, see it hanging over the battlefield in wispy clouds. I could feel the heat of the fires, and hear the rumble of tanks and the screams of the dying men. This wasn't the glorious fight I had been told about; it was a terrible, terrible nightmare of death and waste.

"Karl?"

The voice broke into my thoughts.

"Karl?"

It was only when I heard Opa start up the stairs that I managed to shake the vision from my head.

"Karl?"

"Just coming," I called back, but my throat was dry and the words didn't come out properly. I had to hide the leaflet. I wasn't supposed to have it.

"Are you all right?"

I swallowed. "Yes. I'm coming."

My heart beat faster. Opa was close to the top of the stairs now. He would be here at any moment.

I folded the leaflet in half along one of the creases, my fingers fumbling as if to betray me.

Closer.

Without wasting any more time, I opened the book and slipped the leaflet inside before closing it and pressing it together. I turned it spine out so I could inspect how it looked, and that's when Opa came into the room.

"What are you doing? You've been up here for ages."

"Have I?" I started to slip the book back into its place, but the others had fallen inward, blocking the gap. I used the corners to nudge the others aside to make room. "Sorry. I was thinking about Herr Finkel. Earlier on we saw —"

"I heard about it," Opa said as he came in and stood behind me. "Herr Lang came by; he saw it, too."

"Did he know why they arrested him?"

Opa shook his head. "No idea. Perhaps Herr Finkel said something or sold something he shouldn't have; we'll probably never know."

"Do you think they took him to Headquarters?" I pictured the large gray building by the river. "The other night, when he got angry, Stefan said they torture people there. Do you think —"

"Don't. That's . . ." Opa stopped and cleared his throat. "That's not something you should think about."

"Lisa said people know Wolff from when he was a boy. Did Herr Finkel know him?" Somehow, the idea of it made the arrest seem even worse.

"Most of us do," Opa spoke quietly. "He used to deliver bread."

"And then he joined the Gestapo?"

"He was a policeman first. Not the best, but decent enough. *Then* he joined the Gestapo and, well, things change. People change. Sometimes they do things . . ." Opa let his words trail away and I tried not to think about the shopkeeper's bloodied face.

"I liked Herr Finkel," I said.

"I did, too, Karl." Opa sounded sad. "Now why don't you tell me what you've got there?" He put his hand on my shoulder and looked over to see what I was doing.

"*Mein Kampf*?" He reached over to take the book from my hands. "Hm. Not a great read, I have to say." He twisted his wrist to look at the back of the book, then turned it face out once more so the Führer was watching us. "It's a little dry for my taste. What about you?"

"I haven't read it," I admitted.

"Can't say I blame you."

I looked up so I could see Opa in the mirror that hung on the wall. "I don't think I ever will."

He held my gaze for a long while as if he understood what I was saying, then a gentle smile touched his lips and the creases around the corners of his eyes bunched together. He nodded and squeezed my shoulder. "Let's leave it where it is for now."

He handed it back to me and I put the book in its place among the others. I returned Papa's picture to where it had been, and picked up my silver proficiency badge. I studied it for a moment, remembering the day I had received it — remembering Johann Weber — then I opened the drawer and buried the badge beneath a bundle of socks. When I closed the drawer, I looked at Opa's reflection in the mirror again.

"One day all this will be over," he said. "And I think there'll be a lot of explaining to do."

"What do you mean?"

Opa sucked his teeth and looked up at the ceiling. "Well. I'm no expert, Karl, but one day this war is going to end, and men like that" — he nodded toward the line of books — "men like that can get too big for their boots, stretch themselves too far. And sooner or later, they get what they deserve."

A BAD GERMAN

Opa heated water on the stove, and while I washed my face, he looked for something cold to put on my eye.

"Best not tell Stefan how this happened," he said, handing me a thin slice of pork as I came into the kitchen. "And be careful with that; it's our supper."

I sat at the table and put the cool, sticky meat against my eye.

"It might set him off again like last night," Opa said, "make him more angry. Just say you fell off your bike."

I thought about how Stefan had shouted at me, and Opa must have seen how bad it made me feel because he sat down and leaned back in the chair. "It's not all your fault. Sometimes people get angry about things that make other people sad. Things affect people in different ways."

I waited for him to explain.

"When you think about Papa, how does it make you feel?"

I squeezed my eyes shut and tried to ignore the tightness in my chest. It was like a pain that wouldn't go away. It was always there, even when I didn't notice it. When I was with Lisa, I didn't think about it, but then I'd see something or hear something that would remind me of Papa and the pain would come rushing forward.

"It makes me feel sad," I said.

Opa nodded. "For your mama, it's different. It made her ill."

"But she's getting better now."

"Yes, she is, and that's good." He gave me a sad smile. "But it has made Stefan angry. He wants to blame someone for what happened to Papa."

"You mean he wants to blame the Führer?"

Opa raised his eyebrows and thought about it. "Well, I don't think your brother ever liked the Führer very much. Your father was the same, and —"

"Papa didn't like the Führer?" I asked.

Opa sighed. "Maybe this isn't something to talk about now; we're talking about Stefan, and about why you shouldn't tell him what happened to you. You see, Karl, it might make him do something stupid. You remember how he used to get into trouble at home? And that time he went away for fighting with the other boys? Well, it's the same thing, except times have changed and the consequences are much worse now. Stefan was right when he said that sometimes people are taken away and never come back."

"Like Lisa's papa?"

"Yes."

"And Herr Finkel?"

"I don't know. Maybe." Opa shook his head.

"But how can Kriminalinspektor Wolff be so horrible to people he knows?" Even as the question came out, though, I remembered some of the horrible things *I* had done — like hitting Johann Weber to the ground on the day he received his papa's death notice.

"As I said, Karl, people change." Opa looked right at me. "But not always for the better."

I shifted my gaze and stared at the Nazi party badge pinned to his shirt, the perfect red-and-white circle with the silver lettering and the swastika in the center. "You weren't wearing that the day Kriminalinspektor Wolff came. You used to wear it all the time."

Opa looked down at the badge and shook his head. "Yes, I . . ."

"You don't like him," I said. "Hitler. You don't like him anymore."

Opa didn't say anything. He went to the cast-iron stove and put a pan over the hotplate.

"I won't tell."

Opa looked over his shoulder at me, then took a wooden spoon from the drawer and used it to stir the contents of the pot.

"I don't mean about my eye," I said. "Though, I won't tell about that, either. I mean about anything."

Opa stopped stirring and stood with his back to me.

"About the flower. About Papa not wanting to go to war. About what you really think of the Führer."

Opa turned around and stared at me.

"I promise I won't," I said. "And . . . and I don't think I like the Führer anymore, either. He makes everyone scared and that isn't right. We shouldn't be scared, should we?"

"No," Opa said, "we shouldn't."

When lunch was ready, we sat at the table with a bowl of watery broth. It didn't taste of much, but there was a piece of sausage left, so Opa cut it into tiny chunks and dropped it in. The chewy little lumps sank to the bottom and added only a hint of flavor.

We had hardly started eating, when there was a knock at the front door and Opa put down his spoon to answer it. As soon as I heard Stefan's name mentioned, I went to the window and looked out to see Opa standing on the step talking to two boys. I recognized them right away as the two I'd seen earlier that morning. The same two who had put something into the gas tank of the truck.

Opa was shaking his head as he spoke to them but I couldn't hear what he was saying, so I went to the kitchen door and looked out just in time to hear Opa say, "And don't come here again," before he stepped back inside and closed the door.

"Stupid idiots," he said as he turned around and saw me standing behind him.

"Who was it?" I asked.

"No one."

"Are they Stefan's friends?"

"It doesn't matter; they won't come here again. Now come and eat your lunch before it gets cold."

Back in the kitchen, Opa switched on the "people's receiver" wireless that sat on the sideboard where Oma kept the plates. We had one at home that looked exactly the same. They were specially made so that everyone could afford to have one and listen to the news and programs the Reich put on for us.

There was traditional music playing when we sat down for lunch, but when the song was over, something else came on. I wasn't really listening to it until I heard *his* voice. It was one of the Führer's speeches, something I'd heard lots of times before because they made us learn it at school, but they always played this one part that seemed to be more and more important as the war went on.

"Mr. Churchill may be convinced that Great Britain will win. I do not doubt for a single moment that Germany will be victorious. Destiny will decide who is right."

I knew the words by heart, and I still felt my pride swell when I repeated the words in my head.

Germany will be victorious.

But with the pride, I felt confused. I hated the enemy. The Russians had killed my papa and the British flew over us and dropped bombs and blew up our houses. I wanted Germany to be victorious and I was proud to be German, but at the same time, I didn't love the Führer anymore. I used to think he sounded excited, but now his voice just sounded angry.

"Let's see if there's something else on," Opa said, getting up from the table. "Music is so much better for the digestion, don't you think?"

APACHES

Mama and Oma noticed my black eye as soon as they came home that afternoon, but Opa and I had already agreed on a story. We told them we fixed the bike together, using the old one from the cellar — which was true. Then we told them that once it was working, Lisa and I went out for a ride — which was also true. The only lie we told them was that I had lost my balance and fallen off my bike, resulting in the black eye.

Oma wasn't completely convinced and I suspected she would question Opa about it later, but Mama just looked worried. She hugged me and told me to be more careful. When she did that, my heart lightened and I was happy just to have her almost back to normal.

When Stefan returned, though, he wasn't so easily fooled. He kept looking at me all through supper but didn't say anything more about it until everyone had gone to bed.

"So what really happened?" he asked. "Who hit you?"

It was dark and I was lying in bed, staring at the ceiling.

"Was it Hitler Youth boys? Deutsches Jungvolk? Tell me and I'll make them pay for it."

"It doesn't matter." I touched my face and hated those boys for hitting me.

There was a part of me that wanted to tell Stefan what had happened to him so he would go out and find them, but he would only get into trouble, so I kept quiet and we lay in silence.

Not even the slightest sliver of moonlight broke through the blackout curtains, but if I pressed my fingers into my eyes for a few seconds, I could see bright circles floating on the ceiling. I watched the circles and wondered about Edelweiss Pirates.

"You know, sometimes I wish I was your papa," Stefan said. "Then maybe you'd tell me what happened to you. And I'd have stopped all that Deutsches Jungvolk nonsense, too. Mama should never have let you go."

"I have to go. It's the rules."

"Hmm." Stefan was quiet for a moment. "But you don't have to believe it all so much."

"I don't. Not anymore."

"What changed?"

"Everything," I said. "Papa. You. Lisa. The leaflets from last night."

"The leaflets?" There was an edge to his voice. "What do you know about those leaflets?"

"Nothing." I couldn't tell him that I had one, secreted away inside my copy of *Mein Kampf*. He'd make me get rid of it.

"You know," he said, "if it was older boys who hit you, I can get them back. I have friends who —"

"Edelweiss Pirates?" I said, almost without thinking.

"What? Where did you hear that?"

"I've seen the words on the walls. The flowers, too, like the one in your pocket."

"You can't tell anyone about that." He sounded worried.

"And Lisa found a badge after some boys ran away."

"It's best you don't know anything about it," he said. "If you don't know anything, you can't tell anyone."

"You still think I'll go and tell the Gestapo?"

"It's not that, it's . . . well, it's just that all your friends are in the Deutsches Jungvolk and you're so . . . *into* it all."

"Not anymore. I told you that."

"But if you said something by accident and —"

"I won't."

Stefan sighed. "All right, look," he gave in, "the Pirates are just people. There are a few groups with different names, but they're all Edelweiss Pirates. There was a group in the city called the Navajos —"

"Like the Indians?"

"Exactly. And we're called the Apaches —"

"So you *are* one? That's what the flower in your jacket meant?"

"Yeah."

"But you're not a criminal? I heard they're criminals."

"No, we just like music and having fun."

"And writing on walls."

"Well, there's that, too, and sometimes people get into fights with the Hitler Youth, but mostly we just play music and sing songs and hang out with girls. You remember Jana? The girl you saw me with? She plays guitar and sings with the best voice. You mustn't tell anyone, though; that man from the Gestapo would arrest all of us."

I remembered what Wolff had said about someone putting out the windows at the factory. He had said it was Edelweiss Pirates and I couldn't help wondering if Stefan had been involved.

"Do you really think he does . . . *things* to people at Headquarters?" I asked.

"You mean torture?" Stefan replied.

"Yes. At that place by the river?"

"Of course. That's what the Gestapo is for."

I tried not to think about the soldiers dragging Herr Finkel away. I pushed it out of my mind and stared at the ceiling. Instead I concentrated on what Stefan had just told me; I had finally managed to get him to tell me about the flower. I felt as if I had won just a little of his trust.

I told him about seeing the boys put what I thought was sugar in the gas tank of the truck when Herr Finkel was arrested, and said that they had come to the house to call on him.

"I know them," Stefan said, "but they do things even I would never do. I don't hang around with them."

"Are there many of you?" I asked.

"Not that many in our group, only about twelve in all, but some of the groups are bigger."

It would feel good to be part of a group. That was one of the things I liked best about being in the Deutsches Jungvolk — being with all those brothers — but now I'd decided I didn't love Hitler anymore, it would feel good to be in another group. I imagined myself surrounded by friends and going out to find the boys who had been at the parade. I imagined we found them and confronted them and fought them so hard they begged us not to hurt them anymore.

"How do you join?" I asked.

"You don't," Stefan said. "You're too young."

I pressed my fingers into my eyes once more and watched the colored circles floating like miniature searchlights on the ceiling.

Maybe Lisa and I could make our own group. Our own Edelweiss Pirates.

NIGHT EXERCISE

The next two days were the best I'd had for a while. The weather was perfect, so Lisa and I went for long bike rides in the evening sunshine. Stefan continued to work at the mill and walk home with Jana, the two of them leaving a cloud of flour behind them. Mama looked healthier each day and even seemed happy sometimes.

There were no air raids and the radio told us that our tanks had broken Soviet defenses and would soon be in Leningrad. They were advancing on Kiev, too, and it was only a matter of time before the Russians would surrender. After that, the war would be won and everything would be back to normal.

To make things even better, I didn't see Kriminalinspektor Wolff once — though I did look over my shoulder from time to time, just to see if he was following us.

All of that calm came to an end one night when I heard Stefan moving about in the bedroom. I didn't know what time it was, but it was still dark and felt like the middle of the night. It sounded as if he was getting dressed.

"What's going on?" I sat up. "Is it another raid?" My heart started thumping just at the thought of it, but there weren't any sirens going off and I couldn't hear any planes.

"There's no raid," he whispered. "Go back to sleep."

"I can't," I said. "Not now."

Stefan tutted and crept over to me, patting the end of my bed as he felt his way in the darkness. "Look," he said, sitting beside me, "I'm going out."

"Out*side*?"

"Yeah, but I'll be back soon. And you can't tell anyone."

"Is it something to do with the Edelweiss Pirates?" I asked. "The Apaches?"

For a moment, Stefan didn't say anything, then he sighed. "Yeah, it's something to do with that."

"Can I come?"

"No, you can't. Now promise you'll keep your mouth shut."

"Are you going to get into trouble?"

"I might if you don't keep your mouth shut."

"Then tell me what you're doing."

"Oh, for God's sake, Karl . . ." There was an urgency in his whispering. "Look, I'll tell you tomorrow, but I haven't got time now. I have to go."

The weight lifted from the mattress and I saw a vague hint of him standing there in the gap between our beds. It wasn't exactly his silhouette, more like a darkness within the darkness. He was just a black smudge, moving away from me, melting into nothing.

The bedroom door opened with a gentle click, then, a second later, came the click of it shutting behind him. This was followed by the gentle sigh of his footsteps on the staircase, accompanied by the creaks and groans of the wood beneath his feet.

I strained to hear him reach the bottom, but there was no way of knowing; his sounds faded into nothing, just as his shadow had done when he left the bedroom.

I couldn't help feeling afraid — I didn't know where he was going or what he was going to do — but there was also an excitement that niggled at me. I had the strong sense that I was missing out on something.

I could follow him.

My heart jumped at the thought of it. Even just the idea of sneaking out in the night was exhilarating. Last year we did a night exercise in the Deutsches Jungvolk, and it had been one of the best things we had ever done. The darkness had made it even more exciting than usual, and that's how I felt now, thinking about following Stefan.

I leaped out of bed, threw off my pajamas, and pulled on my trousers and —

You don't have a key.

The thought came like a shot of disappointment. Of course I didn't have a key. Stefan had one because he went to work every day, but I didn't. If I went out, the door would lock behind me and I wouldn't be able to get back in unless I was with Stefan — or unless I rang the doorbell.

I stood there for a moment, half dressed, heart sinking, when a different thought came to me. This time it was a picture instead of words — a picture of the small table by the door, with Opa's key sitting inside the glass ashtray. A dull silver key.

I can take it with me.

With renewed excitement, I pulled on my shirt, just as I heard the door open downstairs. It was hardly much more than a *crrrick*, a long moment of quiet, then a second *crrrick* as Stefan pulled it shut behind him.

I hurried to the window and tugged back the curtain, letting the moonlight flood into the room. I pressed my nose to the glass, and saw Stefan's silhouette standing by the front door. He paused there for a few moments, then turned right and headed past the alley that ran along the side of the house, and continued down Escherstrasse.

Quick, I told myself as I let the curtain fall back into place. *I have to be quick.*

Still fastening my buttons, I crossed to the door and let myself into the hallway. Creeping downstairs, I kept my feet to the very edges of the steps, trying to avoid any that might creak. Once at the bottom, I jammed my feet into my boots and tightened the laces as quickly as I could. I grabbed my jacket and snatched the key from the bowl, sticking it in my pocket alongside my new penknife.

Then I opened the door and slipped into the night.

For a second, I felt like a freed animal. I was both thrilled and afraid. I shouldn't be out in the night. Stefan would be so angry if he knew I was out, and if the police caught me, they might think I was some kind of spy — or up to no good, at the very least. And if the air-raid sirens started up their screaming and the enemy came and the planes dropped their deadly bombs, what then? I would be killed for sure.

Adrenaline raced through my veins, both hot and cold, and I hardened my resolve. There was no going back now.

I walked quickly to the end of Escherstrasse and passed Herr Finkel's boarded-up shop without seeing any sign of Stefan. When I turned the corner, though, there was a group of figures farther along the street, close to the wall. I stopped and drew back around the corner, leaning out just enough to watch them.

They made no sound at all, but stood huddled together like ghosts waiting for someone to scare.

So I waited, too.

The night was cooler than I had expected, and I shivered as a gentle breeze nestled around me. The moon was not much more than a fingernail, but the sky was clear of any clouds, so it gave enough light to illuminate the streets with a silvery gray shimmer. There were white lines painted around the base of the lamp posts and along the center of the road. There were some on the pavements, too, to help people find their way during the blackout, and they seemed to glow in the moonlight.

Still the figures didn't move, and I began to wonder if it was even Stefan at all. Perhaps he had taken a different route. Maybe this was someone else. Maybe this was —

Footsteps.

On the pavement behind me.

Someone was coming.

RUN!

The shape was heading toward me along Escherstrasse. Whoever it was, they were alone and trying to walk quietly, but the night was so silent I would have heard a mouse on the pavement.

Wearing my dark jacket and pressed hard against the bricks, I had to be almost invisible from this distance, but the figure was coming closer and closer, and soon they would be almost beside me. Whoever it was, they were sure to see me in just a few seconds.

It might be a soldier or a policeman who would drag me home by my ear. Or it might be Kriminalinspektor Wolff.

Just thinking his name was like an electric shock running through me and I started moving right away.

Keeping close to the wall, I slipped around the corner and edged along the street toward Herr Ackerman's butcher shop. His doorway was set a foot and a half or so into the wall, forming a small porch that was shrouded in darkness, providing the perfect hiding place.

The figures remained huddled ahead as I crept along the street, then turned, peeling myself away from the wall and slipping into the shadow. I crammed myself into the near corner of the entrance to Herr Ackerman's shop and crouched low.

Then the footsteps came around the corner and someone was right there, close enough for me to reach out and touch them. What surprised me, though, was that it wasn't a pair of trousers I was looking at, but a skirt. And a pair of girl's legs.

I looked up and watched her walk past quickly and quietly. On her back, she carried what could have been a satchel, and it jostled up and down making a swish and bump with each step.

I knew who it was. I couldn't see her face very well, but the moonlight reflected off her golden hair that had been left loose, and I just *knew* that it was Jana — Stefan's girlfriend.

I remained crouched in the doorway, wary that she might not be alone, but leaned out just enough to watch her join the others.

When Jana reached the group, she went straight to one of them and the two shapes joined for a few seconds, as if they were just one person, and I knew it was Stefan. When they broke apart, muffled laughter carried toward me on the breeze, followed by the rhythm of tense but excited speech as they spoke in voices that grew louder until one of them hushed the others.

Jana took the satchel from her back and handed something around, then there was more talking and the group divided. Three of them began walking back in my direction, but Stefan was not in this group and I wanted to know where he was going, so I kept my head peeping out until the last minute, and saw him go farther into town with Jana. Another pair crossed the road and disappeared in the other direction.

I ducked back into the doorway and stayed low while the three passed me, then waited until they had rounded the corner before I set off in pursuit of my brother.

Once I caught up with Stefan and Jana, I trailed them at a safe distance.

They kept in the shadows close to the houses and shops as they moved through the streets, so I did the same as I followed them onto Klosterstrasse in the wealthy part of town. Here, the houses were set back from the pavement, and had front yards behind railings and gates. The road was wide and lined with thick-trunked sycamores and horse chestnuts that were in full leaf and blocked much of the moonlight, making it easier for me to follow.

Creeping after them, scuttling from car to car and tree to tree, I watched as Stefan and Jana let themselves through the gate of the first house. They approached the front door, stopped for a moment, then moved away and did the same at the next house.

I edged as near as I dared, trying to see what they were up to.

They seemed to be taking things out of Jana's shoulder bag and putting them through people's mail slots.

As they were coming away from one of the houses, though, just leaving the path and passing through the gate, the faint whisper of footsteps sounded on the pavement behind me.

I turned to see three silhouettes several yards away. For a moment, I wondered if they were some of the other Apaches, but as they drew closer, it became clear they were not. These silhouetted figures were wearing caps and I knew, right away, they were Hitler Youth, perhaps coming back from a meeting.

The three figures didn't see me, but they saw Stefan and Jana, and they stopped dead.

"Look," one of them whispered. "Who's that?"

"Shh," said another.

Suddenly I was very afraid for my brother. Whatever he was doing, it had to be illegal — otherwise he wouldn't have come out in the dead of night — and he was about to be caught. I wanted to call out to him, to warn him the Hitler Youth was there. I wanted to shout at him and tell him to run, but I was too afraid to make a sound.

I crouched low and watched as the three figures moved off the pavement, into the shadows cast by the trees.

They were like lions stalking their prey.

Over by one of the houses, Stefan and Jana had stopped and come together as if embracing. They had no idea they were being watched.

When I looked back to see the other boys, their shadows were closer.

"What are they doing?" one of them whispered. His voice was like the breeze in the branches as they moved to the shadow of the next tree.

"Keep watching," said another. "Get closer. We'll surprise them."

"And then what?"

"Arrest them."

"Give them a kicking."

My mouth was dry. My hands were cold. This felt very different from the night exercise with the Deutsches Jungvolk — this wasn't fun, it was *dangerous*. My whole body felt heavy with fear as I edged onto the road and lay down along the curb, almost wedged beneath a car. There was nowhere else to go. Nowhere else to hide.

With wide eyes, I looked from the silhouettes of the Hitler Youth, creeping ever closer, to those of Stefan and Jana standing together at the gate.

Why don't you move? The thought screamed in my head. *Move! Run!*

There was only one tree between us now. I could hear the boys breathing, the sound of their boots on the grass, the swish of their clothing, the creak of a leather belt.

Then something snapped inside me, something that made me break through the fear that threatened to paralyze me.

I crawled away from the car, jumped to my feet, and shouted at the top of my voice.

"RUN!"

CHASE

At first, it was as if I hadn't shouted it at all.

No one reacted.

The boys who were sneaking up on us stayed hidden. Stefan and Jana remained where they were. Everything was frozen for a fraction of a second.

"RUN!" I shouted again. "RUN!"

And the world came to life.

"Get them!" said one of the boys behind me, and I took off like a rabbit breaking for cover from the farmer's gun.

I leaped out of the shadows, into a shaft of moonlight that fell between the trees, and sprinted toward Stefan and Jana.

When they saw me coming right at them, closely followed by the group of three boys, they turned and ran.

Now the world was full of the sound of boots pounding the pavement. My own breathing was loud as I pumped my arms and legs as hard as they would go. In front of me, Stefan and Jana ran side by side, the shoulder bag bouncing about on Jana's back.

I could feel the hot breath of our pursuers on the nape of my neck. I imagined their fingers snatching at my clothes, trying to grab me and yank me back into the darkness. It was as if I were being chased by hellhounds, and I ran, ran, ran as fast as I could go.

We reached the end of Klosterstrasse and turned left, dashing along the pavement.

My chest was tight now, my breathing coming harder and harder. My legs starting to tire. My heart was filled with a thousand needles, as if it would explode inside me.

Behind, the Hitler Youth boys grew closer.

They were bigger and stronger and faster than me. They would catch me. Stefan could outrun them, maybe Jana, too, but I had no hope of getting away from them.

I was slowing down. Falling back.

They're going to catch me.

It was only a matter of time. A few seconds and I would be theirs.

As if he could sense me tiring, Stefan looked back. He slowed to come alongside me. "Keep going," he said between breaths. "Be strong."

I couldn't run much longer.

They're going to catch me.

Jana had other ideas about being caught, though. Running just ahead of us, she slipped the bag from her shoulder and slowed down so we were running in a line. Once we were together, she half turned as she ran, holding the bag by its strap and throwing it at the boys, aiming low.

The bag hit its mark, falling at the feet of the first boy, the strap tangling around his ankles.

He went down like a felled tree, shouting in pain as he hit the pavement. The second boy tripped over him, sailing through the night and landing with a sickening crunch when he smashed into the concrete. He rolled as he cried out in pain, and the third boy came to a halt to check on them.

"Get after them," the first boy shouted. "Don't let them get away."

But Jana had already bought us some time, and when I saw the entrance to the cemetery looming ahead, I knew we had a chance.

"Hide," Stefan said as soon as we passed through the gates in the tall iron railings that surrounded the whole place.

I could hardly breathe now; my chest was hurting so much. I had never run so far and so fast in my life.

"Hide, Karl," he said again, coming to a stop and grabbing my arm. "Find somewhere to hide. We'll run."

We were standing on the road that cut through the cemetery, the grass stretching out on either side, broken only by the gravestones.

"Don't . . . leave me . . . on my own," I begged him, my words coming in gasps between breaths. I was almost bent double, trying to recover.

"You can't run anymore and they're coming," Jana said to me.

Sure enough, I could hear footsteps behind us.

"Hide with me," I begged them.

"They'll just look for us," Jana said. "We'll keep running; they'll chase us."

"They'll never find us here," I said. "We can —"

"Do as you're bloody well told, for once." Stefan pushed me away from him, forcing me onto the grass. "Now go. Find somewhere to hide. I'll lead them away." Then he pushed Jana away from him, saying, "You too. Go! Look after my brother."

"What —" Jana started to argue, but Stefan was already jogging away, his boots pounding the path, and behind us, the boys had reached the entrance to the cemetery.

"Come on," Jana whispered as the sound of Stefan's running disappeared farther along the road.

She took my arm as we hurried onto the grass, passed a row of three benches, and headed among the gloomy gravestones. We threw ourselves to the ground and crawled for the darkness around the base of a long, low memorial. There, lying side by side, we watched the road and tried to control our breathing.

The three boys slowed as they entered the cemetery, looking around to see which way we'd gone.

"That way," said one of them, hearing Stefan's footsteps farther along the road. "Come on."

"You go," said a second. "I'll look here. Maybe they split up."

So two of them picked up their pace, continuing their pursuit of Stefan, while the third remained behind.

As the footsteps faded into the night, Jana and I watched the boy standing on the road, turning this way and that in the hope of spotting us somewhere in the park.

I wondered where Stefan was and whether he would be able to outrun the boys chasing him.

The boy who had stayed behind didn't seem to be in any hurry to search for us. He waited for the others to leave, then fumbled in his pockets, and in a few seconds, a flame flared up in front of his face. He lit a cigarette before flicking the match away from him. It arced up and out, dying in the wind.

The boy glanced around, turned around once, then started walking in our direction. My muscles tensed as I prepared myself for more running, but instead of continuing his search, he sat down on one of the benches and leaned back. He tipped his head to face the sky and breathed a long stream of smoke into the night.

Jana nudged me and pointed behind us with her thumb.

I shook my head. I didn't dare move. The boy was so close — no more than fifty feet away.

Jana nodded her head and nudged me again. "Now," she whispered, and started to get to her feet.

I had no choice but to follow her. I didn't want to be left alone out here, and if the boy spotted her, she would be ready to run and I would still be lying on the grass. So I eased to my feet, aware of every sound I made.

The rustle of my jacket was like the driving rain of a thunderstorm. My heartbeat was like the drums of a parade band. When my knees clicked, the noise was like gunshots.

Then Jana nudged me again and showed me the large stick she was holding. It was as thick as my arm and almost as long. She took it in both hands and raised it up, swinging it over her shoulder as if she meant to approach the boy from behind and hit him with it.

I shook my head at her.

If she hit him, she might kill him.

She looked at me, then at the boy, and took a step toward him.

I shook my head more vigorously this time and grabbed the back of her shirt.

No! I wanted to shout.

Jana hesitated, still brandishing the stick as if it were a club, then she lowered it and stood for a moment before backing away.

I was sure that if I hadn't been there, Jana would have hit that boy. She would have swung the stick as hard as she could against the back of his head and she would have cracked his skull in two.

WOLFF AT THE DOOR

Jana and I left the boy sitting on the bench and folded into the darkness. We moved silently along the railings and slipped, unnoticed, through the gate.

"Do you think they caught him?" I asked Jana as we made our way back toward Escherstrasse.

"Not Stefan. He's too quick," Jana said with admiration. "You have a very brave brother, you know?"

I glanced over my shoulder and thought about the boy who had remained in the cemetery. "You were going to hit him," I said.

"That boy?" Her voice changed. "He deserved it. They all do."

"Hitler Youth?"

"Yes, them and all the other Nazis." There was real hatred in her words. "They're killing our fathers and brothers. Ruining our country. Someone needs to shoot Hitler before he leads us all to ruin."

"Shoot him?" I was shocked. "You want the British to win the war? To come here and —"

"No, of course not," she said. "Germany is for Germans. There shouldn't even *be* a war; sending all those German people away to be killed . . . It's all Hitler's fault. And now my papa is dead and my brother, too."

As soon as she said it, I felt as if there was a link between us. "Your papa died? What happened? Was he in the war?"

"I don't want to talk about it."

"Is that why you're an Edelweiss Pirate?" I said to her. "You *are* an Edelweiss Pirate, aren't you? Is it because of what happened to your —"

"I said I don't want to talk about it."

"I want to be one, too. To stop the Nazis from killing our fathers."

"By not hitting them on the head? Anyway, you're too young."

"That's what Stefan said." I couldn't help sounding disappointed.

Jana stopped and sighed before looking down at me. "Thank you." Her voice softened.

"For what?"

"For stopping me from hitting that boy. You did the right thing. And don't worry about Stefan, he'll be fine. He's probably waiting for you at home right now."

When Jana left me on Escherstrasse, I crept home and let myself in the front door.

After replacing the key in the ashtray, I sneaked upstairs to find the bedroom empty. I went to the window, pulling back the curtain to look out.

The street was quiet in both directions.

Across the road, Lisa would be fast asleep in bed. When I'd left to follow Stefan, I had wished that she was with me, but now I was home, I was glad she hadn't come.

I took off my clothes, put on my pajamas, and climbed back into bed. I wanted to wait for Stefan, so I sat up.

The house creaked and groaned as I wondered what had happened to my brother. I could only hope that he had outrun the Hitler Youth boys and that he was on his way home right now. I tried not to imagine him lying in the street, battered and bruised because they had caught him.

I intended to be awake when Stefan came home, but my eyelids grew heavy and I fell into a sleep that was broken only by a loud banging on the door.

Bang. Bang. Bang.

Three loud knocks that startled me.

He must have forgotten his key, was my first thought. *Or lost it.*

Bang. Bang. Bang.

I hope he's not hurt, was the next thing to leap into my head.

Bang. Bang. Bang.

I slipped out of bed, pausing for a moment to hear the sounds of stirring from the other bedroom. Then I hurried across to the door and pulled it open just as Opa was about to go downstairs.

He jumped in shock, putting a hand to his heart.

Bang. Bang. Bang.

"Stay here," he said. "You don't need to come."

When he started down again, though, I followed him, waiting at the bottom of the stairs while he fumbled with the latch, and opened the door.

"Herr Brandt." Kriminalinspektor Wolff took off his hat and came straight in. He looked wide awake, despite the hour.

Opa stepped back. "Would you like to come through to —"

"No need," said Wolff. "Just here will be fine." He flashed a false smile at Opa, then spotted me, standing at the bottom of the stairs. "Ah," he said. "Karl. Did I wake you?"

Opa glanced at me, then turned back to Wolff just as Oma and Mama came downstairs.

"What's this all about?" Oma asked, going to Opa's side. "What's going on?"

"Frau Friedmann." Wolff did a strange little bow. "I'm sorry to hear about your husband."

Mama put an arm around me.

"What . . . what can we do for you?" Opa said. "I've been to the meeting like you said. Look, I have the papers right here." He went to the table by the door and pulled out the drawer.

"No need for that." Wolff stopped him. "It's your grandson I need to speak to."

Mama squeezed me tighter and Opa looked over his shoulder at me again. "You need to speak to Karl?"

Wolff grinned. "No. The *other* grandson."

I thought I was going to fall over.

Stefan wasn't here, and Wolff knew it. The cruel look on his face said as much.

I held on to the bannister and wished there was something I could do. When Wolff discovered that Stefan was missing, he would know he was out in the night and —

"You want to speak to me?"

Wolff looked as surprised as I was when we heard Stefan's voice.

I whipped around to see him coming down the stairs, dressed in pajamas, hair tousled and sleepy-eyed.

It was the first time I'd seen Wolff flustered, but it didn't last long. He cleared his throat and stared at Stefan. "I've had reports of a disturbance tonight; your name was mentioned."

"*My* name?" Stefan rubbed his eyes as he spoke. "Why would my name be mentioned?"

"You've been linked to a group of delinquents calling themselves Edelweiss Pirates."

Stefan shook his head and ran a hand through his hair. "Never heard of them."

"Even so," Wolff said. "Your name has been mentioned —"

"By who?" Mama interrupted, and Oma and Opa looked at me.

"As I say" — Wolff gave Mama hardly more than a glance — "your name was mentioned and there was a disturbance tonight so . . ." He opened his arms, palms up. "Well. I'm just doing my job. I'm sure you understand how it is."

Stefan shrugged as if he couldn't care less.

"But I can see that you are here, at home, where you are supposed to be, so you clearly had nothing to do with it." Wolff glanced down at his hat and brushed a nonexistent speck of dust from the brim. "Well," he said, looking at Mama, then at Opa. "I'm sorry to have disturbed you."

"No, that's . . . that's quite all right."

"Good night, Herr Brandt. Frau Friedmann." Wolff did another odd little bow and I felt a surge of relief. Somehow, Stefan had made it. He had managed to outrun the boys and now he had outsmarted Kriminalinspektor Wolff. I must have fallen into a deeper sleep than I realized and Stefan had come home and slipped into bed without me noticing. This was a small victory for the Edelweiss Pirates.

Wolff turned to the door and put his hand on the latch.

He paused.

Turned back.

Looked directly at Stefan.

"You're not curious?" he asked.

"About what?"

"You didn't ask what kind of a disturbance there was tonight."

Stefan ran a hand through his hair again. "It's none of my business."

Wolff waited.

"All right, then; what kind of disturbance was it?" Stefan asked.

Wolff took his hand from the latch. "Well, I'm glad you asked me that." He put his hat on the table and reached one hand into his pocket. "There's something I need you to look at." He removed a piece of paper. "You see, someone has been delivering leaflets."

Suddenly, I had an image of Jana and Stefan going from door to door, putting something into the mail slots.

"You might have seen them before." Wolff unfolded the paper and came closer, holding it out.

It was a picture of the Führer standing over the bodies of dead German soldiers. One of the leaflets dropped from the enemy planes a few nights ago.

I remembered how afraid Stefan had been when I picked up the leaflet in the street the night they were dropped, and I remembered what had happened to Herr Finkel. The leaflets were trouble. *Big* trouble.

"We can't have this kind of thing on our streets," Wolff said. "I'm sure you agree."

Stefan made a show of peering over to look at the leaflet, but Wolff did not let go of it.

"Terrible," Stefan said with an edge of sarcasm.

Wolff folded the leaflet and put it back into his pocket. "These Edelweiss Pirates — people you have been known to associate with — this is the kind of thing they would do. Delivering malicious propaganda."

"I've got no idea what you're talking about," Stefan said. "I've never heard of —"

"Nevertheless, you have been seen with people suspected of being members." He stared at Stefan.

"None of my friends have said anything about being . . . what did you say they were called?"

Wolff gave Stefan a knowing smile. "Well, sometimes people aren't what they say they are, isn't that right?"

Stefan shrugged.

"Apparently some of these delinquents collected a quantity of enemy leaflets and have been distributing them to people's houses. In the dead of night. One might even suggest they could be accused of spying." Wolff paused. "So, perhaps the thing for me to do is to put your grandparents' mind at rest. Your poor mother, too."

"Sure," Stefan said. "Whatever."

"Then why don't you invite me come up and look at your belongings? To . . ." He made a show of thinking for a moment. "To *reassure* myself that you don't have any of these leaflets just waiting for distribution."

"Gerhard Wolff." Mama's exclamation made him switch his attention to her. "How dare you accuse my son of —"

"It's all right," Stefan stopped her. "I haven't got anything to hide."

We were going to prove him wrong. We would let him look and he'd find nothing and he'd leave empty-handed.

Wolff stared at Mama for a moment, then turned to look at Stefan once more. "Thank you." He smiled and did that strange little bow again, then came to the bottom of the stairs and waited for Mama and me to step aside.

"Really," Stefan said. "It's all right, Mama."

When Mama moved out of his way, Wolff climbed the stairs with slow and deliberate steps. At the top, he paused.

"On the right," Stefan said.

Wolff disappeared into our bedroom.

Oma and Opa came to join us at the bottom of the stairs and we waited in silence, exchanging glances as we heard Wolff's movements. The floor creaked. Belongings were moved. We held our breath.

Stefan looked over at me and winked. It was going to be fine. We had nothing to hide.

Then Wolff emerged from the bedroom and came to the top of the stairs.

He looked down at Stefan, then at me.

"Perhaps the boys would like to join me," he said. "I have something I want to show them."

"What is it?" Oma asked. "What?"

Wolff beckoned to us. "Just . . . come and see."

Stefan patted my shoulder and nodded once for reassurance, then we went up to the bedroom, with Mama following close behind.

When I saw my copy of *Mein Kampf,* faceup on the chest of drawers, my heart stopped and my legs lost all their strength. Beside it, one of the leaflets from the enemy plane lay like the most damning piece of evidence in the crime of the century.

"Perhaps you could explain this." Wolff wasn't speaking to Stefan now, he was speaking to me.

"I . . ."

"This is your book isn't it? It has your name in it."

"Y . . . yes."

Wolff nodded and took his own leaflet from his pocket. He unfolded it and put it beside the one I had hidden in the book. "A perfect match." He stood back as if to admire the pictures of Hitler standing over the bodies of the German soldiers.

He looked at Stefan. "I came suspecting the older but find, in fact, that it is the younger brother who —"

"It's mine." Stefan stepped forward. "The leaflet's mine. I delivered them tonight."

"How noble of you to accept the guilt for your brother's crimes," Wolff said. "But I am not so easily fooled."

"No . . ." I tried to speak up but my voice was faint and thin. "It is mine. I —"

"*I* delivered the leaflets," Stefan said. "I can tell you which streets. Which houses."

Wolff raised his eyebrows. "All right. And I'll need to know the names of your accomplices. You can tell me once we get to Headquarters."

Headquarters. After what Stefan had told me, the very mention of it made my insides churn.

"No." Mama moved to stand between Stefan and Wolff. "You're not taking my son anywhere."

"There's really nothing you can do to stop me, Frau Friedmann."

"Don't 'Frau Friedmann' me. You know perfectly well what my name is," she said. "And that leaflet does not belong to my son. You put it there, Gerhard Wolff. You planted it so you'd have an excuse to arrest him."

"It's Kriminalinspektor Wolff," he said with menace. "And if you don't step aside, I will arrest you, too." He moved closer to Mama and lowered his voice. "I will have you sent to a place from which you will never return."

"What?"

"In fact, I could arrange for your youngest son to lose every member of his family if I so wished."

Mama's eyes widened in horror. There was nothing she could do. Nothing at all. We were powerless.

"It's all right," Stefan said, coming forward. "I'll be all right, Mama." He sounded so brave, but I could see the way he trembled.

"Frau Friedmann?" Wolff put a hand out to one side to indicate that she should move out of his way. "If you please."

Mama kept her head high. She looked right into Wolff's eyes. "What happened to the boy I remember from school? What happened to Gerhard Wolff?"

"I became Kriminalinspektor Wolff, and I have a job to do."

Mama shook her head at him. "How can you sleep at night?"

"I sleep very well," he said as he brought Stefan in front of him. "And I will sleep even better once I know that all of the Führer's enemies have been silenced."

When we stepped back to let them pass, Wolff glanced down at me with a contented and smug look that made me feel so mad.

"Where are you taking him?" Mama asked with desperation as she followed Wolff and Stefan down the stairs toward the front door. "Where are you going?"

"He's just a boy," Opa pleaded. "Only sixteen. It was just some silly prank."

"Open the door," Wolff ordered Stefan, and when he did, we saw two SS guards smoking cigarettes by the small truck parked behind Wolff's car. It was the same kind of truck they had used to take Herr Finkel away.

As soon as the soldiers saw Wolff, they stood to attention, throwing their cigarettes onto the road where they bounced and sprayed a glitter of glowing ash. Coming forward, they glanced at the rest of us standing in the hallway, then took hold of Stefan, walked him to the truck and slammed the door shut behind him.

"You men should be ashamed of yourselves," Mama shouted at them. *"Ashamed."*

Oma took her arm to quieten her down, stop her from saying something we would all regret.

"Please," Opa begged Wolff. "He's just a boy. Don't you remember what it was like to be a boy? To do something stupid? To make a mistake?"

Wolff turned so he was facing into the house, and he looked at each of us in turn. He kept his chin up and his head still so that only his eyes moved. Then he raised his arm and said, *"Heil Hitler."*

Before he could lower his arm, though, Mama stepped forward. She held herself straight and strong and stared Wolff in the eye, curling her lip with distaste. *"You* should be ashamed of yourself, Gerhard Wolff."

Wolff sneered. "It's *Kriminalin* —"

"Shame on you." Mama's hand came up like a flash and slapped him across the left cheek with a loud smack.

Before Mama could hit him a second time, though, Wolff struck her so hard in the face that he knocked her backward. She stumbled away, tripped on the mat, and collapsed to the floor with a crash.

I immediately rushed to her, crouching and holding on to her.

Opa's hands tightened into fists and he started to step toward Wolff, but Oma reached out to hold his arm. Opa stopped, looked at Oma, then took a deep breath and came to Mama's side.

Mama didn't try to get up. She turned so her head was in my lap and she sobbed and sobbed, and I held her and stroked her hair. When I looked up at Wolff, feeling hatred burning in my blood, I saw that he had taken out his pistol and was pointing it down at Mama as if he intended to shoot her right there. His face was no longer calm, but was a picture of fury. His eyes were narrowed, his jaw clamped tight, his breathing heavy.

I held Mama's head as I stared at the dark barrel of the gun, then looked Wolff in the eye, wondering what he was going to do.

He continued to point the weapon at her for a while longer, then, slowly, he lowered it so his arm was hanging at his side. He stood in the doorway like that for a moment, then holstered the pistol and tried to compose himself.

"One Friedmann will be enough for tonight," he said, straightening his hat. "Perhaps I will come for you another time. *Heil Hitler.*" Then he turned on his heels and went to his car.

When Wolff drove away, the truck followed close behind.

BLOOD IS SPILLED

Opa left the door open and stood there, staring into the night as if Wolff's car might come back.

Mama had quieted down and I kept stroking her hair, wanting to make her feel better, but then my hand felt wet and, when I looked down, I realized why she hadn't tried to get up. There was blood. A *lot* of blood.

No one had noticed it in all the commotion, but we saw it now, pooling on the floor, oozing between the floorboards. It was sticky on my fingers and soaking into my pajamas where she'd been resting her head.

"Hannah!" Oma said. "You're bleeding. Quickly, Walther, help me get her up." She took Mama's hand and together they pulled her to her feet.

"I'm fine," Mama was saying, "fine," but she had trouble standing because her legs didn't do what they were supposed to. They kept softening and she sagged as if she were going to drop to the floor again.

The blood was running down her face, along her neck and

soaking into her nightclothes. It was everywhere, and I began to panic.

"Help her," I said. "Please. Help Mama."

They sat Mama at the table, then Opa went to the cupboard and took out the box of medical things, while I stood by feeling helpless and afraid and angry all at once.

Mama still looked woozy as Oma tried to clean away the blood, but she was more alert than before, and when Opa brought her some water, she took the glass and drank every last drop. Her hands were shaking, but she didn't drop it, and when she was finished, she asked for more.

"I can't stop this bleeding." Every time Oma wiped away the blood, more oozed from the gash on the side of Mama's head. "You must have knocked it on the corner of the table when you fell. It's just too deep. You'll have to go to the hospital."

"Come on, then." Opa started to stand. "Help me get her to the car."

"No," Mama said, "you stitch it." Then she looked at Opa. "Go and find out what's happening to my Stefan. That's much more important."

"I don't have what I need for this," Oma told her. "You need a hospital."

"Someone should be here," Mama argued. "What if Stefan comes home and there's no one here?"

"You're right," Opa agreed. "Your mother and Karl should stay here. We can manage on our own."

So Oma bandaged Mama's head to keep the bleeding under

control and Opa drove her away into the night, leaving Oma and me alone.

When they were gone, the house was quiet. Oma and I sat opposite each other at the kitchen table and we didn't speak for a long time.

Mostly, I let my blood boil and thought about what Wolff had done.

I couldn't believe he had taken Stefan away, and I couldn't believe he had hit Mama. I kept seeing it over and over again and I remembered all the times he had smiled that awful smile at me, and how he had asked me to tell him if I ever heard anything about Edelweiss Pirates. Criminals, he had called them, but I bet they never hit women. I bet they never took boys away in the night, like the Nazis did. I bet they never pointed their pistols at defenseless families.

"He's an animal." Oma spoke with tight lips. "I could —"

"Kill him," I finished for her.

She looked up at me.

"I know *I* could," I said. "I hate him."

"Hush now," Oma warned. "Keep those things to yourself."

"Who's going to hear? I could kill him." I raised my voice and stood up, wanting to say it over and over. I imagined ripping that gun out of his hand and shooting him, firing bullet after bullet after bullet. "I want to kill him."

"Don't ever let anyone hear you say that."

"I don't care."

"Well, you *should* care. You've got your mama to think about. And us. Look what's happened already, because your brother's been running around with those Edelweiss Pirates."

"You knew about them," I said. "You knew what the flower meant. You knew who they were."

"We told him not to get involved with them."

"But you hate the Führer just like they do. I *know* it." I banged my hand on the table. "You didn't tell me the truth. You didn't trust me."

"Karl —"

"You didn't trust me." I almost shouted the words. "You thought I would tell."

"And did you?" Oma fixed me with a stare. "Is that how Wolff knew about Stefan?"

I felt a cold shudder run through me. "What?"

"Wolff said someone told him. Was it you?" Her words were slow and deliberate and full of suspicion. "Did you tell Wolff about Stefan?"

"No. Of course not. He's my *brother*. Why would —"

"You reported him once before."

My mouth fell open and I stared, not knowing what to say. The awful secret I had been holding down began to rise to the surface, bringing with it the most dreadful feelings of shame and guilt.

"When he was arrested last year," Oma said. "You reported him. It was you."

"What? No, I —"

"We all know it was you."

Oma's words were like bullets, each one punching through my heart. Each one letting me know what a terrible, *terrible* person I had been.

All I could do was stand there, mouth opening and closing, because she was right and I didn't know what to say.

I had betrayed Stefan. My own brother. He had spent a week in boot camp and come home with his head shaved because *I* had reported him.

Me.

"Why did you do it, Karl? What could you have been thinking?"

I sat down as the overwhelming mixture of feelings drowned my anger. My guilt was coupled with regret, the fear of having been found out, the realization of why no one trusted me, and the relief of finally being able to let go of my secret.

"Stefan knew it was you." Oma looked at me. "The interrogators taunted him with it. They laughed at him for being reported by his own brother. He said it wasn't your fault, though. He forgave you. He knew the Nazis were in your head."

"Not anymore." I put my hands over my face and bit my lip to stop the tears. "Not anymore. I wouldn't do it again."

"You didn't say anything to Wolff?"

"No. I promise." My eyes began to well over. "I've changed. Everything's different now. Everything."

"Really?"

"Yes," I sobbed. "I wouldn't do anything to hurt Stefan. I *wouldn't*. I *promise*."

"I believe you," Oma said, coming around the table to hug me. "I really do."

As she held me, I tried to overcome the terrible knowledge that my own secret was no longer a secret. Everyone knew what I had done. Everyone knew that Stefan had been in trouble because of me. I was afraid that maybe I *had* let something slip this time, that maybe I *had* given Wolff a reason to come looking for Stefan. And I kept thinking about how the leaflet was mine — if I hadn't kept it, Stefan would still be at home.

Some time later, the key rattled in the lock and the front door opened, bringing in a waft of cool night air.

Oma and I hurried into the hall and Mama was there, standing in the doorway with Opa beside her. I couldn't help myself from rushing over to hug her.

Her skin was pale and her head was swathed in the biggest bandage I'd ever seen. She looked like a wounded soldier. There wasn't any blood on her face now, and someone must have washed it from her arms, but there were still crusty bits stuck in the skin of her knuckles and around her fingernails. The front of her nightdress was caked with it, too. A reddish-brown mess that would probably never come out.

Mama hugged me back and we stood like that for a while before Oma told me to let go of her.

"You don't want another fall," she said.

Once Mama was sitting down, Opa explained that they'd been to Gestapo Headquarters on the way back from the hospital. He wanted to bring Mama home first but she was insistent.

"Of *course* I was insistent. I want to find out where my son is and I want everyone to see what that man did to me."

"Was he there?" I asked, trying not to think about Herr Finkel and about Lisa's papa. "At Headquarters?" Just thinking about the place made me feel sick, and I was terrified for my brother.

"He's there," Opa said.

"You're sure?"

"As sure as I can be. They wouldn't let us see him, though. No one would even talk to us, but I saw them bring in two others. A boy and a girl."

"Do you know who they were?" I asked, wondering if they had caught Jana.

"I didn't get much of a look at them," Opa said.

"And how did they know?" I was sure that the Hitler Youth boys couldn't have identified us. It was too dark. "How did they know about Stefan? Who told them?"

Opa gave me a suspicious look, as if he wasn't sure what to say, but I knew what he was thinking.

"No," Oma told him. "We've had a talk. It wasn't Karl."

"Good." Opa let out his breath and nodded. "Good. Well. They just want to scare him, I expect. After that they'll send him home. Stefan will be here in the morning."

"Do you really think so?" I asked.

"Of course," Opa replied, but he didn't sound as if he really believed it.

HELPLESS

Worry and fear kept us all awake that night. In the early hours, I climbed into bed with Mama, because I couldn't sleep. She stroked my hair and we both lay there without speaking, lost in our own troubled thoughts. All I could think about was Gestapo Headquarters, the gray building by the river. I kept seeing Wolff's grin, and my brother being dragged inside, taken into a dark, damp room, and the door slamming shut behind him.

First thing in the morning, Opa and Mama went back to find out if Stefan was there. After all the visions I'd had last night, I couldn't settle until they returned, and when they did, Opa stormed into the kitchen and tore the Nazi party badge from his shirt. He threw it down on the table, saying, "Barbarian!"

"What is it?" Oma asked. "What happened?"

"He won't tell us anything. It's as if we're speaking a different language."

"Nothing at all?" Oma asked.

"Nothing." Mama pulled out a chair and sat down. She picked up Opa's badge and held it out to him. "Put it back on," she said. "We don't want to lose anyone else."

The grown-ups talked and talked until there was nothing else to say, then they went around doing the things they would usually do, but there was a restless tension that fizzed through the house. It was as if we were sitting on top of a bomb that might blow up at any minute. We all wanted to know what had happened to Stefan, but at the same time, we were afraid to know.

I went upstairs to my bedroom and looked at the books sitting on the chest of drawers.

Mein Kampf was still there, faceup, the Führer looking at me with a stern expression.

"It's your fault," I said.

The picture just stared. The Führer's gaze burned through me as if he were there in the room, watching me.

"I hate you." I turned the book facedown. "I hate you."

Downstairs the murmur of voices, and the clatter and scrape of housework and cooking went on, but when I heard the front door close, I went to the window to see Opa striding along the street, and guessed he was going to Headquarters again, to see if he could find out anything.

I glanced across at Lisa's house and wished she were here. I had waved at her when she left for school and I could hardly wait for her to come back. I wanted to get out of the house, but didn't want to go out alone, and I had so much to tell her about what had happened. I hadn't known her for very long, but somehow, it felt as if she was the only person I would be able to talk to about everything.

* * *

Right after school, Lisa came by. I'd spent all day stuck in the house, thinking about what had happened to Stefan and Mama, and about the conversation I'd had with Oma last night, so it was a relief to jump on my bike and ride away from the town.

"Everyone was talking at school," Lisa spoke as she pedaled alongside me. "They said some people were in trouble with the Gestapo last night. I don't know what they did, though. Someone said they got caught helping an escaped prisoner, then Ilse said it was because they were —"

"It was Stefan," I said, almost bursting to tell her. "Stefan and Jana. He and some of the others were putting leaflets through mail slots. You know, the ones that fell from the plane the other night."

"So it was Edelweiss Pirates?"

"Yes. And I went out after them and we got chased by Hitler Youth boys and I didn't warn them in time and —"

"Wait, slow down. *You* were there when he got caught?"

"Yes. Well, no. Well . . . oh, it's all my fault."

As we cycled out of town, I told Lisa everything that happened last night — about sneaking around in the dark and my brother putting things through mail slots and about the chase and the hiding, and Wolff coming to the house and Stefan being there after all, but then Wolff finding the leaflet in my book.

Lisa didn't say anything; she just listened to the whole story.

After a few minutes, we had left the houses behind us. If I'd been at home, in the city, it would have taken much longer. There, the buildings went on forever and we would have passed the antiaircraft guns and the sandbags and the walls draped with Nazi flags. Here, though, everything looked just about normal.

It was as if there wasn't a war at all.

We took the wide road through the cemetery, cycling in the cool of the church's shadow, and I showed Lisa the place where Jana and I had hidden last night. It all felt as if it had happened a long time ago.

Heading along the road by the river, we came to a stop opposite the large gray stone building that had filled my nightmares since Wolff took Stefan away.

Gestapo Headquarters.

There were five shuttered windows on the first floor, and at ground level, a heavy door was set into a shallow porch and flanked by two arched windows on either side. To the right of the building was a lawn, edged by shrubs and trees. A gate in the thorny hedge hung open, and a path led to the door, beside which a Nazi flag hung like a limp handkerchief.

Looking at it now made my skin tingle and my hairs stand on end, and I had to push away images of my poor brother lying curled in the dark somewhere inside.

"Do you think Stefan's in there?" I couldn't help whispering.

"I don't know."

"Maybe I should go and ask?" I was desperate to know if my brother was safe, but I wasn't sure I had the courage to even knock on the door of that place.

"No," Lisa said. "Leave that to your *Opa*. You'd only get into more trouble."

As we cycled away, I tried not to imagine Kriminalinspektor

Wolff watching us from one of the windows, and I pedaled faster to put the place behind me as quickly as possible.

We rode past the train station, through the tunnel, and out into the country, continuing for a mile or so before we followed a track down to an orchard.

There were lines of trees as far as I could see, so we propped our bikes against the nearest one and sat down in the long grass to take off our boots and socks.

The sun was warm and the sky was clear, and the air was so clean and fresh that it felt like we were a world away from everything.

"I would have come out with you," Lisa said. "You should have told me."

"I didn't know he was going, and . . . Where do you think he is? Why won't they tell us?"

"They didn't tell us anything when they took Papa last year. That's the worst thing, not knowing where he is. And not being able to do anything."

"That's exactly how I feel," I said. "It makes me . . ." I tried to think of the right word. "Angry. Like I could explode. I don't know where Stefan is, and even if I did, there's nothing I could do about it. There should be something I could do, but I'm just me and they're the Gestapo and the SS and the army. They just do whatever they like and we have to put up with it and it's not fair."

Lisa listened and nodded and then turned to stare out at the meadow on the other side of the road.

"It's not fair," I said again. "I thought everything was going to be so good and now everything's turned so bad, and it's all my fault." I grabbed a fistful of long grass and twisted until my palm was wet with its juices.

"I used to think it was my fault," Lisa said. "When they took Papa. I thought I must have done something. But it isn't my fault. It isn't your fault, either, you know — about Stefan, I mean."

"So why did Wolff come to our house? How did he know Stefan is an Edelweiss Pirate? He said someone told him and I keep thinking I must have let something slip . . . maybe that day when he saw us at the parade."

"You didn't tell him anything. I was there, remember?"

"So how did he know, then?"

"Someone else must have told him."

"Like who?"

"I don't know. He could have been lying. Maybe no one told him anything. Maybe he knew because he'd seen Stefan with other Edelweiss Pirates. Maybe he just wanted you to *think* someone told him. But it isn't your fault," Lisa insisted, "it can't be."

"I don't know. If I hadn't kept that leaflet in my book, Wolff would never have found it and Stefan would still be at home."

"Then you could just as easily say it was my fault," Lisa argued. "I gave you the leaflet."

"Yes, but —"

"It isn't your fault, Karl Friedmann. If it wasn't for Wolff and the Hitler Youth and that horrible man Hitler, *none* of this would have happened."

I ripped the fistful of grass from the ground, pulling a clump of earth with it. The soil was dry and showered across my leg as I struggled with what I was going to say next. The words didn't want to come out. They seemed to lodge in my throat, making me feel sick, but I plucked up all my courage and forced them out, because I *had* to say them. I *had* to tell Lisa what I had done.

"I reported him once," I confessed in a whisper, staring at the gray dirt on my pale skin.

"What? What did you just say?"

"Stefan. I reported him once and —"

"Your brother?" There was shock in her voice. "Why?"

I twisted the grass in my fist and remembered what had happened, telling it to Lisa with a mixture of shame and relief.

We had been coming back from an exercise with the Deutsches Jungvolk, all of us crammed into open-backed trucks. We hadn't won that day, so we were nursing our bruises and complaining that we'd been cheated out of a victory.

Coming into the city, we had stopped at a crossing, the winners' truck pulling up behind us. Axel Jung, our Hitler Youth group leader, was riding in the cab of our truck, and he started shouting from the open window. A ripple of interest passed through those of us sitting in the back, so one or two stood up for a better look, and it wasn't long before the boys around me were jeering and shouting insults.

When I eased to my feet, legs aching, I saw three long-haired boys standing outside a café, and felt a sudden rush of embarrassment. One of them was my brother, Stefan.

He was standing quietly, watching the truck, with a half smile on his face, maybe thinking that we would move on soon enough. But one of his friends wasn't as patient, and he stepped forward, shouting, "Stupid Nazis."

The boys around me in the back jeered louder, telling them to get their hair cut, calling them Jew lovers, but somewhere in all that shouting, I heard the cab door pop open. Axel Jung stepped down from the truck and crossed to the café in a flash. He raised a fist to hit Stefan's friend, but was met with a solid punch that knocked him to the ground.

In the back of the truck, everyone fell silent. We would never have expected to see Axel Jung knocked down by *anyone*, let alone a long-haired coward like that. But as we stood there and watched, the other Hitler Youth boys jumped down from the cab and went to his side, as did the boys from the truck behind us, so there were six brown-shirted boys circling Stefan and his friends.

At first, they started shoving each other around, trading insults, then one of them stepped in and grabbed my brother, twisting the front of his shirt in his fist. With his other hand, he tried to hit Stefan, but he missed and Stefan hit him back. Right on the nose.

The Hitler Youth boy staggered backward, blood pouring down his shirt, and then the street erupted into a great scuffle of kicking and punching. Some of the Deutsches Jungvolk boys started jumping down from the trucks, eager to join in. Stefan and his friends must have known they couldn't win, so they broke away, sprinting off and disappearing from view. Axel Jung and one or two others gave chase, but it wasn't long before they returned.

When everyone was settled back in the truck, Axel climbed up on the rear bumper and looked around at us, asking if anyone had seen the boys before. I could feel Ralf and Martin looking at me, urging me to tell him, but I couldn't do it. Not because I wanted to protect Stefan but because I was ashamed of him; I didn't want to have anything to do with him. I wanted to be like Axel Jung, not like Stefan Friedmann.

All the way back, though, my friends badgered me, telling me it was the right thing to do. I had to tell Axel. I *had* to.

So I did.

When we arrived back at Hitler Youth headquarters, Ralf and Martin came with me to Axel Jung, and stood beside me as I told the group leader that he had been fighting with my brother, Stefan.

Lisa sat in silence while I told her, and when I had finished, she looked at me as if she felt sorry for me.

"I hate myself for doing it," I said. "As soon as he was sent away, I was ashamed of myself. I never told my family it was me. I didn't realize what they'd do to him. I tried to keep it a secret but everyone knows and —"

"It's not your fault. You had all that silly Deutsches Jungvolk stuff in your head, confusing you. My papa said it's like poison."

"I thought it was the right thing to do . . . but then I knew it was bad, too. I didn't really know what to think."

"Well, you wouldn't do it now," Lisa said. "That's what matters. You're different now."

"I can't believe I ever thought Stefan was a bad German. He's the bravest person I know. It's no wonder no one trusts me."

"*I* trust you."

I looked at her. "Really?"

Lisa smiled and shrugged. "Of course I do, Karl Friedmann. We're friends, aren't we?"

"Yes. We are."

Knowing that Lisa trusted me gave me a good feeling, which settled among all the awful ones swirling inside. There was something else as well: relief. Just like last night when Oma told me they all knew what I had done, there was a sense of being able to get rid of the awful black secret that I had been carrying. It had been hard to find the courage to tell Lisa what I had done, and I had been scared that she would hate me for it, but she didn't hate me, she *trusted* me. And I knew she was right when she said I was different now. I had changed.

I watched her lie back in the grass, then I did the same and we stayed like that for a long time, with the sun on our faces, and our eyes closed. The shadows from the leaves above us danced on my eyelids. The breeze shifted in the treetops, the birds sang, and the whole world felt peaceful. For a moment, I let myself enjoy the light feeling of relief and the thought that I had a good friend beside me. Not a soldier or a comrade, but a friend.

"We should call ourselves Comanches," Lisa said after a while. "If we're going to be Edelweiss Pirates, we should have a name. There's Navajos in Cologne and Apaches here, so we can be Comanches. They're an Indian tribe, too."

She sat up and plucked a daisy from the grass at her feet. She shortened the stalk by pinching it with her fingernail, and leaned over to tuck it into one of my buttonholes. Then she plucked another and did the same to one of her own buttonholes.

"It's not an edelweiss," she said, "but it'll do. And I've been thinking; maybe we're not so helpless."

"What do you mean?"

"Well, maybe there *are* some ways of getting back at Wolff. Especially now that we're Edelweiss Pirates."

"Like what?" I asked.

"Oh." She shrugged. "I have a few ideas."

TRAITOR

Lisa suggested we should visit Frau Schmidt on the way home.

"She might be able to help us find out what's happened to your brother," she said.

"Why would Frau Schmidt know anything?" My voice echoed in the half darkness as we made our way back through the railway tunnel.

"She *almost* told us about Edelweiss Pirates didn't she? She knows about them, so maybe —" Lisa came to a sudden stop beside me, her tires crunching on the gravel beside the railway track.

"Look." She pointed to the wall of the tunnel. It was black with soot, and moss grew from the cracks between the bricks. "See?"

There, beneath the grime, the white letters were faded, but still visible.

HITLER IS KILLING OUR FATHERS

There was something about the flower that made me feel proud now. It was my brother's symbol, and I didn't know anyone braver than him. He had forgiven me for betraying him and hadn't said a word about it, however hateful I had been. He had protected me and been my friend.

We stared at the flower for a long time before Lisa said, "You saw the badge her son was wearing in that photo. Frau Schmidt knows about Edelweiss Pirates. Maybe she even *is* one. Maybe she knows something, or someone who knows where Stefan is."

Once we were in town, we went straight to Frau Schmidt's house. It wasn't Frau Schmidt who opened the door, though; it was Jana.

She held the door with one hand and looked down at us in confusion. "Karl? What . . . what are you doing here?"

I was too shocked to speak.

Jana's expression changed from one of confusion to one of worry as she watched me fumble for words. "Is it Stefan?" she asked. "Is he all right? He wasn't at work today and —"

"What are *you* doing here?" I managed to blurt out.

"What do you mean?" she replied. "I live here. Isn't that why you came?"

"You live here? I . . ." I shook my head and stared at her.

"Yes, of course. Now tell me what's happened."

"They took Stefan." It was all I could think of to say. My mind was still racing from the unexpected discovery that Jana lived here with Frau Schmidt. It didn't make sense.

"Who took him?" Jana asked.

"Wolff," I said. "Wolff took him, but . . ."

Jana scanned the street, looking this way and that. "You'd better come in." She ushered us inside and into the kitchen, where Lisa and I had eaten Frau Schmidt's cookies. I still didn't quite understand what was going on.

"When did it happen?" Jana said as she followed us. "I haven't heard anything."

"Last night." I spoke slowly, still trying to work out why Jana was here. "I got back and Stefan wasn't there, and Wolff came and . . ." My words trailed away as I caught sight of the photos on the sideboard. The first one I noticed was the one I had seen last time, of Frau Schmidt's son Max wearing the edelweiss badge. The last time I saw it, though, I hadn't looked at the other people in the picture. I hadn't seen the face of the girl standing on the end.

Jana's face.

"That's you." I stared at the photograph of Frau Schmidt's children, and everything seemed to fall into place. It was as if someone had shone a flashlight onto the jumbled knot of my thoughts and I had spotted the loose end that would help unravel the whole thing.

"Frau Schmidt is your mama." Now it made sense. Hadn't Jana already told me that her papa and brother had been killed — just like Frau Schmidt's family? And something else started to make sense, too. Wolff must have known Jana was an Edelweiss Pirate, just like he knew her brothers had been. Maybe he had come here last night and done something to make her tell him about Stefan. Maybe it wasn't my fault after all. I *hadn't* let anything slip.

I turned to look at her. "Did you tell him? Was it *you* who told Wolff about Stefan?"

"What are you talking about?" Jana stepped toward me.

"Did *you* tell him?" was all I could say. "Did *you*?"

"I don't understand. What's going on, Karl?"

"What on earth is all that noise?" Frau Schmidt was coming downstairs, having heard the commotion.

"You told Wolff." I spat the words at Jana.

"I didn't tell Wolff anything!"

Frau Schmidt's footsteps came to a stop as she reached the bottom of the stairs.

"So how did he know, then?" I demanded. "How else could he have known?" It was the only thing that made sense, but as I shouted at Jana, she turned to look at Frau Schmidt, who was standing in the hallway, with one hand over her mouth. Her eyes were wide and she was shaking her head from side to side.

For a moment, no one spoke.

"Mama?" Jana whispered in disbelief.

"I had to," Frau Schmidt spoke from behind her hand. Her voice was barely audible. "He was going to take *you*."

"What have you done?" Jana's whole body sagged and she put a hand on the table to steady herself.

"He came last night but you weren't here." Frau Schmidt took a step toward her daughter but stopped when Jana flinched away. "He was going to arrest you for delivering leaflets. He knows your friends, the way you avoid the Bund Deutscher Mädel meetings . . . about your brothers and this Edelweiss Pirates business . . . how many times have I warned you? How many times have I told you? That's why he sent them away and made them join the army. He knows you're an Edelweiss Pirate and that's why he came here. He said he knew a girl was involved, so he came *here*."

Jana shook her head as if she couldn't believe what was happening. "There are other girls —"

"But you weren't here." Frau Schmidt's voice was filled with anger and desperation and regret. Tears began to well in her eyes. "So he knew it was you. He was going to wait for you and arrest you and make you give him everyone's names but I . . . I begged him to leave you alone. To take someone else —"

"So you told him about Stefan?" Jana asked. "But how did *you* know about Stefan?"

Frau Schmidt looked at me and I remembered the first time I had come to the house. I had asked her about the flower. *I* had told her about Stefan.

And she had told Wolff.

It *was* my fault.

"I'm so sorry." Frau Schmidt put a hand to her mouth once again, as if she didn't want the words to come out. "But I had to do something to save my Jana, don't you see? Wolff already took Joseph and Max from me; I couldn't let him take Jana, too." Her voice trembled and her eyes glistened. "I told him you asked about the badge you'd seen your brother wearing, that he would be able to get other names from him, that . . ."

I didn't hear any more of what she said. I couldn't be in that house with her any longer. I had to get out.

Jana called my name and tried to stop me from leaving, but I pushed her away. I barged past Frau Schmidt, knocking her aside, and stormed out into the street.

Grabbing my bicycle, I jumped on and pedaled away as fast as I could.

"It's not your fault," Lisa shouted as she raced to catch up with me. "It's not your fault."

DEATH COMES KNOCKING

Jana came to Oma and Opa's house that evening, asking about Stefan, but I didn't want to talk to her. There was no sign of my brother that day, or for the two days that followed. No one could sleep or eat properly, and all we talked about was Stefan. I kept thinking about how Lisa hadn't seen her papa since he was arrested, and I was gripped by the fear that the same thing would happen to us. I felt as if I was living in a kind of nightmare. Everything had been turned upside down.

Opa and Mama made regular visits to Gestapo Headquarters but came back none the wiser each time. No one would tell them anything.

I helped Opa with his car sometimes — standing in a daze while I washed it or handed tools when he needed them. I even helped Oma and Mama in the kitchen. At first, I thought Mama might get sad again, and go back to bed. She looked tired and scared, but she was angry, too, and that made her stronger and stronger. She didn't have to wear the bandage for long, and the scar on her head wasn't very big at all. I couldn't believe how much blood had come from such a small cut.

The only thing that really happened during the first two days after Stefan's arrest was the arrival of Frau Oster's news. She received a death notice, just like we had, to inform her that her husband — the SS panzer driver — had been killed in Russia. Oma had never liked her very much, but even though we already had enough things to worry about, she and Mama got together with the other women from Escherstrasse and did what they could to make things easier for Frau Oster.

It seemed that as the days went on, the war found new ways into everyone's lives.

I sometimes walked to the shops with Mama, but other than that, I didn't leave the house unless I was with Lisa. As soon as she was back from school, we cycled to our spot by the orchard and talked about our plan to get revenge on Wolff.

On the third night without Stefan, we finally decided to carry it out.

When I went upstairs that night, I stayed awake, watching from the window, waiting for Mama and Oma and Opa to go to bed.

They talked for hours and it seemed as if they were going to stay up all night. I put my ear to the floor. I could only catch snippets of the conversation, but mostly they were talking about where Stefan was and when he might come home.

Eventually, they began to quiet down, then they came upstairs, one by one, and I jumped between the sheets and pretended to be asleep. Mama came in and sat on the bed beside me for a long time. She stroked my head and told me she loved me.

It was hard for me to keep pretending. I couldn't help opening my eyes and telling her I loved her, too.

"Everything's going to be all right," she whispered.

"I know," I replied.

"Stefan will come home soon. You'll see."

"Yeah."

But we were both just trying to make each other feel better.
Neither of us knew what was going to happen, and that was the
worst thing of all.

Mama kissed my head and stayed a while longer, stroking
my hair, and it was so comforting, I had to try really hard not to
fall asleep. I *couldn't* let myself fall asleep — I was supposed
to meet Lisa and there was still something I had to get from the
cellar. I wasn't looking forward to going down there in the dead
of night, but I wanted to do something to show Wolff he hadn't
beaten us completely. I had made an agreement with Lisa, and
a promise is a promise.

It wasn't easy getting downstairs without making any sound.
Every floorboard seemed to creak at night, but I had managed
it once before, so I knew I could do it again.

When I reached the bottom, I waited, listening. There was
no sound from upstairs. No one coming to investigate noises in
the night.

Satisfied that I had made it this far, I crept along the hallway and switched on my flashlight, shining it at the door to the
cupboard under the stairs.

I swallowed and reached for the handle. When I pulled it open and looked down at the cellar door, I tried not to think about the imaginary beasts that lurked in the darkness beyond it.

You can do this, I told myself. *You're as hard as Krupp's steel.*

I didn't feel as hard as Krupp's steel, but I still opened that door. I opened it because I had made a promise to Lisa. I was going to bring something up from the cellar and then I was going to leave the house and meet her. This was all part of the plan, and I didn't want to let her down.

I was doing this for Stefan, too. Wolff had taken my brother away and there wasn't much I could do about it, but I could do *this*. I could carry on spreading the message he and the Edelweiss Pirates were risking so much for.

The blackness of the cellar yawned before me, swallowing the light from my flashlight. The beam barely reached the fourth step before it was smothered by the awful blackness down there.

I crouched and reached for the switch just under the lip of the entrance, putting my hand into the darkness to feel my way toward it.

When I flicked it on, the bulb sparked into life, casting a dull glow into the cellar. It wasn't much better than complete darkness, but it was something, and now all I had to do was go down those steps, get what I needed, and —

Somewhere in the night, way off in the distance, a siren began to scream.

I froze with my foot on the step.

Another siren started up now, still a long way off, but closer this time.

They're coming, I thought. *The planes are coming.*

I had to move.

Everyone would be awake soon and they would want to know why I was here, in the cellar, in the middle of the night. Fully dressed.

With a surge of adrenaline, I backed out of the cellar, flicking off the light and dropping the hatch into place. I bumped into the broom and mop as I hurried out of the cupboard, and they fell to one side with what sounded like a thunderous noise, but more sirens were starting up, all over the city in the distance and here in town — my noise would go unnoticed. It would be forgotten. All I had to do was get upstairs.

I had to hurry.

I rushed along the hallway and took the stairs two at a time. It was too dark to see them, but I had been up and down them so many times I knew exactly where they were and how many there were. I would be in my bedroom in seconds.

The sirens were sounding all across town now, the enemy planes were coming, and I was running the wrong way. I should have been racing to the safety of the cellar, but I was going to my room instead.

My foot slipped as I misjudged the top step, but I caught myself by putting out my hands, then scrambled into my bedroom, just as one of the other doors opened.

"Karl?" Mama called as she came across the landing. "Get up, Karl!" She came straight to my room and pushed open the door. "Hurry!" she called into the darkness.

"Here," I said, standing up. "I'm here."

"Downstairs," Opa said from just outside the door. "Everyone! Now!"

"Oh, what's the rush?" Oma was there, too, somewhere in the darkness on the landing. "They're probably just dropping leaflets again."

"Don't be so sure," Opa replied. "You'll be sorry if it's bombs they're dropping on your head."

"I can't even see where I'm going," Oma complained, then the landing was flooded with light as the overhead bulb burst into life, blinding us all for a few seconds.

"What the hell are you doing?" Opa said. "Turn the light off. You want them to know where we are?"

"They already know where we are," she replied. "Otherwise why would they be making all that racket? And we've got black-out curtains, haven't we?"

"Come on," Mama said, ushering Oma downstairs. "That's enough of that."

In the chaos, no one seemed to notice that I wasn't in my pajamas and I thought perhaps I'd got away with it. There was no time to change now.

The night was alive with the sound of the sirens, as if the whole world was filled with the rise and fall of their wailing, and when we closed the cellar door behind us, they didn't seem as far away as they had the last time we'd been down here.

"Sounds like every siren in the town is going off." Opa brought a bucket of water closer to the table so that it was to hand if there was a fire, and we sat watching each other, all of us terrified of what might be happing outside.

"Cards?" Opa asked, trying to take our minds off it. He began to shuffle a deck of cards that had been lying on the table.

We waited for him to deal them out, pretending not to hear the sirens raging above us.

"When did you get dressed?" Mama asked.

"Hmm?"

"You're dressed," she said.

"Oh. I . . . I was awake," I said, thinking quickly. "I heard the first siren and it sounded like it was miles away but . . . well, then others started, so I quickly got dressed so that when we go outside afterward . . ." I shrugged.

"Don't want anyone to see you in your pajamas?" Mama asked.

"More like he doesn't want *Lisa* to see him in his pajamas," Opa teased.

"Leave him alone," Mama said. "He's growing up. He wants to make an impression."

I was relieved that she had believed my story, but the relief was short-lived because, outside, the eighty-eights began to fire.

Boom b-boom boom-boom. B-boom.

And then in the distance, we heard the steady drone of planes and the terrible faint whistle of falling bombs.

The first explosion wasn't much, really. A dull, flat *crump* somewhere far away, but we all looked at each other, and Mama pulled me close to her.

That first bomb was followed by another.

And another.

And another.

They were raining down on the city. Thudding and thumping and shaking the ground.

"They're getting closer," Oma said.

The eighty-eights continued to fire back with their *boom b–boom boom–boom.*

I could only imagine what it must be like to be outside. It would be a nightmare of fire and explosions and death, as if the world was ending.

"Will Stefan be all right?" I asked, making the grown-ups look around at each other. "Will he be safe?"

"He's probably safer than we are," Opa said, forcing a smile. "Now, Karl can lead," he said, dealing from the deck. He was trying to take my mind off it, but all I could do was stare down at my cards without really seeing them. I was wondering how strong the roof of the house was. I was thinking about what would happen if a bomb landed right on top of us. Would we be blown into dust? Would the house crumble and collapse about us, crushing the breath out of us? Or would it simply destroy the house and leave us trapped down here in the cellar with a bucket of water and a deck of playing cards?

Panic crept over me, filling me up, and I wanted to be outside. I wanted to be in the orchard with Lisa. I wanted to be on my bike with the sun on my shoulders. I wanted to be anywhere but here.

"It's all right," Mama said, wrapping her arms around me. "Don't be afraid."

"I *am* afraid." I dropped the cards on the table.

"So am I," she said. "But it will be over soon."

I looked over her shoulder at the shelf on the far side of the cellar and saw what I had been coming to claim before the sirens began. The plan Lisa and I had put together might have been ruined by the enemy planes — there was no chance of carrying it out tonight now — but looking at the shelf and thinking about Lisa made me feel calmer. I closed my eyes and pretended I wasn't there in the cellar, but away in the orchard. Lisa was beside me and we had taken off our boots and socks to feel the grass between our toes. We were lying back and looking at the sky, watching the clouds and finding shapes in the wisps of white.

Explosions thumped and thudded on the outskirts of town as the bombing came closer and closer. The ground shook beneath us. Dust rained from the ceiling. Death was knocking on our door, but I ignored it. I stayed there in the orchard and ignored it until the last of the bombs fell and the planes finally thundered away and the night became silent once more.

A CHANGE OF PLAN

When we went onto the street, we saw roof tiles littered around the pavement, dislodged by the bombing, but it was the flames that everyone was watching.

An orange halo had risen over the rooftops, flickering and crackling as the fires burned the buildings just a few streets away. The stink of it was thick in the air and sparks rose into the sky, dancing in the breeze like the last fizz of fireworks. The shape of the church tower rose among them, lighting up and then darkening again before glowing once more as the stone reflected the light from the blaze.

It was almost impossible to believe it was happening. Right here in town, buildings were bombed and burning. Probably people dead or trapped in their cellars.

"We were lucky," Lisa said.

I had been too busy staring at the sky to notice her push through the crowd and come to stand beside me.

"Just think," she said, "we might have been . . ." Her words trailed away and I turned to look at her.

The glow from the fires sparkled in her eyes. She had never looked so pretty.

"It's beautiful," she said.

"Yes it is," I replied, because it *was*. It was beautiful and terrible at the same time. The flares and searchlights and embers and flames came together in the night in a magical display, but beneath it all was the horror of what it really was.

"We were so lucky," she said again, and I felt her fingers touch mine.

I glanced down at Lisa's hand, seeing how it waited for me to hold it in my own, so I took it and looked at her, our eyes meeting for the briefest moment before we turned our faces to the rooftops and the display that shimmered over them.

In those seconds it felt as if we were alone in the street, just Lisa and me, then I heard Opa's voice close by.

"Is that Feldstrasse?" he said to no one in particular. "That looks like it might be Feldstrasse."

With that, it was as if Lisa and I remembered where we were and we released each other's hand as if they had suddenly grown hot.

"Maybe they need help," suggested a voice, and I turned to see Herr Ackerman, the butcher, standing close by. "We should go over there." He looked at Opa, waiting for an answer.

Opa nodded once. "You're right."

"Can I come?" I asked.

"Of course not," Mama said. "It'll be too dangerous."

"I'll stay out of the way."

"You're not going anywhere. And *you* shouldn't be going, either." Mama looked at Opa.

"I know what you're thinking," he said. "That I'm too old."

"No, Papa, it's just —"

"Well, the young men aren't here, are they?" he said, standing straight. "Too busy fighting. So the old ones will have to be good enough. And I'll never be too old to help."

"I'll come." One of the other older men stepped up beside him, and soon there was something of a hubbub as the men of Escherstrasse came forward, one by one, until there was quite a crowd of them standing in a group in the middle of the street. The women drifted together, forming another group, offering advice to the men as they began to organize themselves. There were a few children there, too, but their mothers kept them close.

The men agreed to bring buckets and tools, anything that might be needed to rescue survivors, then they hurried back to their houses to get what they needed before setting out toward the flames.

"Are we still going to do it?" Lisa whispered. "Our plan?"

"How can we? It's too late now."

"No it's not," she said. "It's only just after midnight. There's still plenty of time for everyone to get back to bed."

I looked around at all the people, and at the men making their way down the street. "They could be out all night," I said.

"Don't worry about them," she nodded toward the group of men. "It'll be the perfect time."

"But there'll be people everywhere and —"

"— and they'll all be too busy to bother with us."

It was a good point. With everything that was happening, who would even notice the two of us slipping past in the shadows?

"All right," I said. "What time?"

"Two o'clock. And don't fall asleep."

"Two o'clock," I agreed.

"Did you get some?" she asked, and I knew exactly what she meant.

"Not yet. But I will."

"You better," she said. "It's no good without it."

Once the men had disappeared from sight, the women stayed in the street for a while longer, gossiping and tutting and shaking their heads before everything quieted down and they began to drift back to their homes.

"I'll see you later," I whispered to Lisa when Mama called me inside. "Two o'clock."

I went back into the house and Mama closed the door behind me. I was on my way upstairs when I stopped. "I forgot my flashlight. Left it in the cellar."

"You don't need it tonight," Mama said.

"I like to have it," I told her. "Just in case."

"Just in case what?"

I shrugged.

"All right, go on, then. Be quick."

As I went back downstairs, I put my hand into my pocket and held on to my flashlight to stop it from banging around and giving me away. I went straight to the cupboard under the stairs and pulled the door open before lifting the trapdoor to the cellar.

I braced myself and reached under the lip of the hatch to find the light switch.

Climbing down the steps, I could just about see the wonky shelf at the far end of the cellar. And there, right in the middle of it, was what I had come for.

A can of white paint.

HELL

Stefan's key was in the drawer in our room, exactly where I expected it to be. The flashlight picked it out, nestled among the other bits and pieces, and I wasted no time pocketing it. I grabbed my bag that now had the can of white paint stuffed into it, and crossed to the bedroom door, pausing to listen to the murmur of voices from downstairs.

Opa hadn't yet returned from helping with the aftermath of the bombing raid, so Oma and Mama were still in the kitchen, waiting up for him, making it almost impossible for me to sneak out of the house. But then I had an idea. I could climb through a window, and use Stefan's key to let myself back in through the front door later.

The landing between the bedrooms was small enough to cross in a few carefully chosen steps and I managed it without even the slightest squeak of floorboards. Within a few seconds, I was pushing open Oma and Opa's bedroom door.

Not wanting to trip over anything, I clicked on the flashlight and crept across to the window. They always slept with it open, even when it was cold outside.

I peeled back the blackout curtain, and opened the window a little wider so there was just enough of a gap for me to climb down onto the shelter Opa had built to protect his precious car. The construction felt weak as soon as I put my feet on it. It groaned under my weight and I was sure I had to get off quickly or else it would collapse under me.

I went down on all fours and scrambled to the edge, lowering my bag before jumping down onto the grass with a soft thump. Bending my knees as soon as I landed, I rolled onto my shoulder, just how we'd been taught to do when we were training with the Deutsches Jungvolk. Then I was on my feet. I snatched up my bag and jogged across the yard and out into the lane where the darkness was thick and the walls loomed over me. There was only the faintest glow from the fires on Feldstrasse now, and the occasional voice shouting in the distance, but otherwise, it was as if no one else existed.

I swallowed hard and felt the blood thumping in my ears as I hurried along the lane.

"You ready?" Lisa was waiting at the mouth of the alley, crouching in the shadow of the house next door to Oma and Opa's.

"Wasn't easy getting out," I said. "Opa's still not home. And I don't know how I'll get back in without them seeing."

"We'll think of something," Lisa said. "Come on."

Running along Escherstrasse, my mind prickled with excitement and apprehension. We were taking a big risk, and if we were caught, we would be in a lot of trouble, but this wasn't like the last time I came out in the night. This time I was with

Lisa, and even though there were only two of us, we were Edelweiss Pirates and we were going to make our mark.

Closer to the end of the street, the sounds from the area around Feldstrasse grew louder. The searchlights were off, the sirens and the eighty-eights were silent and the fiery glow over the rooftops had dulled, but men's voices traveled on the cool night breeze. There was a smell of burning, too.

"Let's go and look." Lisa grabbed my sleeve and pulled me with her. "I want to see."

We kept to the darkest shadows wherever we could, skulking along the streets as the voices grew louder and louder, but now there were other sounds, too. The crackle and snap of fires, the pop of wood under intense heat, a child crying, a woman wailing.

As we approached the end of a road that met Feldstrasse, the voices became more agitated and I heard someone shout, "Over here! There's one here!"

"Let's see what it is." Lisa tugged my sleeve again and we hurried along the pavement.

That's when we saw the first of the bomb damage.

The corner house must have taken a direct hit, because one side of it was completely gone. There were bricks and timber strewn across the road. Some of the wood was still smoldering, red patches glowing in the night. The smell of burning was strong.

Up close, it looked as though something had bitten a chunk out of the house. Only a small part of the roof remained intact, tiles hanging down into the exposed rooms below. There was a bed teetering on the edge of what was left of a bedroom, and the room beneath was filled with rubble, but I could see traces of the owner's belongings. A lamp sticking out from a pile of broken bricks. An armchair turned on its side. A table leg.

Beside me, Lisa had stopped to stare. "Do you think there was anyone in there?"

I looked up at the house. "Probably."

"Do you think they're dead?"

"I don't know," I said, tearing my eyes away. "Come on, stay low."

I pulled Lisa's arm the way she had pulled mine, and we crept toward an overturned cart in the middle of the road. We crouched behind it, out of sight, and peered over.

Feldstrasse looked like hell.

At each end of the road, one or two of the houses remained intact, but nothing else had escaped the raid. It was hard to tell that there had even been any houses in the middle of the rows on either side of the street, because all that was left was a massive pile of rubble with metal bars and wooden beams poking out at different angles. It was as if someone had dumped a lot of rubbish here and set fire to it. And where there had once been a road between the homes, there was now a huge crater with lazy tendrils of smoke drifting from its darkness.

At the far end of the street, a green fire engine was unable to get any closer to the houses. Firemen had pulled a hose as far as they could and were spraying water on the flames that flickered in the rubble. Other groups of firemen and civilians were dotted around the street, trying to rescue survivors buried in the wreckage. There were the men from Escherstrasse, clearing the mess by passing it along a human chain, and there were soldiers, army and SS, all scouring the twisted remains.

Close to us, one group had gathered around the debris near the crater. Some of them were on their hands and knees, while others waited behind them, issuing instructions.

"They must have found something," Lisa said. *"Someone?"*

The men at the front began shifting broken beams and bricks, passing them back to others who formed a line and handed it from man to man until it could be thrown safely onto the road. Just the slightest wrong move and everything might collapse.

Nearby, a group of small, bewildered children sat in silence on sandbags watching the men work. A group of women stood with them, some of them holding steaming cups, some of them holding each other, sobbing while rescuers searched the ruins for any sign of more survivors.

Over to the right, a woman who was combing the wreckage stopped and raised her hand. "Over here!" she called.

By the crater, the men rearranged themselves so that a group of them, led by a soldier in SS uniform, broke away and hurried to where the woman stood with her hand held high.

"Another one," Lisa whispered beside me, but as she spoke, I saw that the men on their hands and knees at the crater were not men at all.

"Look." I nudged her. "Hitler Youth."

Now that some of the men had moved, I could see that the people digging out survivors were dressed in the unmistakable uniform of Hitler Youth. There were two of them lying on their stomachs, half buried in the rubble. It looked almost as if they were swimming among the bricks and beams, their bodies half under, like they were preparing to dive right down. As I watched, one of the boys completely disappeared from sight. His body slipped away until all I could see were his pale legs, smeared with soot and dirt, and then he was gone.

"He's fallen in," Lisa said.

I put my hands on the edge of the cart and lifted myself up for a better look.

The other boy at the edge of the crater didn't appear to be alarmed that the ground had swallowed his comrade. He remained where he was, half in, half out, and I could hear the faint sound of his voice calling. Then he was backing away, pushing up onto all fours, and dragging something from the hole in the wreckage.

At first I thought it was his comrade, but as the object slipped out, I realized what it was.

"A body," Lisa whispered.

I wanted to close my eyes but couldn't. It felt wrong to be looking at such a thing, but some part of me wanted to see. I wanted to know what it looked like to be dead.

The woman was still wearing her dressing gown. She was facedown, arms outstretched, because the boy had hold of her by her hands. He pulled her clear of the hole, then stepped aside while the men came forward and lifted her. The boy didn't spend another moment looking at the body, but went straight back to his job, lying on his stomach by the hole and calling in to his comrade.

Two men carried the body. One took her feet and the other held under her arms as they struggled through the wreckage.

The woman's head lolled back, her hair hanging down, her arms dangling at her sides. The men took her to a place in the shadows at the far side of the road, close to the houses that had not been damaged. There was another group of survivors huddled there, women and children crying, their moans carrying on the ember-filled breeze. The men laid the body down on the pavement and tried to comfort the survivors, but that's when I saw the other shapes there, lying in a row. I couldn't tell how many there were, but there must have been at least ten bodies on the pavement.

I stared at the dark shapes and wondered if that was how Papa had looked when he died. I wondered if he had been laid out in a line with other bodies.

". . . Karl?"

"Hmm?" I turned to look at Lisa. "What?"

"I said, they've found another." She nodded in the direction of the crater and I looked over to see the Hitler Youth boy dragging a girl's body from the rubble.

When the men took her away, the boy went back to work.

"Let's go," I said. "I don't want to see any more."

SURPRISE IN THE CEMETERY

Do you still want to do this?" I asked Lisa as we left the scenes of horror behind us.

"Do *you*?"

"I'm not sure. I don't . . ." I wasn't sure what I thought. "It's just that, after the raid and . . . and *that* . . ." I looked behind me and felt as if I didn't know what was right and what was wrong anymore. "That could have been my mama," I said. "Or yours. So maybe it's not right to do this. I mean, we should stick up for our country, shouldn't we?"

"Of course we should, but we stick up for *Germany*, not for the horrible people who live here. And there's nothing we can do about the enemy. I hate them, too, but there's nothing we can do. Nothing we can even do to show them we hate them. But we can show Wolff that we hate him."

"You're right," I said, strengthening my resolve.

"Of course I am."

Feldstrasse was close to the church, so we cut through the cemetery, leaving the sounds behind us and making our way into the eerie darkness. The gates were open, just as they had been the other night, so we went straight in, keeping to the road.

"This place gives me the creeps," Lisa whispered. "There's a story about a nun who got walled up inside part of the church and people say you can see her ghost if you come here at the right time. The Shrieking Nun, they call her, because of the noise she makes."

"Oma used to bring us through here on the way to the river to catch fish in our nets and Stefan always used to try to scare me with that story. It never worked, though; there's no such thing as ghosts." But walking through there in the dead of night, it was easy to believe there might be.

"I've heard noises in the night," Lisa said. "Like screaming."

"Probably just foxes."

"They say that if you look into her eyes, she sucks out your soul and you'll never speak again."

"Sounds like garbage to me," I said, but a shiver ran up my spine and I cast a glance over my shoulder to make sure we weren't being followed.

"I've never been in here at night," Lisa said. "Do you think we'll see her?"

"I've been in here at night and I didn't see her." I tried to change the subject. "This is where I hid with Jana. Over there, by the graves." I pointed into the darkness, where the head-stones were just visible.

"Stop!" Lisa grabbed the back of my jacket.

I was still looking over at the dark shape of the gravestones, and had walked a few paces ahead of Lisa, not noticing that she had stopped.

"Stay where you are!" She pulled me to a halt.

"Why? What's the —"

"There," she said. "Up ahead."

"What is it?" I whispered, almost too afraid to know.

Lisa raised an arm and pointed, and I peered into the darkness ahead, half expecting to see the Shrieking Nun, right there, floating above the ground with her eyes glowing red and her mouth open wide as she prepared to suck out my soul.

But there were no ghosts in the cemetery.

Instead, there was something far more dangerous.

Just a few steps away, right in the center of the road, there was a dark shape protruding from the ground. It was thick and almost as tall as me, but set at an angle as if it had . . . as if it had dropped from the sky.

"You were going to walk right into it," Lisa said.

"Is that what I think it is?" I took a step closer.

"Don't," Lisa hissed. "Stay where you are."

"I just want to look."

"You might set it off."

I took another step.

I had seen pictures of bombs at school and I'd heard them whistling in the sky, felt the shudder as they exploded when they hit the ground, but I had never actually seen one close up.

"Come here," I said. "You can see it better." I held my hand out to her and beckoned. "Really. It's all right. They only explode when they hit something."

She hesitated, shaking her head.

"I'm not going any closer," I told her.

After a moment, she sighed and came to stand beside me.

I fumbled in my pocket and pulled out my flashlight, then pointed it at the unexploded bomb and flicked it on.

"What are you doing?" Lisa pushed my arm down so that the beam was pointing at the ground and she looked around in alarm. "Someone will see."

"There's no one here." I pulled my hand away and shone the flashlight at the bomb once more, pointing it at the place where it had thumped into the ground and half buried itself. It wasn't a big bomb; I guessed it would have been about shoulder height to me, but it was probably big enough to destroy a house. As I passed the beam over its length, I saw two words written on the side and, though I couldn't speak English, I was fairly sure I knew what "FOR ADOLF" meant.

"Imagine if it went off now," Lisa said. "We'd be blown to pieces."

"It won't," I said. "Just keep still." I couldn't take my eyes off it. In the back of my mind, I saw the houses on Feldstrasse, reduced to rubble by one of these bombs, but I couldn't stop looking at it. I couldn't move away from it. All that energy closed up inside that metal shell was hypnotizing. And so were those words. It seemed that it always came down to words.

Maybe that's where the real strength was.

"What if it's one of those timer bombs?" Lisa asked. "It might go off at any minute. I think I can hear it ticking."

I listened carefully, but all I could hear was the distant sound of the rescue operation on Feldstrasse. She was right, though; I hadn't thought it could be a timer bomb.

"Please," Lisa begged, so we gently stepped away from the

bomb, moving backward, watching it as if it were a predator waiting for us to let down our guard.

Once we were a safe distance away, we moved onto the grass at the side of the path, intending to carry on with our plan.

"Shouldn't we tell someone about the bomb?" Lisa said. "What if someone else walks down here, or comes in their —"

"No one comes down here at night," I said. "We'll do it on the way back. We'll . . . I don't know . . . we'll think of something, but we need to go now. We need to do this." Too much had already interfered with our plan, and I was afraid that we were on the verge of backing out.

A CLICK OF THE LATCH

Looming out of the dark, Gestapo Headquarters was even more nightmarish in the dead of night.

The building was silhouetted against the river, silent and unnatural. The trees cast twisted shadows across its bricks and I imagined it to be filled with damp rooms and gloomy corners. There would be tools of torture, blood-stained floors, and monsters like Wolff waiting to hit women and drag boys into the darkness.

"There must be loads of them working in there," I whispered.

Lisa shook her head. "I don't think so. Just Wolff and one or two others."

"Why is it so big, then?"

"Papa said it used to be a house, the biggest in town, so they took it. He said they always take the best for themselves."

I stood in the shadow of the wall on the opposite side of the road and stared at the large building. It looked to me like a terrible prison. A place where unspeakable things happened.

When I was in the city, I used to cycle past the official buildings, with Nazi flags draped over them, and hope that one day I would go inside and see the men in their flawless uniforms. I imagined that I would even work in there and that it would be perfect.

Now though, looking at this building, I saw only fear and pain. Nothing here was perfect.

I shivered and tightened my fingers into fists.

"Shall we do it?" Lisa looked at me and then leaned out to glance each way along the street. "It's clear."

My whole body was quaking, but I was determined not to lose my nerve. "Yeah. Come on."

I jogged across the road, where Kriminalinspektor Wolff's black Mercedes was hunched like a beast waiting to spring, and looked both ways, before heading through the open gate. Lisa kept up with me, and as soon as we were in the yard, I tugged the can of paint from my bag.

Lisa stepped into the shadows at the side of the path and scanned the street and house, while I crouched in front of the building and took a screwdriver from my bag, using it to pry open the lid of the paint can. It came up with a small pop, then I fished the paintbrush out of my bag and began to work.

The bricks were rough and difficult to paint on, so I had to rub hard with the brush and keep reloading it again and again.

My heart was pounding with excitement and fear. I was so afraid of this place and of being caught, but at the same time it was exhilarating. I was getting my own back. I was *doing* something. This was my revenge for what Wolff had done to Mama and to Stefan. I was showing them what I thought of them for taking my papa away and letting him die.

In the distance, the faint sounds of activity from Feldstrasse continued, and there might have been a hint of smokiness on the breeze, but mostly I could smell paint and hear the sound of the brush scraping against the bricks.

When I was finished, I replaced the lid on the paint tin and shoved it back into my bag with the brush and screwdriver, then we retreated farther along the path and looked up at my handiwork.

This close, the white letters shone in the night. In the morning, they would glare brilliantly in the sun, sending their message to anyone who happened to pass.

Beneath the words, though, was the part I was most proud of. An edelweiss. Just like the ones I had seen on the walls.

Lisa took a deep breath and nudged me. "Come on, Karl Friedmann, we'd better get out of here."

And that's when we heard it.

A terrifying sound that froze my heart right in my chest.

A sound that snatched the breath from my lungs and made my body numb.

It was a simple sound that in daylight, at home, would not have made me think twice. But in darkness, after what we had just done, the sound of a door opening was the most awful sound there could be.

A rattle of the handle.

A click of the latch.

A squeak of hinges.

The heavy front door of the Gestapo Headquarters swung open and a figure appeared, silhouetted in the dull glow of a light somewhere inside the building.

Right away, I knew who it was.

The shape of Kriminalinspektor Gerhard Wolff was unmistakable.

THE WOLFF'S GRIN

Stay where you are."

He saw us immediately. We were out in the open and the light from inside that dreadful building was enough to spill out and illuminate the short path.

"Stay *exactly* where you are." Wolff's voice was soft and menacing.

Lisa and I were fixed to the spot, as if our feet had grown roots and sent them deep into the earth. My muscles were locked tight. My blood ran cold. I felt as if a million insects were fighting for space inside my stomach.

The light dimmed and then disappeared as Wolff closed the door and came toward us.

"Karl Friedmann." He looked down at me. "And Lisa Herz." Wolff stood straight and stared at us. His face was without any expression at all as he looked from me to Lisa and back again. "Well?" He raised his eyebrows.

We remained silent.

"There must be a reason why I would find you outside

Gestapo Headquarters at this time of night. Has something happened that requires my attention?"

"Umm . . ." I tried to think. There had to be something that would lure him away from this place without looking back. I couldn't let him turn around because then he would see the words on the wall.

"Well, come on. Out with it."

"We . . ."

"Perhaps you need my help with something?" He moved his head as if he were going to look back, and I knew he was going to see it. He was going to look back and see the words and —

"A bomb." Lisa blurted it out so the words almost exploded from her. "There's a bomb."

Wolff looked at her with surprise. "A bomb? But there have been bombs going off all night. Do you think I haven't heard them?"

"Unexploded," Lisa said. "An *unexploded* bomb."

"Ah. I see." Wolff didn't seem worried by Lisa's news, and when he spoke, his expression was suspicious and his tone was disbelieving. "You came out in the middle of the night to" — he raised his eyebrows at us again — "to look at the damage? And you found an unexploded bomb. So, naturally, the first thing you thought was to come and tell me." There was a sense of unpleasantness to what he said, as if every word tasted bad to him.

"I —"

"Please," Wolff interrupted. "Let me tell you what I think really happened. You see, I don't think you came out in the night to look at bomb damage at all."

My stomach tightened.

"As soon as I saw you from the window, I thought to myself, *Ah, the Friedmann boy has come to rescue his brother. Or, at least, to see him.* But now I've changed my mind."

"The bomb —" Lisa started to say, but Wolff held out his hand, one finger extended.

His face darkened into an expression of pure evil, and his next words were laced with venom. "Let. Me. Finish. Don't speak again, young lady."

Lisa clamped her mouth shut.

"Now." Wolff's eyes slipped over to stare at me. "The reason I have changed my mind, Karl Friedmann, is that I see you are carrying something, and because I see you have white paint on your hands . . . *again* . . . and on your jacket . . ." He touched my chest with one finger, pointing to the white splashes that stood out against the dark material.

I said nothing.

"I hope I am wrong," Wolff went on. "I *sincerely* hope I am wrong." He shook his head. "I also hope that when I turn around I don't see anything that will make me want to punish you. It would be a shame to fall out with you. You showed so much promise. The Führer believes the youth is our future; you *do* know that, don't you?"

I swallowed hard.

"But, I suppose there are always those who must be . . . brought into line. Take your brother, for example." Wolff stared at me for a few moments longer, then he stepped between Lisa and me so he was standing behind us. When he turned around, he put one hand on each of us.

Above us, the breeze whispered in the treetops. Behind us, Wolff's breathing was heavy.

"Interesting brushwork," he said at last.

The words on the wall were clearly visible.

Their message was clear, too.

HITLER IS KILLING OUR FATHERS

"I particularly like what you have done with the flower."

Wolff pushed us both forward. "Now, why don't we go inside and you can tell me all about it."

IN THE WOLFF'S LAIR

We stepped into Gestapo Headquarters, the place that had haunted my sleep. The hallway was long and wide, but felt cramped like a coffin. With just a dim light at the far end, the wood-paneled walls closed around us as if they were going to crush us.

Wolff came in on our heels, the door banged shut and my heart thumped hard. It was beating so fast I was afraid it might burst.

"Straight ahead." Wolff was like a devil lurking behind us and I tried not to imagine that hideous grin. "Go on."

Our boots clicked on the black tiles and echoed in that dark space as we made our way deeper into the heart of my nightmare. A strong smell of disinfectant swirled around us, thick and suffocating, but underneath it I could smell something else.

Dirt and sweat and fear.

Terrible things had happened here, things I couldn't even imagine.

My heart pounded and blood swooshed in my ears. I felt weak, and a lump rose in my throat as if I were going to be sick.

I wanted to cry. I wanted to run. I wanted to turn around and beg for my life. But I told myself to be strong.

Like Stefan.

"Stop there," Wolff ordered, and for a moment, there was no sound, as if we might be the only people in the building.

He paused behind us, breathing heavily, then came forward and opened the first door on the left. "Inside."

I could tell right away that his was his place — his *lair* — because it reeked of tobacco and his aftershave.

"Stand there." Wolff pointed to the center of the room, and we did as instructed while he took a seat behind the desk.

He said nothing as he settled into his chair and pulled open a drawer to take out a pack of cigarettes, which he placed on the desktop. They were the same brand he had taken from Oma and Opa's kitchen cupboard. He adjusted the pack so it was exactly straight, the bottom end parallel with the edge of the desk, then placed a gold lighter beside it. He spent a few moments lining them up so they were perfect.

The only other things on the desk were an empty glass ashtray, a small Nazi flag on a stand in one corner, a pen, which was in line with the pack of cigarettes and the lighter, and a brown file with the name "Stefan Friedmann" written on it.

When everything was in place, he opened a drawer to his left and took out two more brown files. He set them on the desk in front of him, then put two forms on top of them and closed the drawer.

The lid of his pen clicked when he removed it, and the nib scratched on the white forms as he wrote.

We waited in silence, shaking with fear, and when he had finished, he turned the papers around and held out the pen.

"Sign here." He pointed with his finger at the bottom of the form. "Now."

I stepped forward and took the pen. My hand shook as I signed.

"Good. Now you." He held the pen out to Lisa, and she did as she was told.

When it was done, Wolff wrote our names on the folders, one for each of us, and slipped the forms inside. He put the folders on top of Stefan's, then sat back.

"My job is not always an easy one." He steepled his fingers and leaned his elbows on the desk. "I don't have anywhere near enough officers for all the work that is building up. There are just so many people to investigate. I have a room here *filled* with files like these." He tapped the folders and his gaze flicked from Lisa's face to mine, and when he looked at me, I couldn't help averting my eyes. I lowered them and stared at the threadbare red carpet.

"Would you like to be me?" he sighed. "Trying to keep order?"

I didn't reply.

"I'm asking you a question, Karl Friedmann."

I looked up and shook my head.

"I thought not."

There wasn't much furniture in the room; just the desk and the seat he was sitting in. There was a bookcase along the wall to my left, but it was empty. The wall to my right was paneled with dark wood and, exactly in the center of it, hung a portrait of the Führer looking serious.

"You have both just signed a D-11. It is an Order for Protective Custody."

Lisa took a sharp breath and I wanted to reach out and hold her hand.

"That means you are mine. You belong to me until I sign a release form. So now I have to decide what to do with you." Wolff snatched up the pack of cigarettes and took one out. He used the gold lighter, flicking it once to ignite a small flame, then leaned back and blew smoke into the air. It streamed across his desk and settled around us like poisonous cloud.

"At least I'm closer to finding all the Edelweiss Pirates in my town." He pointed at me. "Your brother gave me a few names after a bit of persuasion. He didn't mention yours, though."

"The leaflet was mine," I said. My throat was dry and my legs were trembling, but I didn't want to be afraid anymore. I wanted to be angry, and the way he was talking made it easier than I thought.

"I know it was yours." Wolff looked pleased with himself. "But it was your brother I wanted. Now you've decided to follow in his footsteps, though, I have the problem of what I am going to do with you."

"Let us go home," Lisa said. "We won't do it again."

"Oh, you're right about that." Wolff nodded. "You most certainly won't do it again." He leaned back in his seat. The room was beginning to fill with gray smoke. It floated around, catching in the light from the chandelier, mingling with the sickly smell of Wolff's aftershave.

"We're sorry," Lisa said. "*Very* sorry."

"And *you*?" Wolff looked at me. "Are you sorry?"

I wanted to say it, to make him sign a release form and let us go, to get Lisa away from here, but something told me that he wouldn't just let us go. And I wasn't sorry. I was glad I had done it.

"I thought not." Wolff took a deep breath and stared at me. "Open the bag." He pointed with the cigarette. "I want to see what you have in there."

I slipped the bag from my shoulder and approached the desk.

"Not on there," Wolff said. "Over there." He pointed toward the empty bookshelf, so I crossed the room and put the bag on the floor.

I crouched and removed the can of white paint, the paintbrush, and my flashlight.

"That's it?" Wolff asked.

"Yes."

"Turn out your pockets."

I took out the penknife Stefan and Mama bought for my birthday, put it on the floor beside my bag, then turned my pockets inside out so he could see they were empty.

"You too." He looked at Lisa.

Lisa hesitated, then came to where I was standing. She pulled a rolled up paper bag from one pocket and placed it beside my penknife.

"And what is in there?" Wolff asked.

Lisa swallowed. "Sugar."

Wolff clamped his teeth together so that his jaw bulged. "Were you planning on putting sugar in my fuel tank? Is this something you have done before?"

Lisa shook her head and I felt afraid for her.

"Stand there." Wolff pointed his cigarette at the spot in front of his desk.

We obeyed, and without taking his eyes off me, Wolff sat forward and crushed the cigarette into the ashtray. He opened the desk drawer again and took out a leather strap which he folded over once and gripped tight in his fist before standing.

"Put out your hand," Wolff snarled as he came around the desk toward us.

"Please," Lisa said, and there was terror in her eyes.

I felt it, too. I felt the same terror that she felt, but I told myself to be strong. If Wolff was going to hit us, then it didn't matter. I had been hit before; I would survive. Lisa would survive, too. Wolff would sign our release forms and we would go home with sore hands and that would be it.

"Put out your hand," Wolff said again, looking at Lisa. "NOW!" He raised his voice so suddenly that my heart lurched and raced in my chest.

Lisa flinched away from him, squeezing her eyes shut, pushing tears onto her cheeks.

"It's all right," I whispered to her. "It's all right."

When she heard my voice, she opened her eyes and looked at me. Our gaze met and I forced myself to smile. I nodded so gently that I hardly moved, but Lisa understood what I was saying. We were in this together. We would be strong for each other.

Lisa nodded back and raised her arm. Her hand was clamped in a fist but, keeping her eyes on me, she opened it out so the palm was toward the ceiling.

Wolff came to stand in front of her.

He lifted the leather strap to shoulder level and paused.

Lisa stared right at me.

"Perhaps I have a better idea," Wolff said, breaking the silence.

He lowered the strap and reached down to take my right hand. He forced the fingers apart and placed the strap across them before closing them into a fist so I was gripping the cold leather. "You do it," he said. "You hit her."

"What?" I tore my eyes from Lisa's and looked up at him.

"You heard me."

I looked back at Lisa, seeing the confusion in her expression.

"*You* hit her," Wolff said.

Suddenly I had a vision of Johann Weber standing in front of me, the laces on his boxing gloves trailing, boys chanting at me to hit him. But nothing on earth would have made me hit Lisa.

"No," I said. "I won't do it." I threw the strap down on the carpet and stood as straight as I could.

For a moment, Wolff did nothing. Then he bent down to pick up the leather strap and he doubled it over once again. "Who knows you're here?" he asked. "I'm going to take a wild guess and say that *no one* knows. Am I right?"

We stayed silent.

"I don't think you quite understand how much trouble you're in," Wolff said. "My soldiers are helping at Feldstrasse and no one knows you're here. We are alone. You could just . . . disappear. Your mama will wake up in the morning and you will simply not be there. She'll think you must have sneaked out in the night to see the bomb damage. Perhaps you got caught under falling rubble. Or maybe you went into a building and were burned alive." He smiled. "Burned alive. I like that. Maybe that's the best thing for Edelweiss Pirates." He walked behind me. "That *is* what you are calling yourselves, isn't it? Young criminals who hate Germany."

"No," I said. "We hate the *war*. We hate *Nazis*."

"You are a Nazi," Wolff sneered.

"Not anymore." I turned to look at the picture of the Führer. "My papa is dead because of him."

"Put out your hand."

I lifted my arm and opened my hand immediately. I would not let him win. I would not give him the satisfaction of frightening me. I would not —

Swoosh–SLAP!

The whip of the leather strap cutting through the air and the noise of it striking my skin happened simultaneously. They were almost one sound. What followed was an agony that burst in my palm, burned through my fingers, and seared across the back of my hand as the strap curled around.

The pain was enormous and it took my breath away. I clamped my mouth shut, my teeth grinding together, and tears came to my eyes, but I was not crying. I *refused* to cry.

Swoosh–SLAP!

The second was more painful than the first. It felt as if I had thrust my hand into the hottest fire imaginable and I was sure that if I looked down at it, I would see broken skin and blood.

Swoosh–SLAP!

264

The third was the worst. An awful explosion that blossomed in my palm and spread through my fingers, right up my wrist. It made my body cramp and my mind go blank. For a moment, everything went white. Sparks seemed to erupt in the air between me and Lisa and I couldn't help myself from crying out in pain.

I snatched my hand away and bent double, holding it to my stomach, smothering it against my jacket, searching for some way to stop the pain.

"Stand up," Wolff said.

I gritted my teeth and straightened up, refusing to look at him. Instead, I looked at Lisa and tried to smile, to show her not to be worried. But the fear was clear on her face. She was afraid of what was coming next.

"Be strong," I said to her, then I closed my eyes so I didn't have to watch Wolff hit her.

When Wolff had finished, Lisa was holding her hand just as I was, but there was no way to make the pain go away.

"It saddens me to see two young Germans like you dragged into the mess created by these criminals," Wolff said. It was warm in the room and there was a thin film of sweat on his brow that shone in the glare from the chandelier above him.

I looked up at him, letting him see the hatred in my eyes.

"People like these Edelweiss Pirates get under your skin and tell you lies and make you believe them, but it's the Führer who loves you," he said to me. "He loves all his children and he knows they will make Germany strong."

"He sent my papa to war," I said.

Wolff shook his head. "Your father went to war because he loved Germany and he wanted to make it strong. You shouldn't believe what you read in leaflets that fall from the sky."

"Papa didn't want to fight."

"Did your mother tell you that? Did *she* put those ideas in your head?"

"No."

"Your brother, then, and those criminals he hangs around with. They say it's just about long hair and music but they're saboteurs," he said. "They attack the Hitler Youth, daub slogans on the walls. What will be next? Blowing things up? Murdering policemen? And now you listen to their lies," he said, going back to the seat behind the desk. "And I'm wondering what it is I can do to persuade you to be a good German." He sat down and looked at each of us in turn. "Perhaps some time away from home might do you both some good. I know of boot camps that are perfect for children like you."

"No." The word escaped Lisa's lips before she could stop it.

"No?" Wolff turned to her. "You don't want that?"

She shook her head.

"You don't want to go to a camp like your father did?" he said, twisting the leather strap, making it creak. "You know, when I arrested him, he begged me to let him go, but I can't have Communists wandering the streets. That's almost as bad as having Jews running their dirty businesses on our door-steps. Not to worry, though." He leaned back and smiled. "We won't be hearing from him again for quite some time. Perhaps never."

His last words were like deadly bullets. They took away any hope that Lisa might have had of seeing her papa, and her breath escaped her in one quick rush of air. Her body went limp and her knees buckled. Her legs gave way and she toppled like a felled tree.

I reacted quickly, reaching out to catch her as she collapsed. If I hadn't been there, she would have fallen flat on her face. As it was, I wasn't strong enough to stop her, and all I could do was slow her fall. Her weight took me down onto my knees.

When she opened her eyes, Lisa looked about as if she had forgotten where she was, then there was a flash of realization and she turned onto her side, curled into a ball and began to sob.

"I hate you," I said, looking up at Wolff. "I *hate* you."

Wolff stood up, the leather strap still in his hand. "You two will spend the night in my cells while I decide what to do with you. And there's something I want you to see. Something that might make you change your mind about what kind of German you want to be."

NIGHTMARE

It took a while for me to get Lisa on her feet. I helped her up and supported her as Wolff took us out of his office and along the dark hallway where the smell of disinfectant hung in the air like an old ghost. He walked behind, directing us past an office that looked a lot like his, except the only thing in it was a chair, right in the middle of the room. Then we passed another that was stacked with filing cabinets.

We went to the end of the hallway, where a large flight of stairs disappeared into the gloom. I expected to be ordered up into the shadows, but instead, Wolff instructed me to open a door that was set into the wall below the stairs.

"Go down," he said when I revealed the darkness behind the door.

The stink of disinfectant was stronger here, as if this was where the smell was coming from. And I could smell fear, too. My whole body told me this was a bad place, and I hesitated, afraid that if I went down those stairs, I would never come back up again.

"Go on," Wolff snapped.

Still holding on to Lisa, I stepped forward and began to descend into the cellar. This was not like the cellar at Oma and Opa's house, though, these steps were wide enough for Lisa and me to climb down side by side, and there was a sense that I was walking into a very different kind of space.

When Wolff flicked on the light, it became clear this was not a cellar used for storing old furniture and bicycles. This was not a cellar that housed the beastlike furnace that blazed in the winter months. This cellar was home to a very different kind of nightmare.

The room was twice, maybe three times the size of Oma and Opa's cellar and there was no junk in there. Instead, there were six cages, three on either side of the room, set back against the cold brick walls, as if it were some kind of private zoo. A corridor between them gave enough space for a grown man to walk to a door at the far end with his arms outstretched and not touch the metal bars on either side. The floor was stone, unpainted but dotted with dirty patches that someone had tried to scrub away. I knew that they were reminders of other prisoners: bloodstains left behind by people who were long gone.

Each cell contained a wooden bunk close to the floor, but only one of them had a sheet over it because only one cell was occupied.

It was Stefan. My heart leaped.

He sat up as soon as he saw me. "What the hell are you doing here?"

"Painting on walls," Wolff said. "Another Edelweiss Pirate like his brother."

Stefan looked at me with confusion and worry, then started to shake his head. "No. You're wrong. The leaflet was mine. It's me who painted on the walls."

Stefan's bruises were visible as I came closer to the cell. The light was dull in the prison, but the angry marks on his face were clear enough. His left eye was swollen like mine had been when I returned home after the parade, and his lip was fat and crusted with dried blood. His long hair was gone, too, shaved right down to stubble.

"What have you done to him?" I said, going straight to the cell. "What have you done to my brother, you pig?" I turned and glared at Wolff.

"Don't," Stefan said. "Just do what he says. Tell him whatever he wants to know."

"Spoken like a true German," Wolff said. "You see how we can help you to be a better German? When your brother first came in here, all he could do was shout and spit. Now look at him."

"What are you going to do with him?" I asked.

"I haven't decided," Wolff said. "Maybe he's learned his lesson or maybe I'll keep him here a while longer. Or perhaps he needs to go back to a camp for a while."

It was then that I realized Lisa had taken more of her own weight. She felt more sturdy on her feet and there was more strength in her arms. She had stopped sobbing, too, and when I looked at her, standing with her back to Wolff, her eyes met mine.

What I saw there was rage.

The moment I saw it, I knew I had to stop her from whatever she was about to do. Before I could move, though, she opened her mouth and let out the most terrible scream. It was so loud and sudden that it stunned us as it echoed around the stone walls.

As the unsettling noise went on, she turned and threw herself at Wolff, taking him by surprise. She knocked him off his feet, forcing him away from her so that his head snapped back and slammed against the bars of the cell on the other side of the walkway. There was a dull *clang* and he slipped to the floor and Lisa fell on top of him, tearing the leather strap from his grasp and whipping him with it again and again and again.

Wolff didn't make a sound. He just lay there while Lisa hit him in the face and chest, and I hurried over to grab the leather strap as she brought it back for one more strike. When she looked around to see who had stopped her, it seemed like she wanted to hit *me*.

"No," I pulled her to her feet. "Stop."

Wolff was lying completely still on the floor. I hadn't seen him move since he'd struck his head against the bars of the cell.

Lisa stood over him, her shoulders rising and falling with each heavy breath.

"Is he dead?" I asked. "Did you . . . ?"

"No," Stefan said. "He blacked out. I can see him breathing."

I turned to look at my brother. "What do we do?

"You have to get out of here before he wakes up. You've only got a few seconds."

"Then what?"

"Just get out of here."

"What about you? I'm not leaving you. If he wakes up and we're gone but you're still here, he'll . . ." It was too horrible to think about what he might do.

"Don't worry about me," Stefan said. "Just get away from here, Karl. Run home to Mama and tell Opa to take the car." There was panic and desperation in his voice. "Drive away. Anywhere. You have to get away from here."

"I'm not leaving without you," I said, feeling my own rage and panic building. Everything was out of control. This wasn't supposed to have happened. I was supposed to be home in bed, thinking about how clever I was for having written on the wall of Gestapo Headquarters.

"Get away." Stefan gripped the bars of his cell. "Run."

"I need the key," I said, looking around frantically.

"Run, Karl."

"Where's the key?"

"You need to —"

"I'M NOT LEAVING WITHOUT YOU!" I shouted at him. "WHERE'S THE KEY?"

"In his pocket," Stefan said. "You'll have to be quick."

I crouched beside Wolff and slipped my hand into his jacket pocket. He groaned and his eyes half opened as I clasped my fingers around a bunch of keys.

"Hurry!" Stefan called.

The keys snagged on a loose thread when I tugged them from Wolff's pocket.

"Quick!"

I shook them, pulling hard to snap the thread.

Wolff's eyes rolled as he tried to focus on me. "Boy . . ." he managed to say.

The keys came loose with a jangle and I jerked them free, hurrying to the cell door.

"Stop," Wolff said, but the word was slow and weak, and when he tried to push up on his elbows, they gave way and he fell back.

Lisa stood over him, glaring down as if she might snap again at any moment.

"Stop," he repeated. "Stop. I . . . know . . . you . . ."

There were four keys and I fumbled the first into the lock.

"Nowhere . . . to . . . go . . ." Wolff tried to get up, but collapsed once more.

The key didn't work, so I pulled it out and tried the second.

"Hurry!" Stefan said. "He's getting stronger."

The second key didn't open the lock.

"I know you," Wolff said again as the third key turned in the lock. "I'll come for you."

HUNTED

Wolff was growing stronger every second, and his voice was louder as he called after us.

"Get back here!"

Stefan was first to reach the door at the top of the stairs. He barged into it with his shoulder, bursting it open into the corridor.

"Stop!" Wolff ordered.

The door smashed back against the wall, then we were hurrying past the other rooms, heading for the front of the building.

The first shot Wolff fired from his gun boomed in the confined space of the cellar and the sound bounced from wall to wall behind us.

The bullet slammed into the door frame beside me, splintering the wood into tiny pieces that burst into the air at head height and prickled at my cheek as I escaped.

My ears rang and my skin burned and my legs were injected with a fresh boost of energy. I would never have known I had the strength to keep going, but somehow I managed to take it in my stride. I ignored the sting of the splinters and reached out to slam the door shut behind me as I left the stairwell.

A second shot cracked behind us, the bullet punching straight through the wood paneling. It struck the ceiling above, raining plaster dust over us as I sprinted along the corridor, right on Lisa's heels.

"Keep running!" Stefan reached the front door and yanked it open.

We burst out into the night without thinking. All that was in our minds was escape. Nothing else. Just run run run.

There was no more shooting, but we knew Wolff was coming. Like a raging demon, he would be behind us, climbing those stairs as fast as he could, throwing open the doors, storming along the corridor with his blood boiling.

We darted along the path and came out of the yard without slowing, Stefan leading us across to the other side of the road, then we turned right and sprinted along the street.

"He's coming!" Stefan said, but I didn't dare look back. I didn't dare see the face of the man who wanted to kill me. I imagined him not as Wolff anymore, but as a monster, slavering and growling.

Our feet pounded the pavement as we ran.

My chest heaved with exhaustion.

I could hardly feel my legs, they were pumped so full of adrenaline. My vision began to blur and sparks burst in my head as fatigue tried to overcome me. My lungs felt as if someone were squeezing them tight, stopping enough air getting into them, and I knew I couldn't keep running like this for much longer. I was using all my effort, giving every last drop of energy, and soon I would collapse.

And then Wolff will have me.

In front of me, Lisa was beginning to tire, too. The beat of her footsteps on the pavement was slowing.

"Keep going," Stefan said. "Come on. Don't slow down."

I wanted to shout at him, to tell him we couldn't run much farther, but I didn't have the breath. Instead, I looked across at the river, desperate for a place to hide, knowing we were too exposed. Wolff would see us cross the road and —

The sound of a car engine started up and I was certain we were finished.

We'll never outrun his car.

"Down here!" Stefan shouted, and he disappeared from view as he turned left.

A few more paces and Lisa and I were following him into an alley, our footsteps echoing.

Here, the wall rose on either side of us like a tunnel, and any moment now, Wolff would turn down the alley and chase us with his car. With no chance of outrunning it and nowhere to escape to on either side, he would mow us down or stop and shoot us in the back.

I felt my pace slow despite the fear and adrenaline. I couldn't keep running for ever. I could hardly run for another ten seconds.

"The cemetery," Lisa said between breaths.

"What?" Stefan asked, looking back.

"The cemetery," she said again, and I knew she was right. There were a million dark places in there. Gravestones and shrubs and trees and shadows that had hidden me once and could hide me again.

Knowing there was somewhere to go, somewhere to rest, gave me a small burst of energy and I pushed harder.

I can make it to the cemetery. I can make it that far. Then we can hide and rest.

As if to shatter that hope, however, the alley was suddenly flooded with the sound of Wolff's car. A deep growling that grew louder and louder.

He was coming.

"We're almost there!" Stefan called back, and I sensed that even *he* was growing tired now — and if strong, brave Stefan was tiring, what hope was there for Lisa and me?

"Keep . . . going . . ." he panted as we reached the end of the alley.

I stayed right behind Lisa as we ran out into the street.

Wolff's car was gaining on us, picking up speed.

"There!" Lisa managed to shout, and she held out a finger to point.

Not far away, to the right and on the other side of the street, the iron railings that surrounded the cemetery stood uniform along the side of the road. A little farther, and we would be at the entrance.

In the near distance, the silhouette of the church was visible, the vague orange glow of the dying fires from Feldstrasse shimmering around it.

"Hurry!" Stefan shouted, and led the way, feet pounding across the road to the pavement on the other side and then on toward the cemetery entrance.

Behind us, Wolff's car growled like a beast, the engine gunning hard as he reached the mouth of the alley. He came out into the street with a fresh burst of speed and hurtled along the road, just as we made it to the cemetery gates and were swallowed by the darkness within.

We veered away from the road as soon as we could, and ran across the grass, where Wolff would not be able to follow us in his car.

I could hardly see Stefan ahead of me as we darted among the trees and the gravestones, moving deeper into the darkness, heading toward the far edge of the church grounds.

Lisa ran alongside me, the sound of her heavy breathing threading with mine, so it seemed as if we were taking the same breaths.

"Get down," Stefan said as he led us behind a low, rectangular tomb.

I took Lisa's hand and, together, we ducked down beside Stefan, taking cover behind the stone memorial.

I sucked air into my lungs, desperate to feel normal again. My chest was on fire, and my legs trembled beneath me.

On the road, Wolff's tires squealed as he turned into the entrance of the cemetery and came to a standstill, the idling engine chugging in the night.

He must have known we were gone now. His anger would be rising higher and higher.

"We'll go farther back." Stefan turned and began working his way deeper into the cemetery, moving from one gravestone to the next.

Lisa and I followed him, using the same cover, making our way even farther away from the road until we came to a stone outbuilding close to the rear of the church. We made our way around to the back and squatted in a line with our backs against the wall.

More than a hundred yards away, Wolff gunned his engine once more.

"He's leaving," Lisa said.

"Doesn't matter," Stefan replied. "He knows who we are and where we live. He doesn't need to look for us; he just has to go to Escherstrasse."

"Mama." A cold shiver ran through me when I imagined what Wolff might do to her. "Oma and Opa."

"This is such a mess," Stefan said. "What were you two thinking?"

"What are we going to do?"

There was fear in Lisa's voice and I wanted to comfort her, but there was *nothing* we could do.

There was no way out of this.

"I just wanted to be like you," I said to Stefan. "They killed Papa and I wanted to be an Edelweiss Pirate like you, to show them what I think. But now they're going to arrest Mama and Oma and Opa and it's all my fault."

On the road, Wolff's car accelerated through the cemetery and I knew he was heading to Escherstrasse. Everything was lost. There was no hope.

Then, from somewhere down on the road, came the hollow sound of metal hitting metal.

A dull clank that had no echo.

With that sound came an image that flashed into my mind like a bolt of lightning. The silhouette of an object half buried in the ground.

Before that image could fully form though, the unexploded bomb in the road *exploded*. It detonated a fraction of a second after Wolff's car struck it, and the world was filled with noise.

DEATH IN THE CEMETERY

The blast from the bomb swept across the cemetery, flattening shrubs and ancient gravestones. It rushed around tombs and battered the side of the church and the building we had used for cover.

If we had stayed behind the tomb closer to the road, we would surely have died. The shock waves alone would have crushed us.

Behind the stone building, the air was sucked from my lungs in one violent rush, and then more streamed in, hot and heavy with dust. My ears popped, my eyes bulged, my joints screamed in pain, and the cemetery was smothered in a cloud of destruction.

Dirt and branches and pieces of Wolff's car battered the side of the outbuilding like a hurricane. The tiles blew off the roof above us, breaking into pieces as they disappeared into the storm like a thousand deadly knives. Wreckage smashed against the side of the church, shattering the stained glass windows and bouncing back from the walls, filling the night with a whirlwind of debris.

For that moment, there was nothing but noise and pressure and violence and madness.

It was difficult to tell exactly when the effects of the bomb subsided.

I couldn't think straight, I couldn't breathe properly, I couldn't hear, and my whole body hurt.

Dust swirled in the air and my mouth felt gritty, so that when I opened and closed it, I could feel the crunch between my teeth.

The first thing I knew was that someone was shaking me. I was sitting with my back to the wall, hunched into a ball.

The shaking came again and I turned to look at Lisa.

I had to think hard about moving my head. The effort of it was massive. My mind was numb and empty, and when I looked at her, I blinked hard.

She was leaning close and saying something, but all I could hear was a muffled noise and a high-pitched whining. No words. If I hadn't been so stunned, I might have been afraid that I had lost my hearing, but I was too dazed to think much of anything at all.

Lisa leaned closer and shouted in my ear.

". . . alive?"

I stared at her and focused my thoughts. I wiped my eyes and shook my head.

Lisa spoke again and this time the words were clearer.

"Are we still alive?"

I nodded and reached out to touch her shoulder, then turned to look at Stefan.

My brother was lying facedown on the ground, not moving.

I stared at his body, then shifted forward and crawled toward him.

"Stefan," I tried to say, but my mouth would hardly work. "Stefan."

My arms gave way when I came to him, and I fell forward, pressing my face to his shoulder.

"Karl?"

I stopped, not sure if I'd actually heard it. My ears were ringing and it might have been my imagination.

"Karl. You're hurting me."

In one sudden movement, I sat back and an overwhelming sense of relief swept over me. "Stefan? You're all right."

My brother rolled onto his back and looked at me. "What the hell just happened?"

RETURN TO HEADQUARTERS

There was a large crater in the road, and what was left of Wolff and his car was crushed against the trunk of a sturdy oak, but we didn't stay to inspect the damage. It took us a while to recover from the blast and by the time we were on our feet, some of the men from Feldstrasse had come to investigate the explosion.

We left the way we had come in, all of us stunned, our ears ringing and our bodies aching.

"What now?" Lisa asked.

"Home?" I replied. It seemed like the only thing to do.

"I feel like . . . like I should . . . I don't know," Lisa said. "Like I should feel worse. That Wolff's . . . you know."

"Dead?" Stefan said.

Lisa nodded. "It's our fault."

"No it isn't."

"But if we'd reported the bomb . . ." she said. "I don't feel bad, though. Is that wrong?"

"I don't feel bad, either," I said to her. "Anyway, you *did* try to tell him, remember? When he caught us outside. You tried to tell him and he should have listened to you."

Lisa nodded again.

"So let's go home." I reached out and held her hand.

"You have to take me back first," Stefan said.

"What?"

"You have to come back to Headquarters with me. You have to lock me back in the cell."

"No. We —"

"Don't you see, Karl? I can't be out of that cell. They'll think I escaped and then I'll have to hide and you'll still be in danger, and Mama and Oma and Opa . . ." Stefan shook his head. "I *have* to go back."

"I won't lock you in."

"He's right," Lisa said.

"But what if they do something to you?"

"I can't just run away, Karl. They'll come after me. After you, too. And Mama. You need to lock me up so they can release me like they released the others."

"What if they don't?"

"They will."

I couldn't help thinking about how he had been taken away the last time, though. Maybe, if they took him away again, he wouldn't come back.

"No one knows what just happened," Stefan argued. "No one but us. Don't you see? If I run away, they'll come after me, but if you lock me back in the cell, no one will *ever* know what happened. They'll just think Wolff went out in his car and hit an unexploded bomb. You'll all be safe."

I tried to argue, but as always, Stefan was right. So we headed back to Gestapo Headquarters and went down into the cellar. Stefan hugged me and returned to his cell.

The key was still in the lock, and the bunch jangled when Stefan helped close the door. He turned and looked at me through the bars.

"Lock it. Then get your things from upstairs and leave the keys. No one can know you were here."

"What if they don't let you out?" My mind was filled with doubt. "What if they do something to you?"

"Like what? They've already beaten me and shaved my head. What else are they going to do?"

"I —"

"Go," he said. "Now."

"Come on." Lisa took my arm and pulled me away from the cell. "Before someone comes."

I nodded and wiped my eyes, and followed Lisa up the stairs. At the top, I stopped and turned to look at my brother for what I thought might be the last time. I wanted, more than anything, to let him back out, but that would only lead to trouble for everyone.

He looked so brave when he raised a hand to us and we left him.

"Get our things," Lisa said, heading straight to the front door. "I'll keep watch."

With a heavy heart, I jogged to Wolff's office. The Führer watched from his picture on the wall as I got my bag and shoved everything inside. My hands were shaking and I was fighting back the tears. I couldn't stop thinking about Stefan in the cell downstairs.

When I had gotten everything, I turned to leave, but stopped when something caught my eye. There, on the corner of Wolff's desk.

Three brown folders.

I hesitated, looking from the folders to the door, then back again.

Take them.

I ran to the desk and grabbed the folders. I flicked each one open, seeing the arrest forms we had signed, then stuffed them into my bag along with everything else.

And that's when I had an idea. If only there was enough time.

Do it.

Rushing around the desk, I pulled open the top drawer on the left and rummaged through the empty brown folders and documents.

Nothing.

"Hurry up!" Lisa shouted.

Without pausing, I slammed the drawer shut and yanked open the one below it. Another pile of papers nestled in there, but they were of no use to me.

"Karl!"

I tugged open the bottom drawer and immediately saw the forms I was looking for. I could hardly believe they were real.

"Karl! What are you doing?"

I snatched one from the top of the pile and put it on the

desktop as I kicked the drawer closed. Leaning down to look at the document more closely, I reached out for Wolff's pen.

This was my chance to do something right. Perhaps —

"Quick!" Lisa ran back from the front door. "Someone's coming. We have to go."

"One minute." It was a risk, but there might just be time.

"Now!" she hissed. "I can hear them coming!"

A KNOCK AT
THE DOOR

We managed to slip from Headquarters without being seen. The soldiers were returning from Feldstrasse, tired and dirty, and we hid in the shadow of the thorny hedge until they had disappeared inside the Gestapo building.

When everything was quiet, we sneaked away from that awful place and Lisa and I finally made it back to Escherstrasse, but our street felt like a different place now. *We* felt different.

As soon as I was home, I washed my hands and face, and hid my dirty clothes before climbing into bed. I didn't sleep at all. Lying there, staring at the ceiling, ears ringing, I couldn't shake the fire and explosions out of my mind, and I kept seeing images of Stefan locked in that horrible cell. His bruises and the dried blood on his face. I was frightened that putting him back behind bars had been the wrong thing, that maybe he would be taken away and I would never see him again.

The next morning, Oma put breakfast on the table in the kitchen. She talked with Mama and Opa about the bombing, and about Stefan, but I kept quiet. I didn't say a word about what had happened to me last night, even though it pressed down on me like a terrible weight.

I picked at my bread, not feeling hungry. I was too scared to eat anything. Too scared to say anything. All I could think about was poor Stefan, and how I had locked the cell and left him in that horrible prison.

When three knocks came at the front door, my heart jumped.

Everyone looked around at each other, worry and fear clear in their eyes.

The knocking came again and Opa pushed back his chair. "I'll get it."

Mama stood up, too, lifting a trembling hand to her mouth as she spoke. "Who is it? Is it him?"

We followed Opa into the hallway and watched him unlock the door.

He glanced back at us before pulling it open.

Standing on the step, flanked by two SS soldiers, Stefan looked even worse in the early morning light than he had in the dull electric glow of the bulbs in the prison last night. His eye was swollen shut, bruises shone on his face, and his short hair made him look like a prisoner from a camp.

One of the soldiers stepped forward and held out a piece of paper.

Opa took it from him, fumbling it open with shaking fingers. He looked at it for a long moment, then turned to show it to Mama.

"A release order," he said.

Mama let out a gasp and hurried straight to Stefan. She

wrapped her arms around my brother and stood there on the step, holding him as if she would never let him go.

"You're safe," she sobbed. "You're safe."

The soldiers didn't say a word. They turned and walked away, boot heels clicking on the pavement.

Opa took Mama's elbow and guided her inside with Stefan, closing the door before bringing them into the kitchen where he sat them at the table. Oma and Opa then pulled up chairs so that they were all sitting around Stefan. They checked his bruises and asked him question after question. They wanted to know where he had been and what had happened to him.

Stefan looked over their shoulders to see me standing by the door and our eyes met. He nodded once at me and I felt a massive sense of relief. It was as if an enormous weight had been lifted from my heart.

I watched them fussing over Stefan, then went upstairs and took my copy of *Mein Kampf* from the top of the chest of drawers.

I stared at the face of the man I had come to hate, and thought about all the things that had happened since my twelfth birthday. It had only been a matter of days, but it felt as if it had been years, and my world was not the same anymore. All those games and parades and uniforms and medals weren't exciting now; they were not things to be proud of, but things to be afraid of. They were the things that had made us laugh at Johann Weber and beat him to the ground, things that caused Stefan to get arrested and Lisa's father to be taken away.

They were the things that had killed Papa.

"Only one thing to do with you," I whispered as I picked up the book and went outside.

The sun had not been up for long and the air was cool outside. There was still a faint smell of burning drifting on the breeze, but otherwise, it was a beautiful day.

I placed three brown folders on the grass at the far end of the backyard, and put *Mein Kampf* on top of them so the Führer was looking at the sky, then I doused him with kerosene from Opa's supplies.

As I took a match from the box, I heard footsteps and turned to see my brother coming across the lawn.

"I was so scared," I said when he stopped beside me. "Last night."

"Me too."

"I thought I might never see you again."

Stefan looked down. "Are those our files?"

"Yes."

"And the release order? That was you, wasn't it? You filled it out."

"There was only just enough time, the soldiers were coming back. I left it on Wolff's desk, but I didn't know if it would work; the signature was really bad."

"The signature was really *good*." He looked at me. "And when they couldn't find my file and Wolff was gone . . ." He took a deep breath. "Thank you, Karl."

"You're welcome."

"You're braver than you look." He smiled, then shifted his eyes toward the files and the book. "And you've really finished with all this?"

I nodded.

"But you know you'll still have to go to Deutsches Jungvolk meetings? They'll still try to get inside your head."

"They won't be able to. Everything's different now," I said. *"Everything."*

When I put a match to the book, the flames burned blue and flickered in the wind. The folders went up well, but the book was thick and it took a while for the fire to work through it. The pages blackened and curled as the Führer turned to smoke.

"I should go and tell Lisa," I said without taking my eyes off the fire. "She'll want to know you're home."

"She's a good friend," Stefan said.

"Yes, she is."

Stefan and I watched the paper burn for a while, then he put his arm around my shoulder and we went back into the house.

Mama was still in the kitchen with Oma and Opa.

"What were you two doing outside?" she asked as Stefan went to sit with her.

I looked at her for a moment, then shrugged and smiled. "Just taking out some trash."

EDELWEISS PIRATES

The Edelweiss Pirates was a loosely organized youth movement that arose, mainly among the working classes, in towns and cities across Nazi Germany. Many groups had different names but they all considered themselves to be Edelweiss Pirates, named after the edelweiss badges that many of them wore. The groups arose in response to the strict, paramilitary nature of the Hitler Youth, and rebelled, initially, against the government's control of leisure time.

One of their slogans was "Eternal War on the Hitler Youth."

Groups of Edelweiss Pirates were mostly peaceful, engaged in hiking and camping trips, and defying the laws restricting free movement. They were known to paint buildings with anti-Nazi graffiti and to distribute propaganda leaflets dropped by the Allies. As the war progressed, however, some groups became more defiant by attacking Hitler Youth patrols, and harboring army deserters, Jews, and even prisoners of war.

Much later in the war, Edelweiss Pirates were even suspected of involvement in the murder of Gestapo officers.

In October 1944, Heinrich Himmler (the Chief of German Police and Minister of the Interior) ordered a crackdown on the group.

On November 10, 1944, thirteen youths were hanged at a public gallows in Ehrenfeld train station in Cologne. Six of them were, or had been members of the Edelweiss Pirates.

The youngest was sixteen years old.

ACKNOWLEDGMENTS

You'd be amazed how much work goes into bringing a novel to life, so I'd like to take a moment to acknowledge all those who have helped make *My Brother's Secret* what it is. Thanks to my agent, Carolyn, for all her honest words and advice, and to Bella for her fantastic editorial work. I can't stress enough how brilliant everyone is at Chicken House — their passion for good stories is unequaled and I have felt well and truly supported every step of the way — so thanks to Barry for making it all happen, and to Rachel L. and Rachel H. and Elinor for all their hard work. Thanks also to Tina (who never seems to rest), to Laura and Becky, and to Emellia for working so hard on the US edition of this book. Big thanks have to go to my good friend Graeme, who has been helping me with promotional materials for the past few years. My biggest thanks, though, is for my first readers and best supporters — my wife and children. Thanks for always being there and for putting up with me when I'm lost in Danworld — which is most of the time.

I'd also like to acknowledge the bravery of those who resisted.